THE HOUSE ON PUNISHMENT CORNER

She wears tight black calf-length boots with high heels as spiky as an ice pick. Her long legs are sheathed in the sheerest nylon that shines like wet paint. The jet black stocking-tops are held taut by the suspenders of a black satin-and-lace basque, its cinched waist clinging tightly to her curves. Her breasts billow out of the low-cut lacy bra. She does not wear panties.

She is Clarissa Peacham, boss of Peacham Associates, and her employees do just what she tells them at her house on Punishment Corner . . .

The House on Punishment Corner

Becky Bell

First published in 1995
by HEADLINE BOOK PUBLISHING

A HEADLINE DELTA paperback

10 9 8 7 6 5 4 3 2 1

ISBN 0 7472 5223 8

Typeset by CBS, Felixstowe, Suffolk

Printed and bound in Great Britain by
Cox & Wyman Ltd, Reading, Berks

HEADLINE BOOK PUBLISHING
A division of Hodder Headline PLC
338 Euston Road
London NW1 3BH

The House on
Punishment Corner

Chapter One

WILLIAM

She always wore boots, tight, black, calf-length boots with high heels as spiky as an ice pick. Above them her long legs were sheathed in the sheerest nylon, nylon that shone like wet paint. The jet black stocking-tops were held taut by the suspenders of a black satin-and-lace basque, its cinched waist clinging tightly to the natural contours of her body. Her breasts, big orbs of flesh, billowed out of the low-cut lacy bra of the basque, the upper hemispheres of her areolae just visible. She was not wearing panties. Her sex, covered in thick curly hair, was exposed.

She stood with her legs apart, and her hands on her hips. 'How dare you?' she said. 'How dare you?' The expression on her face was imperious. The scorn in her eyes was absolute. He was worthy only of her contempt.

She always wore long gloves too, made from black satin, pulled, like a second skin, well above her elbow. The tops of her arms, like the tops of her thighs, looked impossibly soft and creamy in contrast to the slick material stretched so tautly below them.

1

'How dare you?' her voice barked again. She was able to read his thoughts, to know all his secrets.

'I can't help it,' he said. He fell to his knees in front of her.

Two steps forward. It was always the same. Her stockings rasped against each other, her spiky heels clacking on the floor. He could see her so clearly, her breasts quivering, her nipples so hard now they had escaped the constraint of the lace altogether, and poked above it. She shook her head as though to cast off some irritation and the mane of her long chestnut coloured hair flew as if caught by the wind. He could smell the heavy, musky perfume she always wore. If he dared to look he could glimpse the lips of her sex between her legs.

That was how it always began. That was always the image he saw first. That was always what made him erect, often before he'd even touched his penis.

He would have to be punished for his impudence, for daring to look at her nakedness. He knew that. She reached for the riding crop. Her fingers, gloved in black satin, closed around the braided handle and she slashed it experimentally through the air into the open palm of her other hand. He flinched, and his cock spasmed.

'How dare you?'

She raised the whip high, her breasts lifted out of the corset by the movement. It was always the same. But the whip never landed. The image was frozen as a white string of semen arced out from his cock, and spattered down on to his belly. Inevitably the image began to fade. In its place he was left with its trigger, the full colour reproduction of Clarissa Peacham, dressed in a peach coloured suit, her legs crossed, her calves held parallel, sitting behind the massive desk in her office. It was the official photograph of the Chairman and Managing Director of Peacham Associates printed on the back cover of the published yearly report and accounts. It lay on the pillow next to William, the image that sparked all his fantasies.

He did not like to admit to himself that he was obsessed by her. He liked to pretend that his masturbation rites could be driven by any woman he chose. The fact that it was always Clarissa Peacham he conjured up was something he hid from himself, a secret he kept in a separate compartment of his mind, just as Ms Peacham's photograph was kept in a separate drawer in his bedside table. He did not like to admit either, perhaps because he didn't understand it, that his fantasies concerning her always involved her disdain and the idea of his being punished for daring even to look at her.

He *did* admit to himself that she was undoubtedly one of the most beautiful women he had ever seen. She had strong, well-proportioned features: a straight nose, cheekbones that looked as though they had been sculpted in stone, a firm chin and a fleshy, rich mouth with very red lips. Her hair was a torrent of thick glossy chestnut, tumbling over her shoulders in soft, flouncing waves. But it was her eyes that were her most stunning asset. Almost the same colour as her hair they were large and bright with a hypnotic quality that made it impossible not to stare at them. They sparkled with life, the windows of a soul that danced to a rhythm that was unmistakably sensual.

Her body transmitted messages on the same wavelength, radiating a flow that was quite obviously sexual. She was aware of its effect, walking with the self-conscious elegance and haughtiness of someone who knew every head turned to watch as she passed by, women envious of her looks and style, men desirous of her body. She was tall with long legs that were contoured by well-defined muscles and a sleek, taut figure toned and firmed by a regular exercise regime that made her capable of catlike grace. The narrowness of her waist seemed to emphasise the line of her full, jutting breasts above it, and the generous swell of her hips and buttocks below delighted the eye.

Her attitude to the world was as clear as her sexuality. She displayed an arrogant confidence in her own ability and a total lack of concern as to what others thought of her. She dressed accordingly, flaunting her spectacular body and seeing no reason to disguise it. The way William imagined her was not far from the reality. Clarissa Peacham favoured tight, abbreviated skirts, that clung to the flat plane of her stomach, and exposed her long supple legs, always sheathed in the sheerest of nylon, more often than not woven with Lycra to give a glassy sheen. She wore tight, figure-hugging blouses with plunging necklines that revealed the dark tunnel of her cleavage and the rich curves of her breasts as they wrestled with the restraint of her bra. And, as William knew only too well, she frequently wore boots with the highest of heels, making no concession to her height, so she would tower over other women and a good few men.

In fact, William hadn't seen her that often. While Clarissa ran Peacham Associates, one of the biggest advertising agencies in London, and was a majority share holder, William Briton was only a minion. The gulf that divided them was unbridgeable. Her office was at the top of the building, on the sixteenth floor, his on the sixth. Very occasionally she would come down to wander around among the lesser mortals in the open plan office they all shared and then his eyes would be rooted to her, unable to do anything but stare, drinking in the details of her appearance, until, like strong liquor, they intoxicated him.

He could remember every separate occasion he had seen her, how she had looked and what she had worn. How many times had he tried to imagine what her body was like under those expensive clothes? How many times had he conjured up an image of her breasts, had watched them spill from the cups of her bra as it fell away, or imagined silky panties being skimmed down those wonderful legs? How many nights, lying naked in bed, had he tried to picture her pubis nestling at the bottom of her almost concave belly? Would it be thick with chestnut hair – as he had imagined tonight – or nearly hairless, barely covering the slit of her labia? And what of her sex? He had tortured himself with thoughts of that too. Would it be loose and fleshy, like an over-ripe fruit, or as tight and thin-lipped as a leather purse?

Every single occasion he had seen her had provoked him. Each had seen him hurrying to his bedroom the moment he got home needing to deal with the almost unbearable frustration her presence had caused in the only way he had available to him. And each time would disturb him in a way he simply did not understand. Clarissa Peacham was not just a beautiful woman he lusted after but knew he would never have. Her effect on him was much more profound. She inspired something he did not understand, stimulated something that was buried in the dark, hidden depths of his psyche. He knew it was there but for the life of him he could not bring it out into the light.

The phone on his desk rang only once before he picked it up.

'Mr Briton?' It was a man's voice.

'Yes.'

'This is Ms Peacham's assistant.' The voice had a tone of authority acquired, no doubt, by association with the ultimate power in the company.

'Ms Peacham?' he queried. In his three years with Peacham Associates he had never received a call from the sixteenth floor. There was no reason to. He was a computer programmer whose primary job was to feed market-research information into the machine that would, in turn, use it to produce charts and graphics and easily digestible forecasts that the agency's clients could paw over and discuss and often, inevitably, discard. He was not responsible for the research or for the conclusions. 'Yes?' he said trying to keep his voice from faltering despite the fact his heart was pounding due to a rush of adrenaline.

'Could you come up here at once. Ms Peacham wants to see you.'

'Me?' The word came out with a high-pitched squeak.

'Yes, you,' the man said disdainfully before slamming the phone down.

William got to his feet. He was sweating, perspiration beading his forehead and upper lip. What did she want with him? He started towards the lift then remembered his jacket. He went back for it, grabbing it from the back of his chair and putting it on. The lift was on the floor below. He pressed the call button anxiously. What did she want with him? Though he knew it was completely illogical and totally impossible he felt guilty, as if she had discovered the purpose for which he had been using her official company photograph.

In the lift he straightened his tie and combed his hair,

checking it in the large mirror that covered the back wall. He wiped the sweat away with his handkerchief and tried to calm himself by taking deep breaths.

The lift doors opened directly on to a large reception area with floor-to-ceiling plate glass windows on two sides. A desk made from rosewood, the size of a billiard table, stood barring the way to the corridor that led to the directors' offices.

'William Briton,' he said to the receptionist who sat behind the desk. She was a gorgeous brunette in a light blue suit who looked at him as if he were something distasteful that had attached itself to the sole of her shoe. 'To see Ms Peacham,' he added.

She typed something into the computer terminal on the desk and waited for a response from the screen. Apparently it was affirmative. 'Double doors at the end of the corridor,' she said without looking up at him again.

William shuffled uneasily down the corridor. There was an oil painting by Miro on one side of the white walls and a large Hockney oil on the other. He knocked on one of the double doors. It was opened by Ms Peacham's male assistant whom William recognised. He had always trailed behind her on her infrequent visits to the lower depths.

Without a word the man, a weedy-looking twenty-year-old who was already going bald, ushered William across the outer office. Neither of the two secretaries in the office interrupted their typing to look up at him as he was led across to a large oak panelled door which was already ajar. The assistant opened it without knocking and allowed William through. He closed it so rapidly he made William jump.

'Mr Briton.'

7

Today she was wearing a peachy silk blouse, its cut so tight he could clearly see the outline of her bra and its wired cups. The light from the window behind her shone onto her hair, bouncing from its waves and flounces so it seemed to dance with shades of chestnut and orange. She was sitting behind a large modern desk – the desk in the official photograph – of polished walnut inlaid with strips of brass. The nails of her long rather bony fingers, painted the exact same colour as her blouse, beat out an impatient tattoo on the desk top in front of her.

'You wanted to see me?'

'Yes, I did,' she said, getting to her feet. Her skirt was short and peachy too and flared out from her hips. He was unable to stop himself feasting his eyes on the nylon-sheathed thighs it revealed. He had never been this close to her. 'There's something I have to discuss with you. Not now, I don't have the time.'

'Erh . . . right . . .' He wasn't sure what he was expected to say.

'Tomorrow evening. Say at seven.' She did not ask him if that was convenient.

'Seven,' he repeated gormlessly, sure his mouth was opening and closing like a fish. She was wearing a strong musky perfume that he seemed to inhale through every pore of his body.

'But not here. Not in the office. I want you to come to my home.'

'Your home?' Again the repetition came out as though he were witless. 'But I . . . why . . . ?'

'Thank you,' she said sitting down again and dismissing him with a wave of her hand.

8

There was a string of questions he wanted to ask, but as if by some sixth sense, the assistant opened the panelled door again and he was ushered out. What did she want to discuss? Why her home? It simply didn't make sense.

'You'll need this,' the assistant said in the outer office, thrusting a small white card into his hand as he opened one of the outer doors.

William was in a daze as he stood outside the office, his mind churning. What did it all mean?

'William. What are you doing up here?' The voice brought him back down to earth. He recognised another occupant of the sixth floor walking down the corridor towards him. Gloria Price was a brunette, pretty enough, but with a habit of wearing rather dowdy clothes.

'I was sent for . . . to see Ms Peacham.'

'Me too. What's it all about?'

'God knows,' he said unhelpfully. Gloria had as much reason to be called to Ms Peacham's office as he did. For some reason he didn't want to volunteer any information about what had happened to him. 'I think it's probably just routine.'

Gloria gave him a funny look, knowing full well routine was the last thing it was, but as she was about to challenge him the door opened and Ms Peacham's assistant beckoned her in.

William walked to the lift. As he waited for it to arrive he looked at the card the assistant had handed him. Neatly printed in black letters it read: 10 Punishment Road, London W.1. Written in the top right hand corner in a bold italic script was: 7.00 p.m. Sharp.

William lay in bed unable to sleep, his mind torn between

excitement and anxiety. Ms Peacham had not given him the slightest clue, in her manner, as to what she wanted to see him about. Her face, and her amber eyes, had been expressionless, which had given him room to read into them every possible emotion from anger to lust.

As the night grew longer and the streets outside lapsed into silence, William tossed and turned. He was developing increasingly more elaborate theories as to what Clarissa Peacham wanted with him and, just as puzzling, why it had to be at her house. Though he kept telling himself it was impossible, that a woman of her sophistication, elegance and wealth, would never have had any reason to notice him, let alone pick him out, in the small hours of the morning he was in such a state of high anxiety even this unlikely scenario assumed the status of the possible.

It was not, he told himself, that outlandish. He wasn't unattractive. He was tall and kept himself reasonably fit. His face was well proportioned with a straight nose, a square jaw and slightly hollow cheekbones. He had dark brown eyes and very thick, curly black hair, matched by a dark complexion.

But just as he convinced himself that Ms Peacham was quite capable of selecting a male partner as casually as she could select a new pair of high-heeled boots, his mind would swing to the other side of the pendulum. He would convince himself that the only reason she wanted to see him was purely connected to work. She had called for Gloria Price too hadn't she? Perhaps that was for the same reason and she too had been asked to her home. He had tried to see Gloria that afternoon but had been told she was out at a meeting and wouldn't be back until the next morning. If she had been issued with the same invitation there would have been no room for doubt: Ms Peacham's summons was no reason for excitement.

What if she hadn't, however? The pendulum swung back. What if Gloria's visit to the sixteenth floor had been coincidental, had been for an entirely different, and possibly trivial, reason and she had not been invited to the house? Then, William could well imagine, that Ms Peacham's strong and powerful personality would see no reason to abide by social convention or out-dated morality. She would do as she pleased. If she had seen William on her ambles around the sixth floor, and had decided she wanted him, she would certainly not hesitate. Of course her invitation had been brusque and charmless. But that was entirely in character. Clarissa Peacham had a habit of taking what she wanted without unnecessary pleasantries.

The odd thing was, considering the number of times the presence of Clarissa had made him reach into the drawer of his bedside table and extract the official photograph of the Chairman and Managing Director of Peacham Associates, William didn't want to begin his time-honoured ritual. In the darkness he seemed to be able to see Ms Peacham's eyes staring at him intently, watching his every move. Though it was totally illogical, he did not want her to discover the secret of his masturbation rite.

The first fronds of daylight had crept around the bedroom curtains before William's mind – and Ms Peacham's eyes – allowed him to drift into an uneasy sleep.

'Come in.' He'd expected servants. But Clarissa opened the

11

front door herself. 'This way,' she said turning and leading him down a long corridor. There were pictures on the walls that looked like Gillray cartoons except they all featured men with enormous erections sticking out of their eighteenth-century breeches. One in particular caught William's eye. The penis was the size of a horse's head and had been bridled around the glans with reins held firmly in its owner's hand. He was trying to pull it back but unsuccessfully as great splashes of semen, lashed out towards the female who sat in a chair opposite, the look of surprise on her face mixed with very definite excitement.

'In here.'

The bedroom was small and featureless. There was a double bed with a single bedside table and an Anglepoise lamp that only lit the area around the bed. The rest of the room was veiled in shadow. Heavy red velvet curtains were drawn across the window. The mattress was covered with a white sheet. William thought this must be a special room, a room she reserved not for sleeping but for sex.

'I've been thinking about you, William. I've been watching you.'

Clarissa sat on the bed. She was wearing a dark blue satin robe, tied at the waist with a matching belt. She crossed her legs and the satin fell away to reveal her thighs. She looked up at him steadily, her tongue just visible between her lips.

'Watching you,' she repeated.

She slipped the robe from her shoulders. She was wearing a dark green bra and tiny thong cut panties. Her long bony fingers undid the clasp of her bra and it slid off her breasts. They quivered at their freedom. They were big and round and seemed to defy gravity, her nipples tilting upward. She took them in her hands and began to knead them roughly, pushing and pulling at the spongy flesh.

'Do you like my tits, William?'

She lay back on the bed, opened her legs and bent them at the knee. She was wearing black silk-covered, high-heeled slippers and the heels dug into the sheet. Her hand stroked the triangle of her sex covered tightly by the gusset of the panties. He could see the thick bush of chestnut hair under the green silk. She pushed her finger, covered in the dark green silk, into her vagina and then withdrew it leaving the panties sucked into her sex.

'Take your clothes off William.'

'I thought . . .' He did not know what to say.

'You thought what? That I got you here to talk business? That I wanted to know what you were doing in the office? I brought you here to fuck me, William. No other reason. If you don't like the idea you'd better go.'

Hurriedly he pulled off his clothes. His cock was already erect. It *felt* as big as the one in the picture in the hallway.

'What you're going to do William is lick every inch of my body. Every inch. Do you understand?'

'Yes.'

'Good. Then, when you've got me properly worked up, when you've got me all wet and aching and my clitoris is all swollen, you're going to fuck me. Or should I say I'm going to fuck you.' The last remark made her laugh. Her laughter was a strange hollow sound that seemed to echo around the room despite its size. She looked at him with those chestnut eyes. He could see the flame of excitement dancing there and her determination that she would get her own way. 'This is for my pleasure, William. My pleasure. Do you understand?'

He looked at her long lithe body. 'You're so beautiful,' he said.

'Do you understand?' she repeated. 'You are not here for your benefit but for mine. You are not permitted to come.'

'Not permitted . . .'

'Not permitted, William. Afterwards, if you give me what I want I may permit you to wank for me. But that would be a privilege and like all privileges it will have to be earned.'

William didn't understand. She couldn't mean what she said, she couldn't expect him to enter her, fuck her, be pressed into her beautiful body and be surrounded by her slick, clinging sex and not come. It was impossible. Of course she didn't know how obsessed he was with her, how many times he'd come just trying to imagine what her naked body would look like, but even so surely she couldn't expect him to have that much control?

'Come on, come on,' she chided. She stretched out her left foot and dug the heel of the black slipper painfully into his thigh. 'Start with my legs, William. Start to lick my feet.'

He sunk to his knees at the foot of the bed and took her left foot in his hands, pulling off the slipper. Her toenails were varnished a deep crimson red. He leaned forward, feeling his bone hard erection prodding against his belly as he brought his mouth down on to the arch of her foot, kissing it, then licking it.

'That's where you belong isn't it?' she said.

He didn't know what that meant.

He licked the side of her foot and along to her toes. He could see right up her long slender legs. He could see her sex, barely covered by the gusset now that most of it had been drawn up into her vagina. The material had puckered and was a much darker colour than the rest of the panties, moistened by her juices.

'Now the other one,' she said irritably as though annoyed she had to tell him.

He transferred his mouth to her other foot. He felt his cock pulsing with excitement as he saw her hands gather up her big breasts again, her fingers digging into the pliant flesh.

'Right up between the toes . . .'

William's whole body was taut, every muscle rigid. Her flesh felt wonderful against his lips. It was all he'd dreamt of, all he wanted. She was magnificent. He had never seen a more beautiful woman. Her sex seemed to be breathing, sucking the material in and out. She was playing with her own nipples, pinching them. She fed the right nipple into her mouth, then took it between her lips. He could feel the effect this had on her. Her body quaked. He'd never seen a woman do that to herself.

He had too much spunk. He was full of it. He should have masturbated last night. Then he would have been all right. But he hadn't and his cock was so full he knew he'd never be able to hold out. He could feel the slick of wetness it had produced rubbing against his belly. He wanted to sit up so his cock wouldn't rub against it any more but he couldn't because there was still acres of her flesh he had to cover with his tongue.

It was no good. He tried everything. He tried not to look at her, tried not to feel her silky soft skin against his lips, but it was no good.

'No, no,' he cried as his semen brimmed up out of him,

spattering against the white sheet and his body.

'What have you done?' she said at once. She pulled her foot away from his mouth and used it to send him sprawling back on to the floor. 'What have you done?' she repeated looking at the semen that had spattered over his stomach.

'I didn't . . . I couldn't stop myself.'

'How dare you? How dare you? How dare you?' Her voice was as cold as ice. It was so cold he shivered and the convulsion woke him, the stickiness on his belly the only thing he had not imagined.

GLORIA

She was too worried to concentrate on the meal, or on him for that matter. If she could have thought of a good excuse to cancel, or any excuse, she would have done. But she had no way of phoning him. They had arranged to meet at the restaurant and she remembered he was driving straight there from some sales conference so he wouldn't be in his office or his home to take her call. She tried both just in case his plans had changed but got answerphone messages, as she'd expected.

There was no alternative but to go through with it, though her interview with Clarissa Peacham had left her in no mood for going out. It was not what Ms Peacham had said that had disturbed her so much but what she hadn't said. The interview had been short and enigmatic. She had puzzled over it ever since.

Gloria worked as an assistant in the department that prepared the storyboards for filmed commercials. Her ambition was to work her way up to the creation of advertising campaigns. At the moment she could not think of a single aspect of what she did that would involve Clarissa Peacham, let alone need a personal interview at her home. It made no sense. In her two years with the company she couldn't remember exchanging even the most casual greeting with the woman.

Not that Clarissa hadn't always fascinated Gloria. To her Clarissa was like a film star; sophisticated, elegant, rich and remote. She found it hard to imagine a more beautiful woman. She was, Gloria thought, what every modern woman should aspire to. Clarissa appeared to be totally in control of her own destiny, she had conquered the world on her own terms. She had done what most women – and most men for that matter – only dreamt of, and done it without losing her femininity or the very obvious sensuality she seemed to exude with every step.

'So we reckon we can increase the overall sales at least four-point-five percent in the first year alone,' he was saying as he chomped on mouthfuls of sherry trifle. 'And that's only on the model with the articulated limbs.'

Derek Taylor was a toy salesman. They had met two weeks ago in Gloria's local supermarket where he'd asked her for advice about which brand of soap powder to buy. She had agreed to go out with him because he was relatively attractive and had a nice smile, but mostly because she was bored with sitting at home on her own.

'When we get the full moving body the sky's the limit. I think we might be looking at ten percent growth year on year . . .'

He droned on as they drunk coffee and Gloria accepted his offer of a brandy. She needed it. As he continued to tell her the merits of the new super-doll his company was importing from the States, her mind focused again on Clarissa Peacham. She could see Clarissa's eyes, and the way they had looked at her as her male assistant had ushered her into the office. They had bored into her like X-rays and she had had the curious idea that Clarissa had been trying to imagine what she looked like without her clothes. What had provoked such a strange thought she did not know; nor did she know, even more peculiarly, why the thought had created a very definite flush of excitement in her.

Though Clarissa had given her not the slightest clue in terms of what she had said or the manner in which she had said it, Gloria was sure, instinctively, that whatever was going to be discussed tomorrow evening it was not going to be pleasant.

Derek drove her home, apparently oblivious to the fact she had hardly said a word, and still determined to give her a run-down on every aspect of the toy business. Gloria, in the meantime, let the words roll over her, unable to forget the curious way Clarissa had looked at her.

'We're home,' Derek said as he parked his car outside the Victorian terraced house that had been split into two flats, the top one of which belonged to Gloria.

'Do you want some coffee?' she said.

'Yes, please,' he said enthusiastically. They had only been out once before and on that occasion he hadn't got past the front door.

Gloria led the way into her small, neat flat. Derek had bored her all evening but she didn't want him to go home. It was not that she hoped he would take her mind off Clarissa: he had already failed to do that. She had a baser motive. Despite the Sword of Damocles that hung over her head – or perhaps, because of it – she felt unaccountably randy. It was a feeling caused by that look in Clarissa's eyes, though how that translated into the pulsing sensations, the little trills and thrills of excitement that sparkled, like bubbles in champagne, in her body now, Gloria did not know. Derek was no Adonis, not the great hunk of muscular manhood she might have hoped for, but he would have to do.

'I don't want any coffee,' she said boldly in the hall.

'No?' he said. 'What do you want?'

Gloria found herself imagining what Clarissa would do in this situation. How would she behave? What would she say to get a man into her bed? She had a vision of her standing in a long black silk dress that clung to every curve of her tall, elegant body, its skirt split almost to the hip. What would she say?

'I want you to take me to bed.'

Derek's eyes lit up. 'Really?' It sounded as though he couldn't quite believe it.

Without answering Gloria turned and walked into her bedroom. She could imagine Clarissa doing the same, the long black dress swishing as she moved. Derek followed her.

'Unzip me,' she said without turning round. She could have got out of her plain beige dress without undoing its zip but she knew this was what Clarissa would do.

Derek came up behind her and pulled the zip down.

Gloria shook her shoulders and let the dress fall to the floor. She was wearing a rather worn, cream coloured bra and tan coloured tights with no panties. She hadn't anticipated a sexual encounter tonight. Clarissa, she knew, would have been dressed in slinky black satin and lace, but though she didn't have the money for expensive underwear she had nothing to be ashamed of when it came to her body. She was not as tall as Clarissa but had a slender figure and her legs were shapely and firm.

Turning to face Derek she reached behind her back to the clasp of her bra, undid it and leant forward so the cups would fall away from her breasts. She had very round, firm breasts that jutted proudly from her chest. Her nipples, she realised, were already hard.

'Aren't you going to get undressed?' she asked him. Gloria had never behaved like this before and knew it was because she wanted to be like Clarissa, to have the same determination, the same attitude of not caring what the world would think. It excited her.

As Derek hurriedly pulled off his clothes, in such a hurry he forgot to take off his shoes before taking down his trousers, and becoming tangled up as a result, Gloria stripped off her tights then pulled back the counterpane on the bed. She lay on her back, propping her head against the wall with the pillows, watching Derek's attempts to extract himself from his trousers.

Eventually he was naked, his uncircumcised cock still flaccid. His body was not unattractive though he had a roll of fat on top of his hips. Gloria wanted to maintain the initiative. She extended her leg so she could brush her toes against his cock.

'You'll have to do better than that,' she mocked, knowing she shouldn't say such a thing but not caring. Isn't that the sort of thing Clarissa would say?

He sat on the bed and leant forward to kiss her. She allowed his tongue to penetrate her lips but broke the kiss off quickly. Kissing wasn't what she wanted. She sat up, pushed him back on the bed and dropped her head into his lap. Circling his cock with her hand she jerked back his foreskin so sharply it made him moan. She slipped his glans into her mouth, running her tongue around the rim of it and feeling it instantly engorge.

'Better,' she said pulling her mouth away as soon as his erection was complete. She swung her thigh over his hips and positioned her sex above his cock. With her hand she pulled the tip of his glans to and fro against the furrow of her labia until she felt it pressing into her clitoris. It was her turn to moan. For a second she teased herself, feeling the juices flowing in her sex, but avoiding the temptation to sink down on the hard phallus she held firmly in her hand. She looked at Derek's body but not at his face. His face didn't matter. It didn't matter who he was. She was enjoying her role, playing the part of Clarissa, her face, she knew, bearing the expression of distant disdain Clarissa Peacham had perfected.

Gloria's sex life had never really been satisfactory, if she were honest with herself. She had rarely achieved orgasm and had never reached the shattering climaxes that other women seemed prone to achieve. Consequently she had never been that interested in sex or in men. She had had affairs but often preferred her own company. She had never felt like this before, her body seething with sensation. It was all to do with the way Clarissa had looked at her. She felt Clarissa had somehow looked into her soul, and knew something about her she did not know herself.

Sinking down on her haunches she buried Derek's cock in her body. He moaned loudly. She pulled herself up again. She could see Clarissa's eyes so clearly it was almost as if she were in the room.

'No,' he mumbled as she pushed down for the second time.

He gripped her thighs to prevent her rising off him again.

'You feel good,' she said. It was true. His cock was big and hot. She felt her sex clinging to it, her juices cascading over it.

'No,' he repeated, tossing his head from side to side. She saw his muscles go rigid. 'No.'

Inside her body she felt his cock jerk and kick. He was coming. A sticky wetness spurted out into the very centre of her.

With no thought for him, pulling against the hands that tried to hold her back, she bucked up off his body and back down again, riding him relentlessly before it was too late and his cock began to soften. It was enough. In four or five strokes she was on the brink of an orgasm that she knew would be stronger than anything she had ever experienced before. Suddenly, unaccountably, unbidden by anything she was conscious of, she had a crystal clear image of Clarissa, her long fingers snaking around the back of her neck, pulling her head until her lips were ground against that full rich mouth.

'God, God,' she breathed as she ground herself down on Derek's erection, trapping her clitoris between their bodies, as the orgasm took hold of her. She knew it was not Derek's cock that had plunged her into these unaccustomed pleasures but the thought of kissing Clarissa's inexplicably exciting mouth. She used every ounce of her strength to push his cock deeper, determined to enjoy the wonderful sensations for as long as possible.

It was difficult to work. All day Gloria found her mind drifting away from the storyboard on which she was trying to concentrate, and back to last night, trying to work out what had happened to her. Something had been set free, something that had been locked up in her mind and hidden away. Its release had caused her to have an orgasm more extensive and profound than anything she'd experienced before, of that she was positive. There could be no other cause. Derek's sexual prowess, and sudden ejaculation certainly hadn't been responsible. Much to Gloria's relief, he had made a feeble excuse and left quickly, scrambling into his clothes and out of her flat – and she suspected out of her life – minutes after his flaccid cock had been squeezed from her sex. No, the metaphorical bee that had got into Gloria's sexual bonnet was nothing to do with Derek.

It was everything to do with Clarissa and the enigma of the invitation to her house. Gloria had been convinced that Clarissa's motives were entirely to do with work, but now she was not so sure. Why, if it was work, should she want her to come to her home? It was a question her subconscious had answered for her, though it was an answer she found hard to accept.

It was mid-morning when William Briton arrived at her desk. She knew him from the company Christmas party last year. They had shared a corner, neither particularly interested in joining in with the group festivities. Gloria had been grateful that he had made no attempt to grope her or do anything but pass the time. It was only as he walked across the open plan office that she remembered the conversation they had had outside Ms Peacham's office.

'Well,' he said with no preliminaries, 'what did she say to you?' There was no need to ask who the 'she' was.

Gloria told him.

'Same here, exactly the same.'

'She asked you to her house?' Gloria asked.

'Yes. That's what I don't understand.'

'What do you thinks she wants?' The fact that William had been included in the invitation swung Gloria back to thinking it could only be a business matter.

'What do *you* think it's all about?' he asked.

'God knows.'

They went around in circles with ideas for awhile, William's apprehension and puzzlement as great as her own. In the end they decided there was nothing to do but wait and see.

The rest of the day passed slowly. At lunch Gloria thought of going to see William again but decided against it. She had tried to figure out if there was any connection between the two of them, something they shared in common, which might give a clue as to why they had both been selected for the same treatment, but could think of nothing, except perhaps that they were similar personalities. William, like her, had no family and few close friends, frequently preferring his own company, or so he had told her over the Christmas punch. How that coincidence related to Clarissa's invitation she did not know.

At five-thirty Gloria went to the ladies' room, washed her hands and touched up the very little make-up she wore. There wasn't time for her to go home first if she was to arrive at Clarissa's house at the appointed time and she definitely didn't want to be late. So she left the Peacham Associates office building and walked to Punishment Road, which was not that far away.

At six-fifteen she found a pub just around the corner from Clarissa's house and sat drinking an orange juice, so her breath wouldn't smell of alcohol, killing time. She had bought an *Evening Standard* on route and flicked through its pages without taking in a single word.

It was six-fifty-five when she rang the bell of the impressive Regency house on the corner of Punishment Road. As she heard the bell ring, deep somewhere inside her overriding feeling was one of excitement.

Chapter Two

WILLIAM

He stood outside the house, gazing up at it apprehensively. It was ten minutes to seven. The house was impressive. Standing on the corner of an immaculate Regency terrace, the tall, white painted walls and symmetrically placed windows formed a classic facade. Walking a little way down the street which intersected with the terrace William could see that it obviously had extensive grounds to the back of the building. A large back addition almost doubled the size of the original house. There was a high wall all the way along the back, topped with discreetly hidden razor wire. Security cameras were mounted on the side and front walls and under the columned portico that sheltered the front door.

William waited anxiously, hiding behind an ancient horse chestnut tree, not wanting to be seen from the house. He felt tired after his relatively sleepless night and had a tight knot in his stomach caused by an unshakeable conviction that what Ms Peacham was going to say to him – and to Gloria – was not going to be pleasant.

He saw Gloria walk down the street and mount the steps

that led up to the front door. For some reason he decided not to go in with her and shrunk back behind the tree until she had disappeared inside. She was early anyway, and he didn't want to be early.

At least now he was sure that the wild sexual scenarios he had imagined in the deepest watches of the night, and his incredibly vivid dream, were merely a figment of his over-wrought imagination. Gloria's invitation had confirmed that. Any idea he had harboured that Clarissa Peacham had somehow lighted on him as an object of sexual longing, was purely fanciful. The visit to the house had to be to do with business, though, for the life of him, (and having spent all day searching his recent work load looking for a cause) he could not imagine what business. Nor could he think of a reason why Gloria should be involved. She worked in a different department and their jobs did not overlap. There was no reason for them to be summoned together.

At precisely seven o'clock William came out from behind the tree and walked up to the black-painted front door. He heard a tiny whirr of electric motors and saw the security camera lens focus on him. There was an old-fashioned brass bell pull set in a circular recess to the side of the front door. His hand was trembling slightly as he pulled it. Somewhere in the depths of the building a bell sounded.

'Yes?' The large, panelled front door had opened and a woman in a plain black dress and white frilly apron stood in the doorway. She was slender but rather ungainly, her shoulders large, her waist thick and her legs, covered in black opaque stockings, lumpy. She was wearing what was very obviously a blonde wig and her face was caked in a thick powdery make-up

28

that did little to disguise her rather coarse complexion. Her expression was as blank as a stone wall.

'William Briton. I have an appointment . . .'

'This way,' the maid snapped before he could finish, her voice throaty and gruff. She stood aside so he could enter, then closed the door behind him. The vestibule was tiled in black-and-white marble, a sweeping staircase on the right-hand side leading up to a gallery on the first floor. Without another word the maid led the way down a long corridor, towards the back of the house. Her flat, clumpy black-laced shoes did nothing to improve the shape of her thick ankles.

At the end of the corridor she opened a plain door and indicated that he should go in. She closed the door smartly as soon as he had done so, the suddenness of the sound making him jump.

Gloria was there waiting nervously, perched on the edge of an uncomfortable wooden chair. The room was small and barely furnished. There were two other wooden chairs and a small table. The single window was glazed in frosted glass. It was a room designed to increase anxiety, where it was impossible to relax or be distracted.

'Hi,' William said weakly. He did not want to meet Gloria's eyes.

'Hi,' she said apparently not wanting eye contact either.

By some mutual and unspoken agreement they said nothing else, each wrapped up in their own private apprehensions as to what was about to occur, neither willing to voice their fears, the companionship they had shared this morning melted away by the proximity of the event.

Sitting in a chair opposite Gloria, William looked at her

surreptitiously. She was a woman more interested in her career than her appearance and he had never really looked beyond her rather dowdy clothes, and uncompromisingly plain make-up, but now he saw that she was attractive. Her hair was short, dark and rich, and cut in layers, a style that suited her rather round face. She had large brown eyes, a slightly retroussé nose, a small but beautifully formed mouth and bones that made distinct ridges high on her cheeks. She had a slender and curvaceous figure and shapely legs.

Gloria was sitting with her elbows on her knees, her face cradled in her hands and she was wearing the same clothes she had worn in the office: a plain brown suit with a cream blouse. William could just glimpse the outline of a white bra supporting a full bosom. Her skirt was knee length and, as she sat primly with her knees together, he could see her finely contoured calves, clad in tan coloured nylon. She wore brown shoes with a low heel.

Half-an-hour passed in silence, each of them finding it more difficult to contain their nervousness, fidgeting uneasily on the hard chairs but unwilling to communicate their anxieties or make eye contact, their mutual apprehension obvious from their body language, their conviction that the interview to come was not going to be pleasant becoming more and more deep-rooted.

The door opened with no warning, making them both start.

'This way,' the blonde-wigged maid said eyeing them both, William thought, with a look of undisguised disdain, before striding off down the corridor, expecting them to follow.

By the time they had caught up with her she was standing by another door in the long corridor not far from the marble floored vestibule. She knocked on the panelled door twice.

'Come.' The voice from inside belonged to Clarissa Peacham.

William glanced at Gloria as the maid opened the door. For the first time the brunette met his gaze, the expression of trepidation written in her face an exact reflection of what he knew she would be able to read in his own.

The maid stood aside to let them into the room but did not enter herself, shutting the door again as soon as they were inside.

The room was a complete contrast to the austerity of the one they had just left. A thick burgundy red carpet was matched by the burgundy colour of the walls. Dark blue drapes were tied back at the side of two large casement windows. One whole wall was fitted from floor to ceiling with oak shelves piled high with books. To the side of this was a massive walnut desk, two boards of solid wood sandwiched together and supported on a chromium metal frame. In front of the desk were two steel chairs in an ultra modern design, their ebony seats almost as narrow and uncomfortable as the saddles of a racing bicycle. There was a long, low sofa upholstered in brown leather, an occasional table also made from walnut and two futuristic speakers, though William could not see any other hi-fi equipment in the room. In one corner, recessed into the wall was a glass cocktail cabinet.

Clarissa Peacham sat behind the desk in a high-backed swivel chair, its brown leather the exact match of the sofa. To one side of her, on the desk, was an antique solid silver tray, on which was set a silver ice bucket. The bucket contained an open bottle of Perrier Jouet champagne packed in ice cubes. A

31

half empty champagne flute, a long cigar shape in plain glass, was being twirled by its stem between Clarissa's fingers.

'Sit down,' she said indicating the steel chairs, her voice betraying no emotion.

As they obeyed she took a sip of the champagne. She was wearing a pale yellow dress made from the softest suede, its scooped neckline revealing a deep cleavage and the billowing upper surfaces of her breasts, its skirt, unusually, covering most of her thighs. Her chestnut hair had been gathered in a pleat and pinned at the back of her head, giving her an air of severity.

'Well . . .' She put the glass down on the table, reached for the bottle, carefully refilled her glass before crushing the bottle down into the ice again. Leaning back, she looked from William to Gloria, as though they were interesting exhibits in a museum. She was in no hurry. She smiled and licked her top lip with the tip of her tongue.

'First let me thank you for coming here. I think this sort of thing is better done out of the office.' That gave no clue as to what 'this sort of thing' might turn out to be. She paused again.

William had the impression she was enjoying herself, toying with them, like a cat with an injured mouse.

'I have here,' she said as she opened a buff coloured folder, 'assessments of both your performances in the company over the last six months. I have to say, it makes very depressing reading.' Clarissa looked at the file once more, then flipped it closed and put it aside. She rested her head on the back of the leather chair and ran a finger under the neckline of the dress and over the top of her left breast. 'You see I'm sure you understand it's a very competitive environment out there. I have to insist on certain basic standards. If I find that my employees fall below these standards . . . well to be blunt, under the circumstances, I really cannot afford to keep them on.'

'What?' Gloria said.

'I don't understand . . .' William blurted out simultaneously.

'What don't you understand, Mr Briton?' Clarissa snapped, leaning forward again and staring straight into his eyes.

'I've not been told my work was unsatisfactory,' he persisted despite the fact that the intensity of her gaze had made his knees go weak.

'Nor mine,' Gloria added at once.

'Is that relevant?' Clarissa replied calmly.

'Yes I think . . . I mean, shouldn't we have been warned first if something was wrong?' William said.

'I take the view, Mr Briton, that if someone is not up to the job that's an end of it. I see no point in prolonging the agony as far as they are concerned.' She picked up the champagne flute and sipped at the wine.

'I don't think that's fair,' Gloria said.

'If you are considering a complaint for unfair dismissal I don't think we would have much trouble in establishing your work is lazy and slip-shod,' Clarissa snapped, picking up the buff file then slamming it down on the desk again. 'But, of course, that is your prerogative. You may go now.'

'Just like that?' William snorted.

'Yes, just like that, Mr Briton.' Clarissa smiled, a rather odd crooked smile.

The words began to sink in. He was fired, out-of-work,

33

sacked. Of all the things William had imagined would come up this evening being told that he was out of a job was not one of them. He couldn't believe it. He couldn't believe there was anything wrong with his work. Worse still, the employment market was flooded with computer programmers. It might be months, even years before he found another job. He could see that Gloria was as flabbergasted as he was.

'Look . . . isn't there . . . isn't there anything we can do? I'm sure I speak for both of us. Couldn't we be given another chance?'

'Yes. Please,' Gloria said sounding equally desperate, the prospect of unemployment obviously just as bleak for her.

'No,' Clarissa said simply.

'Please . . .' William's heart was pounding, a film of sweat breaking out on his upper lip. He would have thrown himself at her feet if he'd thought it would do any good.

'Please, Ms Peacham, I need this job. If I've made mistakes I only need to be told what they are. No one's said anything. I just need to be told . . .' Gloria was close to tears.

Clarissa Peacham got to her feet and walked over to the window. The room overlooked the gardens of the Regency square in front of the house. She gazed out at the big horse chestnut trees that dominated the greenery. It was a long time before she came back to the desk, a deliberately long time, so they would be able to ponder the severity of their situation. It was part of her calculations.

Clarissa had worked it all out, selected them carefully, just as she'd selected all the others. They were loners. No family. Few friends. No one to ask questions. They were average

34

performers, not high-flyers, not the sort of people another company would snap up the moment they became available. For them the prospect of unemployment was all too real. In her experience it was better if they had experienced difficulties with the opposite sex – as she knew both William and Gloria had. William's wife had run off with another man and Gloria had never established a long-term relationship. Clarissa had had them investigated thoroughly. It had not been difficult. Their regular assessment interviews had contained more personal questions than was usual for this very reason. Clarissa studied the files of all personnel for her own purposes.

William Briton and Gloria Price were the perfect candidates for what she had in mind. Naturally there was nothing wrong with their work, but they were not secure enough or confident enough to challenge her on that point.

'If there was any way . . .' William said right on cue.

'Yes,' Gloria agreed. 'Anything.'

Clarissa enjoyed the moment like a hunter about to spring a trap. She sipped her champagne, savouring the fear she had inspired in their faces, and the power she had over them. That was all part of the fun after all. She allowed herself to smile, a soft, kind smile this time.

'Well . . .' she said slowly, 'I suppose . . .'

'Yes?' They hung on her every word, their faces lit up with hope.

'No, no it's not appropriate,' Clarissa said sharply. She had shown them a glimmer of light at the end of the tunnel, then slammed the door in their faces. She almost laughed as she saw their expressions change to despair again. 'You may go,' she said curtly.

'Please . . .' William was begging now. In the last few minutes he had obviously convinced himself he would never get a job ever again.

The moment had arrived. Clarissa let them wait a little longer, teasing them, stretching their emotional limit.

'Well, I suppose . . .' She counted to ten, the feeling she always got in this situation coursing through her veins, a pleasure as pure as sex, toying with lives like the Emperors of ancient Rome. How she would have loved *that*, the turn of a thumb sending the gladiator to his death or his freedom. This was less dramatic but just as thrilling. 'Perhaps something could be arranged. As you see this is a very large house. It needs a very large staff to keep it in order. Let us say, for the sake of argument, that you were prepared to come and work here for me, for a period of time, say one month . . . then . . . assuming your work was satisfactory, you could return to your jobs in the company. Your work would have to improve, of course, out of all recognition, but you would be reinstated.'

She saw the blank look on their faces, as they struggled to digest what she was suggesting. She attempted no clarification, not yet at least.

WILLIAM

'You want us to work as servants?' William asked. His heart was thumping. For some reason he could not understand it was thumping with what he could only describe as excitement.

'Yes.'

'But then we get our jobs back?' From the tone of her voice it clearly didn't make any sense to Gloria.

'Yes.'

'I suppose I wouldn't mind,' Gloria said.

'Right . . .' William agreed hesitantly still not really sure what was going on inside his head.

'Of course,' Clarissa sat down in the brown leather swivel chair and leant forward, her elbows on the desk, her chestnut coloured eyes sparkling, 'I shall demand absolute obedience.'

There was something about the way she said the word 'obedience' that made the hair on the back of William's neck prickle.

'Obedience?' he queried his voice faltering.

'It is only fair to tell you that besides your normal household chores, there would be other more onerous duties.' She leant back in the chair, swung it around to the side and crossed her legs.

'What . . .' William's voice was so hoarse he had to clear his throat. 'What other duties?'

Clarissa Peacham smiled a wicked smile. She looked from one to the other.

'You are both attractive. You will be required to perform services of a somewhat personal nature, both for me and for my guests.' The finger was tracing along the line of her bosom again.

'I don't understand,' Gloria said. William shook his head in agreement.

Clarissa laughed. 'What – did you think I'd give you your jobs back in return for a little cleaning and dusting? That's barely credible is it?' she scorned.

'What then?' William said fearing the answer.

'Perhaps a little demonstration would be the best way to

illustrate the point.' Clarissa rested her head against the back of the chair and closed her eyes for a moment, as if she were enjoying a wave of physical pleasure. She opened them again and looked directly at William. 'Mr Briton . . . William . . .' she used his Christian name for the first time. 'Let's see if you can demonstrate your . . . willingness.'

The intense glare from Clarissa's eyes was like the beams of two powerful headlights. William felt himself drawn towards them, like a frightened rabbit.

'Take off your jacket. Lay it over the back of the chair. I want you to clean my shoes, William. Come round the desk here.'

William got to his feet. He was wearing the suit he always wore for work, a rather shabby brown check. He pulled the jacket off and folded it over the back of the chair then walked round the desk. He looked down at Clarissa's shoes. They were yellow to match the dress, with a spiky heel and black piping decorating the top edge. They were perfectly clean. As usual her legs were sheathed in very sheer hosiery.

'Get on your knees,' she said quietly.

William obeyed. He experienced another jolt of excitement he did not understand. He looked around for something to clean the shoes with, expecting her to produce a duster or a brush.

'What are you waiting for?' she snapped irritably.

'What do you want me to use?'

'You are slow aren't you? I want you to use your tongue.' She showed not a flicker of emotion as she said the words.

'My tongue!' His exclamation was a reflex. 'You must be joking.' He looked into her eyes. They told him she was in deadly earnest.

38

'Do it,' she said quietly.

'I . . . you can't . . .' He looked at Gloria but oddly, though he could see surprise in her eyes he could not see any distaste. In fact it was almost as though she was enjoying the spectacle.

'I don't want a conversation, William, I want your obedience. If you are not prepared to do as I say you must leave immediately. It is your choice.' Clarissa watched him carefully. William knew that the flame of rebellion in his eyes had died, quenched by the thought of the future that awaited him if he did not obey. He also knew that she saw something else there too, something he could not disguise – a glimmer of excitement.

Her legs were still crossed. She flexed the upper one and pointed her toe. 'Don't disappoint me William,' she said.

William looked at her long legs. He had never seen them this close before. They were superb, curved and contoured and sleek, the well-defined muscles of her calves tapering into her narrow pinched ankles. He needed to bend forward only very slightly to reach the leather of her shoe with his mouth.

'William . . .' The voice was harsher, impatience mounting.

What else could he do? Without further hesitation he pressed his lips against the yellow leather, then, self-consciously, began to lick it. Almost immediately his cock stirred. It was the last thing he had expected to happen. He suddenly remembered his dream and how she had demanded he lick her feet.

'Good boy,' Clarissa said. 'Isn't he a good boy Gloria?'

Gloria was staring at him. 'Yes,' she said barely audibly.

The words seemed to engorge his cock further. He felt it fighting to escape the constriction of his pants and trousers. He tried to concentrate on what he was doing, moving over the toe of the shoe and then right around to the heel.

Without a word Clarissa uncrossed her legs then crossed them again, bringing her other shoe up to his mouth. The view this action produced made William's erection swell further. The suede of the dress had lifted and he had glimpsed her thighs. She was not wearing tights but stockings, their tops pulled taut by long black suspenders. But more than that, much more, he had seen above the stockings, to the very apex of her thighs. No panties covered her sex. In that momentary glimpse he had seen the dark slit of her labia fringed thickly by brown pubic hair.

Her shoe tapped against his cheek as a reminder that his work was only half completed. He started to lick the leather again, at the same time trying to look up under her skirt. He could just see the tops of the stockings and the clip of one suspender but the view above that had disappeared.

'Stand up,' Clarissa said suddenly.

It was the one thing he couldn't do. His cock was fully erect. He didn't think he'd ever felt it so hard. If he stood up it would tent his trousers unmistakably.

'Stand up,' she snapped again.

'I haven't finished,' he mumbled trying to continue to lick her shoe.

Clarissa snatched her foot away.

'I'm not going to ask you again.'

He had no choice. He got to his feet. His cock stuck out from the front of his trousers, its shape outlined under the material.

'I thought so,' Clarissa said with satisfaction.

'I didn't mean to . . .'

'Shut up. Did I give you permission to look at my legs?'

'No, but I couldn't help it.' William had thought the situation might deflate his erection. Instead it seemed to be getting harder.

'Well what do you expect me to do now?'

'It's just . . .' He couldn't think of anything to say.

'Can you see this Gloria? Look at the state of him.'

Gloria nodded.

'Well since your cock is so intent on drawing attention to itself we might as well see the whole thing.'

'What!'

'Take it out.'

'I'm not . . .' William stopped as he realised what he was saying. 'I really didn't mean to look. It just happened. It won't happen again.'

'I want to see it William. Do as I say.' The words rang out like shots from a gun.

William felt his pulse racing. Short of walking out, into certain unemployment, what could he do? He was in no position to refuse this implacable woman however embarrassing her requests. He unbuckled his belt and unzipped his flies. Taking the waistband of his trousers and briefs together he dropped them down to his knees. He straightened up. His cock, freed at last, sprung out from his belly. He'd hoped it would shrivel up under Clarissa's withering glare. Instead it throbbed and jerked with excitement.

'Bend over the desk,' Clarissa said calmly pushing the leather blotter along the surface until it was in front of him.

'What for?'

'Don't dare to answer me back,' she snarled. 'If you are to serve me in this house you have to learn to obey without

41

question. Is that clear? You must learn you will be punished for any failure to do so. If you refuse to be punished you will be thrown out and that will be the end of your chances of reinstatement in your careers. Is that clear to both of you?'

What alternative did he have? 'Yes,' he said.

The chestnut eyes turned to Gloria, the question lingering.

'Yes,' Gloria said.

'Are you going to bend over then?'

He had never been in a more humiliating situation in his life, but apparently, and to his amazement, his cock was harder than he could ever remember it being. Dancing in front of his eyes too was the memory of the tantalising glimpse of stocking tops, suspenders and hair fringed labia. It seemed to have burnt into his mind like a brief glance at the sun imprinted on the retina.

He folded his arms on the walnut desk and rested his head on them, his trousers and briefs dropping to his ankles as he bent over. His naked buttocks felt incredibly vulnerable.

Clarissa got up from the swivel chair. Lying on the surface of the desk was a long thin strip of metal. It might have been a ruler but had no markings and was twice the usual length. Clarissa picked it up and flexed it against the desk. It bent into a semi-circle.

'Start as we mean to go on,' she said.

'Look I really didn't mean . . .' A dagger of fear had stabbed into William as he saw what she obviously intended to use on him.

Like a cat springing on its prey Clarissa's hand lashed out and grabbed William by the hair. 'Don't think,' she snapped lowering her face so their eyes were no more than six inches apart. 'Just do.'

She released her grip looking at Gloria, her crooked smile changing the symmetry of her face again.

'Six, I think,' she said.

William saw Clarissa's fingers, their nails varnished a dark blood red, curl around the ruler. His cock was pressed between his navel and the desk and he could feel it twitching, like an animal trying to escape a trap. His emotions were running riot. The humiliation of being in this position, bent over a desk like a naughty schoolboy, was making him seethe with anger: he wanted to tell Clarissa Peacham what she could do with her job. He wanted to get up and storm out. But he knew he wasn't going to do that, partly because of his fear of unemployment, but also, he began to realise, for another reason. That reason was excitement, sexual excitement, of an intensity he could not remember experiencing before. It made his pulse race, his mouth dry and his cock so hard he thought it might burst. In fact he was so excited, his cock throbbing so much, he had the terrible thought he might not be able to control himself, that he might shoot his semen all over the leather blotter. The image of her labia, nestled at the top of her fleshy, stockinged thighs, popped into his mind again.

'You want it don't you?' she whispered as if she could read his mind. 'I knew. I knew William.'

He didn't understand what she meant. Knew what? Knew that being treated like this would excite him? How could she have known that? He didn't know it himself.

Thwack. A sudden stripe of pain seared across his buttocks, so unexpectedly – he hadn't even realised she had lifted her arm – he reared up from the desk and grabbed his buttocks in both hands.

'Get down,' Clarissa's voice was firm but not angry. She knew he was reacting to pain not trying to rebel.

For a moment William looked into her eyes. She was looking at him like an indulgent teacher with a pupil who had to learn something new and difficult.

'William,' she said.

He lowered himself back on to the desk-top, the pain that had coursed through him seconds before turning to waves of heat, heat that was streaked with pleasure. He realised with astonishment that he wanted the second stroke. He didn't know what was happening to him, and didn't want to work it out. He just wanted to feel another stripe of pain translate itself to burning pleasure.

But Clarissa made him wait.

GLORIA

'Now I think you should participate in our little demonstration.' Clarissa was looking across the desk at Gloria. 'You I think, are a very different animal.'

Gloria was not at all sure what that meant. Her reaction to what had happened to William was very similar to what he was only too obviously experiencing. She felt an almost sickly excitement which she did not understand. She knew her sex had moistened but she did not know why.

'Stand up.'

Gloria looked into Clarissa's eyes. She found nothing there but the unwavering demand that she comply. Slowly she got to her feet.

'Good. Now take your jacket off.'

Almost in a trance, Clarissa's fierce eyes hypnotising her, Gloria obeyed, folding it over the back of the steel chair just as William had done.

'Now your blouse.' Clarissa demanded.

'What?' That request jolted her out of her reverie.

'Your blouse, take it off.'

'I don't think—'

'Gloria. Do I have to remind you of your circumstances? If you do not wish to obey me you may leave. Go now.'

'No.'

'Then do as I say.'

Gloria's hands were trembling as she reached for the little buttons on the front of her blouse. She undid them one by one, then pulled the material from her skirt. She looked into Clarissa's eyes and remembered the way they had looked at her yesterday: she couldn't get rid of the idea they had wanted to see her naked. Now it was quite obvious from the expression on Clarissa's face that Gloria's intuition was right. Clarissa's eyes sparkled with excitement.

Gloria stripped the blouse off her shoulders. Though William was still bent over the desk she could see his eyes looking up at her.

'Now your bra,' Clarissa said, her voice cool and calm.

Gloria knew it was now her turn to cross the line that William had crossed. She must either grab her things and storm out – or meekly remove her bra and display her breasts.

Slowly Gloria reached behind her back for the clip of the white bra. She felt as though someone else was performing the movement, not her, as though she were watching from above, seeing a stranger's hands undoing the little hooks, slipping the thin straps off her shoulders, hugging the bra cups to her breasts before finally, and decisively, throwing the white lace aside. Her breasts were very round and firm, her nipples, puckered and hard. What she had felt about Clarissa last night seemed to have re-asserted itself in spades.

'I think you would enjoy doing the honours now, don't you?' Clarissa said. Gloria could see her eyes looking at her naked breasts.

'What do you mean?'

'You know what I mean Gloria. Take your skirt off, you'll be more comfortable.'

'My skirt?'

'Yes,' Clarissa said gently. 'Don't be shy. You've got nothing to be ashamed of. You're very attractive. Take your skirt off now, let me see your legs. Don't make me angry.'

Gloria unfastened the zip of her skirt and let it drop to the floor. She stepped out of it but didn't pick it up. She was wearing pretty white lace panties under her tights. They matched her bra. The expression in Clarissa's eyes as they roamed her body was exactly the look that had haunted and provoked her last night. Once again she had the strange feeling that Clarissa knew more about her than she knew about herself.

'Very pretty,' Clarissa said. 'A little more attention to what you wear and a little more make-up and you will be quite lovely. Now come round here.'

Gloria walked around the desk a little unsteadily, as though the strong emotions she was experiencing had intoxicated her. She looked down at William's naked buttocks. A red weal, scarlet in some places, pink in others, crossed his white flesh.

She could hear him breathing shallowly, his embarrassment overcome by excitement.

Clarissa extended her hand and stroked Gloria's cheek with the back of her hand. She looked straight into her eyes. 'What are you feeling?'

'I don't know,' Gloria said without thinking. The touch of Clarissa's hand made her shiver. She had an almost irresistible urge to kiss her fingers but managed to stop herself.

'You will know soon. You'll know everything. Here.' She handed her the thin strip of metal.

Gloria still had the feeling this was happening to someone else, as though it was a stranger's hand, not hers, that grasped the cold metal.

'Put your hand here,' Clarissa instructed touching the small of William's back and making him start. 'Come on,' she chided when Gloria did not respond at once.

Gloria rested her left hand at the bottom of William's spine, the ruler in her right. She had never done anything like this before but clearly there was no choice. Whatever was going to happen to her in the next month she would have to learn to accept it. Trying to keep her mind blank she raised the metal ruler and brought it swinging down on William's buttocks. The blow was ineffectual. There was no thwack as there had been with Clarissa's stroke and William hardly reacted at all.

'No, no, harder than that,' Clarissa said.

Gloria felt the chill of Clarissa's annoyance like a blast of cold air. She had been unemployed for two years before getting the job at Peacham Associates and did not want to be unemployed again. Quickly she raised her right arm, took aim this time, and slashed the ruler down with a satisfying reverberation of steel on flesh. William gasped, the stroke much harder than Clarissa's blow. A red weal appeared immediately.

'Better. Again now,' Clarissa said.

Gloria experienced an odd sensation, like a rush of blood to the head. It was as though something had snapped in her and released a crimson flood of raw emotion, a little like the sensation she had experienced last night. She raised her hand again and smacked the ruler down, wanting to make William gasp, wanting to see his flesh crawl and feel the heat from another weal radiating up from his buttocks.

'No,' he cried, the second blow from Gloria even harder than the first. But he did not rear up from the desk.

'That's right,' Clarissa said approvingly.

But Gloria wasn't doing it for Clarissa's approval now. She was doing it for herself, though she was not sure why. Perhaps it was a way of relieving her own anger at her situation. In quick succession she rained three more strokes down on the prone buttocks and then, when Clarissa did not stop her, delivered a fourth and a fifth.

William's whole body was trembling, she could see. He was moaning continuously. Though she did not know how, never having done anything like this in her life before, Gloria knew the stripes that criss-crossed his white buttocks were provoking him beyond endurance. She knew he was going to come. She looked up at Clarissa wanting to be told what to do. She didn't know whether she would be grateful or disappointed if she was ordered to stop.

'You can see it can't you?' Clarissa said. 'Do it then.'

It would only take one more blow. She raised her right hand

and swung it down harder than any of the other strokes. The thwack seemed to echo around the room. Without thinking Gloria threw the ruler aside and used her hand to caress the raw, super-heated flesh, responding to an instinct she didn't know she possessed. William quivered at the touch of her cool fingers. As she ran her hand over the incredibly hot weals on his buttocks she felt him shudder.

'No,' he gasped. His body shuddered twice in rapid succession then slumped forward on the desk in complete collapse.

Clarissa Peacham smiled to herself. She had not missed a thing. Her eyes moved from William to Gloria. She had chosen well. Both her victims were perfect. Both had responded exactly as she had thought they would. Both would be easy to train, pliant and suggestible, putty in her hands.

'You did well,' Clarissa said. 'Tell me what you feel now?'

'Excitement,' Gloria said unequivocally because it was true. Her sex was wet and throbbing.

'Good,' Clarissa said.

Gloria looked into Clarissa's eyes. What she saw there shocked her. It was desire, sexual desire, need even. Desire and need for her. No woman had ever looked at her like this so blatantly before. Clarissa raised her hand and she watched it descend, as if in slow motion, to her naked breast cupping itself around the perfect sphere. Without taking her hand away Clarissa moved to stand behind Gloria, cupping her other breast too, then hugging the brunette to her, as she lowered her mouth to her neck and kissed it.

'I can feel how excited you are,' she whispered. 'I know what you want.'

'Please . . .' Gloria moaned not knowing whether she was begging for more or for less.

Clarissa's right hand left her breast and delved below the waistband of her tights. In less than a second, as though drawn there by some invisible magnet, her middle finger had slipped though Gloria's thick black pubic hair into the furrow of her sex. It found her clitoris.

'God, God . . .' Gloria muttered. No woman had ever touched her there. The finger pressed the tiny clit against the hardness of her pubic bone. Her mind was in a whirl. This was so sudden. There were so many things she had not experienced before and each, it appeared, was more exciting than the last. She felt Clarissa's heavy tits pressing against her shoulder blades. Despite the suede dress she could swear she could feel her nipples, hard as pebbles, trapped between their bodies. What she had felt last night was like a premonition of what she was feeling now. She shouldn't be enjoying it, she shouldn't be responding in this way, but it was beyond her control.

'Please, please,' she moaned as the finger started to move, dragging her already engorged clit from side to side. The touch was perfect, the right pressure, the right tempo, in exactly the right place. She couldn't remember a man who had ever touched her so tellingly.

As unexpectedly as everything else that had happened to her, she knew she was going to come. She could feel her wetness soaking into her tights and her body melting over Clarissa's single finger. She threw her hand back until it rested on Clarissa's shoulder, the tendons of her neck stretched taut. As Clarissa's lips fastened on her neck again, and the fingers of her left hand pinched gently at her nipple, the two feelings arced down to join the electricity generated in her clit. That trinity of sensations produced a spark that lit up every nerve in her body. She felt a rush of pure pleasure, her body quivering from head to toe, the force of her orgasm surpassing what she had felt last night.

Clarissa held her tight, letting her climax run its course. Finally, feeling all her energy leech away, she released her. 'That was only the beginning,' she said softly in her ear.

It must be true. She was prepared to believe everything Clarissa told her. Twice in twenty-four hours she had experienced orgasms so rich and so rapid she could hardly believe her body was capable of such responses, after years of frustration. But she knew the responsibility lay with Clarissa. Last night it was the memory of her eyes that had brought her to a shattering climax. Tonight the cause had been more direct. But either way Clarissa had found a way through her body's defences, given her the ability to experience sexual gratification the like of which she had never known.

Clarissa saw it all in her eyes. The moment was right to take things further.

'Touch my breast now, Gloria,' she said turning the girl round to face her.

'Your breast?' Gloria said, still not down from the highs she had reached.

'You must learn to obey. You must learn to please me.' Clarissa's voice was quiet and gentle. 'You want to please me don't you?'

'Oh yes,' Gloria said. But her feelings were confused. As she came back to reality it was difficult to accept it was a woman who had given her such incredible sexual satisfaction.

'You can tell yourself that you are doing it because I have ordered you to do it,' Clarissa said. It was quite obvious from Gloria's reactions she had never had a woman before.

Gloria told herself exactly that. She simply had no choice. She extended her hand and cupped it over the yellow suede on Clarissa's left breast. She thought she could feel Clarissa's heart beating but it might well have been her own, her pulse was pounding so strongly in her veins.

'What do I do now?' she said her voice like a child asking an adult for advice with a problem they could not understand.

'What do you want to do?'

'Kiss you.' She blurted it out before she realised what she was saying. But to her astonishment Gloria realised it was true.

Clarissa laughed, throwing her head back and producing a strident sound that rattled around the room. 'You do learn quickly don't you?' She traced her finger over Gloria's small mouth. 'Lovely mouth,' she said. 'Lovely delicate lips.' Then in an entirely different tone of voice she said brusquely, 'You may put your clothes on now. And you,' she added, tapping William's buttocks. 'Get up.'

Her mood had changed. She walked around William and sat back in the swivel chair, crossing her legs.

'Listen carefully,' she said.

Gloria, in an almost trance like state, groped for her clothes as she saw William pull his trousers and briefs up around his hips. His cock was flaccid. The white blotting paper on the leather blotter had absorbed his semen.

'You have until six o'clock tomorrow to put your affairs in order,' Clarissa continued. 'I will tell your supervisors at work you will not be reporting for one month. You will have to make whatever arrangements you need to make bearing in mind you will not be permitted to leave this house again until you have fulfilled your . . .' she searched for the right word, 'obligations here. You will return to this house at precisely six o'clock tomorrow evening. If you are late, or if you do not turn up, your employment with Peacham Associates will be terminated forthwith. Naturally in that event you will not be given references. There is no need for you to bring any clothes, or toiletries. Everything you need will be provided.'

As if by some pre-arranged signal, there was a knock on the door and the maid entered unbidden. Clarissa picked up another file and laid its contents out on the desk, studying them carefully. They were clearly dismissed.

'This way,' the maid said in her odd, husky voice. 'Come on,' she said when they didn't react immediately.

Gloria started towards the door her emotions in turmoil. It felt like a bucket of cold water had been thrown over her, dousing the extraordinary passion she had felt. But it had only been partially successful. Her body still quivered with the aftershocks of her orgasm and her mind was reeling, unable to dismiss the desire she had felt, nor cope with it. She couldn't work out how she had been able to feel such intense need for a woman when she had never even dreamt of such a thing before. The idea of being attracted to a woman was preposterous and yet that was precisely what she had felt.

She had still not buttoned up her blouse and was holding her jacket in one hand as they were ushered to the front door. William's shirt, she noticed was hanging out of the back of his trousers.

In seconds they found themselves outside on the street, the contrast between the intimate activity they had been engaged in only minutes before, and the real world reinforcing Gloria's feelings of confusion. Clouds had gathered and it was beginning to drizzle with rain.

Curiously she had no desire to discuss what had happened with William and fortunately he seemed to feel exactly the same way. They both stood looking out at Punishment Road, dazzled and disorientated.

'See you tomorrow,' William said, the first to move.

'Yes,' Gloria replied.

Gloria took the opposite direction to William as he walked off down the road. She badly wanted to be on her own. As she walked a movement caught her eye and she looked up at the front of the house. Clarissa stood in the window gazing out. She gave no sign that she saw Gloria, just stared ahead, appearing to see nothing.

Chapter Three

WILLIAM

What did it mean? That's what he kept asking himself. What did it mean? How could it have happened? Like an automaton he had gone to bed almost as soon as he'd got home and, to his surprise, had fallen asleep immediately, the sort of sleep that comes from exhaustion, deep and apparently dreamless.

In the morning, he had woken with an erection so hard it felt as though it were made of steel. As he rolled onto his back consciousness only partially returned, a sting of pain from his backside bringing everything that had happened flooding back in a rush, the sensation only serving to further enlarge his already rampant cock. He moved on to his side and used his right hand to explore his buttocks, withdrawing hastily as his fingers found the weals the metal ruler had made, and produced another sharp stab of pain.

He got to his feet and stared over his shoulder in the mirror opposite the bed. His buttocks were criss-crossed with marks, some light pink, some a deep scarlet, and with every shade of red in between, along at least four distinct lines. Gingerly he touched them again, but found they reacted angrily.

His erection was as uncomfortable as his buttocks. Usually his early morning erections subsided the moment he got up but today's showed no sign of diminishing. He took it in his hand and looked at it in the mirror. It felt strangely insensitive, like a thing that had been attached to his body, the lever of some machine the function of which he did not understand. He wanked it gently a couple of times but it did not respond. He ran his finger around the rim of the circumcised glans, a movement that usually produced a spasm of feeling, but got none. He suddenly saw Clarissa's eyes. They were looking at him with a stern admonition, as if he were not allowed to touch his cock. He took his hand away. He stared at it in the mirror. He had the strangest feeling it did not belong to him any more.

It did not take him long to make the necessary arrangements to leave his flat unattended for a month. His neighbour was willing to water his plants and his bills were all paid by direct debit. He had no close friends to tell, his ex-wife would certainly not care, and his only family was a maiden aunt he only saw once in a blue moon.

What did it mean? The experience with Clarissa, kneeling at her feet and licking her shoes, had left him with a whole panoply of emotions he did not understand. He had never been so humiliated in his life. It had been bad enough getting an erection under such circumstances, but having to stand up and display it, in front of two women, had added insult to injury. And yet the whole experience had excited him: that is what he could not understand. Admittedly, it was partly to do with Clarissa. After fantasising over her for so long it was not surprising that any contact, however bizarre, had caused him to have an erection, and the glimpse of her sex and her long

56

legs sheathed in sheer stockings had only reinforced it. But he would have expected the way Clarissa had subsequently treated him, the contempt and disdain she had shown him, to pour a damper on his excitement, not to inflame it further. But it had, and he could not deny it.

Her treatment of him had touched a nerve in his sexual psyche that had never been touched before. And the strokes of the metal ruler had had the same effect. What Clarissa's contempt and his humiliation had provoked, the metal ruler had intensified to such an extent, and so surprisingly, that there was nothing he had been able to do to prevent his ejaculation. He had never been beaten at school, and, though he was perfectly aware that it was a common sexual fetish, it was never something he had imagined would bring him sexual satisfaction. But he could not forget the way the stripes of pain had exploded across his buttocks, and how the heat they had generated had turned to intense, squirming pleasure.

In fact he could forget nothing about last night. He reviewed everything that had happened and, instead of feeling shame at his humiliation, felt only arousal. From what he had seen of Gloria's performance, and the way she had reacted to Clarissa's ministrations, the super-charged atmosphere had affected her in exactly the same way.

As to what was going to happen to them both over the next month, what services they would be required to perform, and to whom, William preferred not to speculate. He only knew he clearly had no choice. Clarissa had trapped him.

He suspected that there had been nothing wrong with his work – or Gloria's for that matter – and that the whole scenario had been manufactured for Clarissa's own reasons. But what could he do? A complaint to an Industrial Relations Tribunal would take months and he'd still be out of work. There was simply no alternative to going along with Clarissa's demands. He needed his job at Peacham Associates and Clarissa Peacham knew that only too well.

At five o'clock he locked the front door of his flat and walked down to the street. It would take him forty minutes to get to Punishment Road and he didn't want to be late. As he walked to the tube station he felt a knot tying itself in the pit of his stomach. He might have expected it to be apprehension but, if he were honest with himself he knew that, as the appointed hour approached it was excitement that dominated his feelings.

GLORIA

'Sorry, he's not here.'

'Can you get hold of him?'

'I doubt it.'

'You don't know where he is?'

'No.'

'Well can you leave a message in case he comes back. Ask him to ring Gloria.'

'Gloria. Got it. Has he got your number?'

'Yes.' But Gloria gave it again.

'Right,' Derek's flatmate said, reading the number back to her.

Gloria put the phone down. She was desperate. She must have been desperate to try and get hold of Derek. She hadn't ever imagined wanting to see him again. She'd prayed he would be in but his flatmate said he'd gone out at eight and he didn't know when he'd be back.

It wasn't that Gloria had a sudden desire for him. She didn't. But he was all that was available and she *did* have a sudden and unbelievable desire for a man, any man. To be more accurate she needed a cock, a hard, pulsing cock to fill the enormous void she felt inside her. It was, she knew, a feeling that Clarissa had created.

Her sex demanded all her attention. It had from the moment she'd got home. She had stripped her clothes off and taken a shower, and the sight of her naked body, in the bathroom mirror, had caused her to tremble from head to toe. Wrapping herself in a towelling robe hadn't helped. Her nipples, rubbing against the rough material, were alive with sensation, taut and corrugated. But they were only an extension of what was happening in her sex. That was seething. Not only was her clitoris throbbing wildly – the impression Clarissa's finger had left on it so strong it was almost as though it were still there – but her labia were lubricated by a flood of juices that would not stop. Above all, Gloria was aware of her vagina contracting relentlessly as though longing to be filled. Some of the contractions were so strong they made Gloria moan with their intensity.

She had to have relief. She had to have a man. Sitting on her double bed she dialled the number of her previous boyfriend. They had had a desultory and casual affair with no great passion or feeling and had just drifted apart. But he was better than nothing. She would ask him if he'd come over and fuck her, and hope her boldness would be a turn on.

'Hello?' It was a woman's voice that answered his phone.

'Is Mark there?' Gloria asked.

'Who's calling?'

'Gloria.'

Gloria heard the woman say something but her words were muffled by the fact she had obviously put her hand over the mouthpiece. She thought she heard a man's voice too.

'Apparently he's just gone out,' the woman said coldly.

'Who is this?' Gloria snapped.

'I'm his fiancée,' the woman said sharply and put the phone down.

Gloria sprung to her feet. Mark was her last hope but she was determined to do something. She opened the top drawer of a pine chest she used for her underwear. She found a pair of black panties, no more than a triangle of shiny black nylon supported by thin black straps. She pulled them up her legs and over her sex. They barely covered her thick black pubic hair, and the strap between her legs immediately disappeared into the furrow of her labia. Ignoring the bras, neatly stacked next to panties in the same drawer, she took out a white T-shirt and pulled it on. The cotton clung to the shape of her firm breasts and the outline of her hard nipples was only too clear but that was the effect that she wanted. Quickly she took a short black skirt from her wardrobe and a pair of high heels. She stepped into the skirt and smoothed it over her hips. It was tight and emphasised her pert bottom. The high heels further exaggerated the contours of her buttocks shaping the muscles into a definite pout. She looked in the mirror and was surprised by what she saw. She never normally wore anything so obvious.

She brushed her hair and applied a shade of lipstick she rarely used, a dark red that had been given to her on her birthday by a girl in the office. She grabbed her small handbag and was out of the flat and down the stairs before she had time for second thoughts.

The wine bar was no more than a four minute walk. She swung into it and marched up to the long bar that ran the whole length of the room. The bar was busy, crowded with people with a large preponderance of men, sticking together in groups of three or four, the lesser number of women doing the same thing, seeking protection in numbers. There were few couples. This was a place for meeting, not for romance.

At the bar Gloria found a free barstool and ordered a glass of red wine. She was intensely conscious of her clothes rubbing against her body. In her over-active imagination she could see the strap of her panties sawing against the pulsing nub of her clitoris. The T-shirt too seemed to be grinding into her nipples.

She saw men looking at her, their eyes moving from the clear shape of her breasts under the white cotton to the contours of her thighs, not sure which was the most alluring and glad they didn't have to choose. She, in the meantime, returned their gaze, anxious to get on with what she had in mind. One man caught her eye. He was blond and tall, with a very square jaw, large blue eyes and a small scar on his right cheek. He was wearing jeans and a blue denim shirt which was open at the neck, revealing a mass of blond hair on his chest.

It was not difficult to catch his eye as he was staring right at her, in common with the other two men he was with.

Gloria had never behaved like this before, but needs must when the devil drives. With a crooked finger Gloria beckoned him over. This produced a roar of delight from his companions, who slapped him on the back enthusiastically as he started towards her.

'Hello,' he said smiling broadly as he got to the barstool. 'Excuse my friends, they've had rather too much to drink.'

'And you haven't?'

'No. Can I buy you one?' His accent was slightly Cockney.

'Not really.'

'What then?'

'Do you find me attractive?' Gloria was in no mood for small talk. She didn't want to have a conversation with the man. She didn't even want to know his name.

'I didn't mean to stare,' he said defensively.

'I like it. But is that all you want to do?'

'What do you mean all?'

'Isn't there somewhere we could go?'

She saw the penny drop. She didn't have to draw him a diagram.

'My place?' he suggested grinning.

'Takes too long,' she said. Her need was urgent and overwhelming.

'Too long?'

'Come on.' She took his hand and wriggled off the barstool. She led him along the bar to the back of the room ignoring the smirks of his friends. Two signs indicated that the toilets were down a narrow staircase. She led the way.

'Is this a wind up?' he said as they reached the bottom.

'Do you think *this* is a wind up?' Gloria said. She pushed him back against the pine cladding that lined the wall and kissed him full on the lips, grinding her hips against him, plunging her tongue deep into his mouth and hugging him tightly. She felt his cock unfurl instantaneously. 'Well?' she said as she broke away.

'No,' he said. He looked at her steadily, convinced now that she was serious.

There was a door marked PRIVATE between the two toilet doors. Gloria tried it. It wasn't locked. She pulled the blond through and into a tiny storage room. There was a Hoover and a stack of cleaning equipment in one corner, leaving hardly enough room for both of them.

Gloria's heart was thumping against her ribs and her breathing was shallow. She hitched up her skirt. He stared at the triangle of black nylon, and the black pubic hair that escaped from around its edges. She attacked the belt of his jeans, then his zip, freeing them and tugging the denim down over his hips together with the light blue underpants he wore. His cock sprung free. It was circumcised and erect, not very long but very thick. At last Gloria had what she so desperately needed.

Bracing herself against the wall, Gloria tugged the white T-shirt up over her breasts and splayed her legs open. Up to now the blond had allowed her to take the initiative but suddenly his mood changed. He reached forward and hooked his fingers into the panties, pulling them up and to one side. Taking her by the shoulders he took a step forward and bent his knees, feeding his cock down between her legs. He had not expected the wetness he found there. Almost accidentally, on the tide of her juices, his cock slid right up into her vagina.

Gloria moaned gratefully and writhed down on his phallus, her sex contracting against the penetration it had yearned for, testing its hardness.

Straightening up he plunged his cock deeper, almost lifting her off her feet. His hands moved to her breasts, kneading them roughly then pinching at her nipples.

'This is what you want is it?' he muttered through gritted teeth.

'Yes, give it to me.' Gloria felt a surge of sensation coursing through her body as the man began pumping his cock up into her.

And then a curious thing happened. The surge of pleasure had closed Gloria's eyes and on the blank screen of her mind she suddenly saw Clarissa. She was looking at Gloria unblinkingly, those chestnut eyes flaring with anger. At exactly the same moment Gloria felt the sensations from her sex change. Where before it had been alive with feeling, her clitoris throbbing, her vagina stretched by the width of his cock, it became numb and lifeless as suddenly as if someone had thrown a switch.

Desperately Gloria bucked her hips against the man, pushing her clitoris against the base of his shaft, while her hands grabbed his muscled buttocks to drive him deeper. But she produced no reaction. Her sex refused to respond. Everywhere she looked, in her mind with her eyes closed, or in the storage room with them open, she saw Clarissa watching her.

The man's phallus swelled as he hammered into her. He was much better than Derek, much better, ironically, than almost any man she could remember. He was powerful and energetic and it was a long time before she felt his cock start to spasm. He moaned softly against her throat, a trickle of sweat running down his face and onto her T-shirt, and his spunk jetted out into her. But though she could feel the power of his penetration and the heat and wetness of his semen spattering into her, even this provocation could not break the hypnotic spell Clarissa's eyes seemed to have cast on her.

Gloria closed her eyes, wanting to see Clarissa more clearly. She was smiling now, her anger gone. Gloria could hear her voice. 'What do you want to do now?' it said over and over again. And Gloria knew the answer. 'Kiss you,' she replied though she wasn't sure she actually said the words.

WILLIAM

The black front door opened. William had expected the maid but standing in the doorway was a very different type of woman. She was large and strong looking with a deep bosom and large hips, but despite her size she was girlish and feminine. She had a large-boned face which was not unattractive and brown hair cut just above the shoulders. Her eyes were green and her mouth fleshy. Her grin revealed two rows of very regular and very white teeth. Her meaty arms and shoulders and substantial bosom were exposed by a sleeveless V-necked, knee-length beige dress. As far as William could see her legs, sheathed in rather coarse nylon, were as muscled and powerful as her arms. A bunch of keys hung from a brown leather belt strapped tightly around her broad waist.

'We are expecting you,' she said in a German accent. 'Please to come in.'

She closed the door after him.

'Follow you must,' she said. She crossed the vestibule and opened a small door under the stairs. 'My name is Olga. You call me Olga,' she said. There was a long passageway behind the door and she led the way along it, into what was obviously the back part of the house. There was a single door at the far end which she opened to reveal a flight of steps down into a cellar. 'Please . . .' Olga said indicating he should go first.

The stairs were carpeted and the cellar walls painted white. At the bottom William found himself in another narrow corridor at each side of which was a series of doors to what looked like wooden cubicles. Screwed to each door was a metal number from one to eleven.

Olga took him down to the door marked five, took a key from her key ring and unlocked it. She indicated he should go inside. The cubicle was a little bigger than the double bed that it contained. The walls were made from wood and the floor was covered in the same cord carpet as the hall and stairs outside. Apart from the bed there was no other furniture. There were two sturdy metal hooks bolted into the wall about three feet apart and at head height a single light bulb hanging from the ceiling, but, William noticed, no light switch. The bed was covered with a single dark brown sheet but otherwise had no bedding, not even a pillow. On the foot of the bed was a neatly folded, heavy-duty black plastic bag.

'Home,' Olga said, grinning. 'Home for one month. You put these,' she tugged on William's jacket to indicate what she meant, 'in here.' She picked up the plastic bag then dropped it again. 'All, understand?'

'All my clothes?' William said, astonished.

'Of course your clothes,' she said as if it were the most natural thing in the world. Clearly in *this* world it was. 'Quick. Quick,' she added.

William hesitated. She obviously had no intention of leaving the room but what alternative did he have? He pulled off his jacket and began to unbutton his shirt as Olga sat on the bed watching, her grin widening.

'Is good,' she said as his shirt came off.

William tried to keep his emotions under control, but it was difficult. The excitement he had felt as he'd set off was very definitely mixed with apprehension now. He hadn't expected this strange accommodation.

He kicked off his shoes and stripped off his socks. Reluctantly he undid his belt and unzipped his trousers, allowing them to fall to the floor. He picked up the black plastic and started to stuff the clothes inside.

'All I say,' Olga snapped, pointing to his briefs.

'I thought . . .'

'*All*,' she said firmly the grin gone.

William skinned the briefs down his legs and put them in the bag with the rest of his things. He saw her eyeing his penis.

'And the watch,' she told him. He unclipped his watch strap and dropped that too into the plastic bag.

Olga got to her feet. She took a small white plastic tag from the pocket of her dress and tied it around the neck of the bag. Attached to the tag was a label. William saw, written on it, the date and his initials.

'Good, good,' Olga said. She bounced out of the room with the bag but almost before the door had closed she was back again. 'Hands here,' she said picking up his arm and indicating he should put his hands at the back of his neck. 'Quick, both.' When he did not react as fast as she thought he should she smacked him with the flat of her hand on the top of his thigh.

'You must learn to do things quick, you understand?'

'Yes, sorry.'

He did as he was told lacing his fingers together behind his head and feeling slightly ridiculous and very vulnerable, especially as she dropped to her knees right in front of him and picked up the shaft of his penis between the thumb and forefinger of her right hand, staring at it intently as she moved it around as though she were examining some alien creature she had never seen before. He felt it stir.

She pulled the shaft up and used her other hand to cup his balls, squeezing them slightly. His cock pulsed again beginning to engorge despite himself.

'That is good,' she said. 'Come on, come on.'

She made a circle of her thumb and forefinger and looped it around the ridge at the bottom of his glans, as her other hand pulled down on the sac of his balls.

'Come on,' she urged.

He looked down at her. The V-neck of the dress revealed a long line of cleavage. It was deep and dark and the cream coloured bra she was wearing pushed her two mountainous breasts together. She looked up at him and their eyes met. She had an expression of almost childlike glee at what she was doing. His cock surged in her hand. He found himself inexplicably attracted to this strange woman.

'Yes,' she said at once. She wanked his erection energetically. 'It is up now yes?'

'Yes.'

'Very good I think,' she said. She pulled his cock forcefully this way and that. 'Is good,' she pronounced apparently satisfied. Taking her hand away she got to her feet. 'Hands down,' she said brusquely. She smiled looking straight into his eyes again. 'You like me?' she said with a girlish grin.

'Yes,' he said thinking that there was no point in antagonising her.

'I mean sexy like?'

'Yes,' he said, the state of his cock ample testimony to the truth of the statement.

'You like big girl yes?'

'Yes.'

She laughed, a hearty guttural laugh. 'You like to see my bosom. Very big tits. You like to do me?'

'Yes.'

'Very bad,' she said. 'You very bad man.' She lashed out her hand and smacked it painfully against his erection, then laughed again. 'Maybe I ask mistress permission. Maybe,' she said coquettishly letting him see again the girlish woman that lay hidden in her large frame.

She turned on her heels and walked out of the door without another word or glance. William heard the door being locked and footsteps going up the stairs. He thought he heard the door at the top of the stairs close too.

Not at all sure what to do he sat on the bed. The mattress was thin and uncomfortable.

Whatever William had expected it certainly wasn't Olga or the treatment she had meted out to him. He supposed he thought he would be given a tour of the house and a list of his duties, not to be stripped down and examined and left locked in a featureless cubicle in a cellar. It had come as a shock. It had been all too obvious that part of his duties would be sexual but he had assumed that would be in the privacy of Clarissa's bedroom. What had happened suggested his sexual services were to be much more public and much higher on the agenda.

Alone, naked, in what he could only describe as a cell, William's mind was spinning. His erection showed no signs of diminishing, fed, no doubt by the fact that this new set of circumstances, as unexpected as they were, undoubtedly excited him. The way he had been treated by Olga provoked the same responses as the way Clarissa had used him in her study. Being forced to strip in front of Olga was just as embarrassing and, at the same time, just as thrilling. Whatever else was going to happen in Clarissa's house it was entirely removed from anything he'd experienced before.

Time passed slowly and without his watch he had no way of telling how long he sat on the bed waiting. There was nothing to do. Eventually his cock softened. There was nothing to look at in the room, no visual interest and he was sure that was deliberate. He lay back on the bed and closed his eyes.

Occasionally he heard sounds. There were footsteps coming down stairs and the doors of the other cubicles being opened. Somewhere he thought he heard what sounded like a lift and he certainly heard the sound of someone taking a shower. He heard voices too, female voices but he could not hear what they said. On several occasions he heard the sound of a key being turned in a lock.

He thought of Clarissa and tried to imagine what she was doing somewhere up above him. He wondered about Gloria too. Had she been subjected to the same humiliating ritual? Was she one of the women he had heard being taken into the cubicles? He had only partially glimpsed what had happened between the two women in Clarissa's study but he had seen and heard enough to know Gloria had experienced the same uncontrollable sensations he had. Whether she was used to the sexual attentions of a woman he did not know but, from her reaction, he suspected that she was not. Just as Clarissa had read his own sexual secrets and released something in him, he suspected the same thing had happened to Gloria.

Thwack. The sound was distinct and unmistakable. *Thwack.* It echoed through the basement. *Thwack.* The third stroke was accompanied by a muffled cry of pain from a female voice. *Thwack.* The cry was louder this time. There was a pause. William thought he heard another voice but could not hear the words. The voice was cool and hard. *Thwack. Thwack.* Two more blows in quick succession both followed by muffled wails of pain. William heard a scuffle of feet and one of the cubicle doors being locked.

Almost immediately he heard a key being inserted into the lock of his cubicle. The door swung open and Olga stood in the doorway. There was a film of perspiration on her forehead and upper lip and her hair was slightly dishevelled. She held a thick leather riding crop in her hand.

'Come,' she said.

Self-consciously, only too aware of his nudity, William shuffled out into the hall.

'Follow,' Olga said. She had changed her clothes and was now wearing a sort of uniform, a military style jacket in a dark grey and matching riding breeches. Her feet were clad in highly polished black boots. The clothing made her look stern and forbidding and her attitude seemed to have changed too. The amusement she had displayed earlier had completely disappeared.

Turning on her heels she led the way down to the other end of the corridor of cubicles. At the far end the corridor turned to the right. They passed a shower room and a toilet before they arrived at a modern lift. She pressed the call button and the single lift door opened. She gestured that William should enter, then followed him in.

There were four numbers on the panel of buttons in the lift. Olga pressed the button marked one. The lift rose noiselessly with only a slight jolt as it reached the first floor.

'Out,' Olga said, clearly not going to get out herself.

William found himself in a small alcove about the size of a telephone box on one side of which was an opening into a much larger room. The carpet was thick and cream coloured and there was a full length mirror immediately opposite the lift door. The naked man standing apprehensively in front of it appeared like a total stranger to William.

'In here.' The voice was unmistakable. It was Clarissa Peacham.

William turned the corner into the main room. It was a lavishly decorated and luxurious bedroom, its large windows draped with thick cream and white curtains that matched the material of the counterpane on the extra large bed and toned perfectly with the carpet. The walls had been lined in off-white silk and there were several oil paintings, individually lit. All, it appeared, were by the same artist and were devoted to scenes of a forest in autumn. The burnished golds and chestnut of the leaves echoed the colour of Clarissa Peacham's hair as she sat on a modern brown leather and chrome chair, one of four drawn up around a circular rosewood breakfast table.

Apart from the bed, the table and chairs, there were two

bedside chests in burr walnut with large ceramic lamps and dark red lampshades. Two large white sofas faced each other at the end of the room nearest to the windows, a coffee table, also made from burr walnut, dividing them. On one of the side walls was what William guessed was the main door into the bedroom from the first floor landing and beside this was a French bow-fronted secretaire with floral marquetry. To one side of the bed were three identical doors standing side by side. Two were closed but one was ajar and William could see a bathroom in dramatic black marble beyond.

Clarissa Peacham was wearing a black satin robe. She was sitting with her legs crossed, the robe revealing most of her thigh. William stared at her feet. She was wearing the black silk high heeled slippers he had seen in his dream.

'Come over here,' she said.

On the table in front of her was a crystal glass wine cooler. It contained a bottle of Louis Roederer Cristal, swathed in ice. Two champagne flutes stood at its side, one empty the other half full.

William approached the table feeling more self-conscious than ever. Clarissa was staring at him but he did not want to meet her eye. It was the first time he had seen her looking anything less than perfectly immaculate. She looked a little flustered, her make-up slightly smudged, her hair slightly mussed. She picked up the champagne flute and sipped the wine.

'I am only going to say this once. Whenever you are summoned to see me you must get on your knees. You must kiss my feet, both of them in turn, the left foot first. Is that understood?'

'Yes.' He didn't understand it at all.

'Do it then William. Now.' Her voice snapped like an elastic band.

For some reason the words produced a strong surge of sensation in his cock. Immediately, wanting to make a good impression, he knelt in front of her; just as quickly he felt his cock begin to unfurl. He put his hands in his lap to try and hide it and found himself blushing.

'Take your hands away,' Clarissa said, not missing a thing. 'Clasp them behind your back.'

He did as he was told.

'Well now, look at that.' Her eyes stared at his cock. He felt it rise further under her gaze. 'What's the cause of that?'

'I don't know,' he mumbled.

'You don't know! Don't be ridiculous. You must know why you get an erection William.' She raised her leg and prodded her foot against his thigh. 'What did I tell you to do William?' she chided.

Immediately William leant forward, a little awkwardly with his hands clasped behind his back. He pressed his lips against her foot and felt his cock surge again.

'Take my slipper off,' she said.

He pulled the slipper off her foot then kissed her toes. He moved up to the arch of her foot. It was ludicrous, grotesque even, he could hardly believe he was actually doing it, but it was also profoundly exciting and he couldn't understand why.

Clarissa pulled her left foot away, slipped her foot out of her other slipper and presented him with the right.

'Hands behind your back again,' she said.

He obeyed then kissed her right foot. She wriggled her toes against his lips.

'Do you find me attractive William?' she said when she was finally satisfied he had done enough and took her foot away.

'You're beautiful,' he said sincerely.

Clarissa got to her feet. The folds of the robe floated around her legs as she took one step towards him and the black satin brushed against his body. Almost unconsciously he inhaled the heavy, musky aroma of her perfume. He thought he could also detect the inimitable scent of sex. He stared at her satin covered belly. The robe was held together by a sash of the same material knotted loosely at her waist. Slowly Clarissa pulled the sash from one side. The silky satin whispered as it rubbed against itself and the knot parted. The front of the robe opened. William found himself staring at Clarissa's belly, covered in black French knickers, their sides split to the hip, her thick chestnut pubic hair escaping from the loose fitting crotch.

'Well now William . . . what can you see?'

'Your body,' he said his voice hoarse.

'What part of my body?'

'Your legs, your stomach . . .'

'Not my cunt?' The word sounded strange on her lips.

'Yes, that too,' he agreed, gulping.

Clarissa extended her hand around to the back of his head and pulled his face forward on to the black satin. 'You're very lucky aren't you William? Lucky to be able to see me like this? Lucky to be able to serve me?' Her fingers gripped his thick, curly hair, and pulled his head back again, staring down into his eyes.

'Aren't you William?' she insisted.

'Oh yes.'

She stepped back and walked behind him. He heard a door opening and the distinctive noise of a cord operated bathroom light switch being pulled on.

'Come here,' she ordered, after some minutes had passed.

He got to his feet and walked into the bathroom. Clarissa was sitting at a dressing table that had been built into one corner of the room, facing a large mirror. She was taking off her make-up with pads of cotton wool dipped in some sort of cream. The bathroom was impressive, a huge white tub with a jacuzzi, a large glass shower cubicle and two hand basins as well as the toilet and bidet. Everything was tiled in black marble except for the wall behind the bath, which was covered from floor to ceiling in mirror tiles. William stared at his naked body in it, his erection pointing directly at Clarissa.

'Run me a bath,' she said.

He obeyed immediately, glad of the distraction of having something to do. He closed the plug of the bath by means of a knob under the taps then adjusted the mixer until it produced a flow of warm water.

Clarissa got to her feet. 'Come and stand behind me,' she said, moving away from the stool and standing in front of the wall of mirrors. He did as he was told, careful not to let his projecting erection touch the black satin. But that was not what she had in mind. She stepped back and pressed her buttocks into his stomach, trapping his cock between their bodies. 'Take my robe off,' she said looking at his eyes in the mirror as she moved her buttocks, almost imperceptibly from side to side.

William had to remind himself to breath. He took the material in his hands and slipped it off her shoulders. She wasn't wearing a bra and he watched in the mirror as her big, melon-shaped breasts emerged. They supported their own considerable weight without drooping and jutted from her chest proudly. Their nipples were like large buttons, wider than any he had seen, though the areolae that surrounded them were narrow. William felt his cock twitch against her French knickers.

'Does that excite you William?' she said.

'Oh yes.'

'You like my breasts?'

'They're beautiful.'

'Pull my knickers down now,' she said turning to face him. He reached out to grasp the waistband. 'No,' she said at once. 'Kneel down.'

William did as he was told. His erection was as hard as it had been last night in her study and a tear of fluid had formed at the slit. Clarissa was looking at it with what William could only interpret as disdain. He reached up and grasped the waistband of the French knickers at both sides of her hips and pulled them down. As they descended he found himself staring into the apex of her thighs. Though the triangle of pubic hair on her vulva was thick and fluffy, he could see that the hair between her legs was distinctly damp and plastered against the folds of her labia.

She raised each foot in turn so he could disentangle them from her ankles.

'Do they feel nice?'

'Feel nice?' He wasn't sure what she meant.

'Rub them against your cheek.'

'Oh no,' he said realising she meant the silky knickers.

'Do as I say,' she snapped angrily.

Reluctantly he brought the silk up to his face. He could smell her perfume and the aroma of her sex, mingled together to form a unique musk. He stroked the material against his cheek. It felt warm and incredibly soft. His fingers slipped on to the crotch. It was unmistakably damp.

'Well?' she said. Her naked sex was only inches from his face. William guessed it was all deliberate, all calculated. She wanted to tease him, to make him suffer. Perhaps she wanted him to do something she could punish him for, something that would teach him the first lesson in the discipline of her house. He knew it would not be difficult.

'So soft,' he almost whispered.

'They've been next to my sex William. Rubbing against my cunt. Don't tell me that doesn't excite you?'

'It does.'

A lot of the others had broken at this point, lost control and lunged for her, trying to finger her breasts or her sex, an easy victory. They had soon learnt their mistake. But William remained still though it was quite obvious he was wrestling with himself to maintain control, his whole body trembling.

'Is my bath ready?' she said in a different tone, walking away from him.

He scrambled to his feet, glad of the chance to escape from her teasing, and turned off the taps, his erection banging against the side of the bath. Clarissa climbed into the tub and lay down.

'Fetch me a glass of champagne,' she ordered.

William trooped back into the bedroom. He poured the chilled wine into the flute and took a deep breath before picking it up. This was hell. If this is what Clarissa had meant in her study by 'more onerous duties' he wasn't sure he could stand it. She was deliberately taunting him with her body, making him look at it, and perform little intimate functions, like pulling off her knickers, while making it quite obvious he was not to be allowed any real satisfaction.

'William.' Her voice was angry.

He ran back into the bathroom.

'When I ask you to do something you must do it at once,' she snapped. 'Do you understand?'

'Yes,' he said. 'I'm sorry.' He handed her the glass.

'Yes what? I think it should be "yes Ms Peacham" don't you?'

'Yes . . . yes Ms Peacham,' he said.

'That sounds better.' Clarissa sipped the wine, then put it down on the tiled ledge that ran all the way around the bath. She allowed her body to sink into the water then tilted her head back so her hair was submerged too and only her face was not covered. Her big breasts floated loosely in the soapy water. 'Tell me about Gloria.'

'I don't know anything about her, Ms Peacham,' William said.

'Don't you? You've never slept with her then?' Clarissa knew full well that he hadn't.

'No, Ms Peacham.'

'Do you think she is a lesbian?'

'No, Ms Peacham,' he said though he hadn't forgotten what had happened in Clarissa's study.

'I've just had her up here with me. It was very interesting.' She erupted from the water, her breasts quivering, her hair plastered to her head, water cascading off her in every direction. 'I should have allowed you to watch. Would you like that?'

'No, Ms Peacham,' he said definitely.

'No? No?' She sounded astonished. 'How can that be? I thought you said you found me attractive?'

Clarissa got to her feet. She took a bar of soap from a dish on the ledge and started rubbing it over her body. William watched as she lathered her breasts and her stomach, then worked the soap down between her legs. His cock throbbed.

'I do, Ms Peacham,' he said wishing she would stop.

'But you wouldn't like to see me with Gloria, see her kissing me, see her kissing my body, kneading my breasts.' She was watching his cock, seeing the effect the words had on him. 'Licking at my cunt?' She never used a euphemism for that part of her anatomy it seemed.

'No, Ms Peacham,' he said shaking his head from side to side, trying desperately not to imagine the picture her words conjured up.

Clarissa picked up a big natural sponge and used it to rinse the soap off her body. 'I'm very disappointed in you William. And I thought we were getting along so well together.' Satisfied all the soap was gone she stepped out of the bath. 'Get a towel,' she said.

There was a heated towel rail loaded with large white towels. William snatched one and held it out to Clarissa.

'No, you fool. Use it to dry me.'

'Oh no,' he said. It was expecting too much.

'What?'

He thought his cock had been hard before, but that was nothing to what it felt like now. It was so hard and so full he began to believe it was capable of coming of its own accord, without being touched. He *knew* having to rub Clarissa's body would be the last straw.

'Please, Ms Peacham. I just can't, please don't make me.'

'William.' Her voice rattled around the bathroom, imperious and implacable. 'This will not do at all. I don't expect to be disobeyed on any occasion, but on your very first night. It does not bode well does it?'

'I'll do anything else, I just can't do that.'

'And why not?'

William blushed a crimson red. He couldn't say the words.

'William, if you do not use that towel in ten seconds you will be out of this house in ten minutes. Is that understood? You are already in trouble for disobedience. Don't make it worse.'

William saw he had no choice. Clarissa's eyes stared at him, her determination absolute. He took the towel and rubbed it around her neck and arms. He didn't understand what was happening to him. He had seen naked women before but they had never produced this effect. She was undoubtedly one of the most beautiful women he had ever seen, and one that had obsessed him and been the object of his secret sexual fantasies for a long time, but that did not explain the intensity of passion that he felt. There was only one explanation: what excited him most and what he had never experienced before was the way he had been treated.

'Harder,' she complained.

He rubbed her collar bone and her big, spherical breasts,

trying to ignore the way the firm yet supple flesh wobbled in his hands. He moved down to her stomach and the front of her legs trying not to look at her pubic hair as he dried it.

'Now the back,' she said turning around.

He rubbed her shoulders and her long spine. Her buttocks rose sharply from the small of her back, as round as an apple, the cleft that bisected them deep and dark. He rubbed the towel over them and felt his cock jerk wildly.

'There,' she said. 'What was all the fuss about.' She caught his towel covered hand and drew it around her body to her stomach. 'But you've missed a bit.' She opened her legs and pulled the towel down between them. Then, quite deliberately, she pulled the towel away so his fingers were uncovered, pushing her buttocks back at him at the same time, so his tortured cock was pressed into the silky cleft of her bottom. The double impact of feeling her soft, yielding, wet labia against his hand, and the rich, supple curves of her buttocks encasing his cock was simply too much for him. He gasped and shook, reflexively jamming his fingers hard up against her vagina, as a string of spunk jetted out of his cock, and over her bottom, spattering up almost to her shoulder blades.

'How dare you!'

The words were far away, so distant he could hardly grasp their meaning.

'How dare you!'

How often had he heard her say that, as his spunk jetted out of his cock held tightly in his own hand?

'How dare you!'

The intensity of his orgasm had been so great it was some time before he got a grip on himself and realised that the words he had so often heard in his imagination were real, as real as the naked body in front of him, spattered with his spunk.

'You'll pay for this William, you'll pay for this!' Clarissa said.

Chapter Four

GLORIA

It had been a beautiful day, the sun shining in a clear blue sky. Though it was still only June by the time Gloria walked into Punishment Road the pavements seemed to be radiating heat. She looked at her watch. It was ten minutes to six. She mounted the steps of number ten and tugged on the old fashioned bell-pull. Clarissa Peacham had told them not to be late. She had said nothing about being early. It was a tiny gesture of defiance, though, in truth, defiant was the last thing Gloria felt. As she heard the bell ring deep inside the house she tried to keep her mind blank, desperately not wanting to remember what Clarissa had done to her last time she entered this house.

The door opened. A large woman in a beige cotton dress, belted at the waist with a brown leather belt, from which hung a bunch of keys, smiled at her sympathetically. 'You are expected,' she said in a heavy German accent. 'Please to follow me.'

The woman stepped aside to let her in and closed the front door behind her with a loud bang.

'I am Olga. You call me this,' the woman said, leading her

across the black and white marble tiles and up the sweeping staircase to the first floor. Gloria noticed her hefty calf muscles as she followed her.

They walked down a wide corridor at the end of which was a single door. Olga opened it without knocking and ushered Gloria inside. The large bedroom beyond was lavish, toned in various shades of cream and white with a huge double bed. But Gloria was not given much time to admire it. Olga marched to the back of the room and opened one of three identical doors.

'In here,' she said.

Gloria found herself in a small rectangular room. The walls were painted a very dark blue, and the carpet was the same colour. There was no window and the only light came from an opaque glass fitting screwed into the ceiling. In the middle of the room there was a black leatherette examination table, exactly like those found in doctors' surgeries for examining patients. The wall opposite the door was taken up by a large built-in storage unit with cupboards and drawers, all with small brass locks.

A neatly folded black plastic bag sat on the end of the examination table.

'You must put your clothes in here,' Olga said pointing to the bag. 'All in here.'

'All my clothes?' Gloria queried.

'Yes, all.'

'I don't understand.' Gloria couldn't make sense of the words.

'Undress.' Olga said losing her patience. 'Then clothes in this bag.' The smile had melted away to be replaced by a much harder expression, one that brooked no argument.

Gloria hesitated. She had not been expecting this. If she were honest with herself she had hoped Clarissa was anxious to resume where she had left off in her study and if that were not going to happen immediately she'd imagined being shown to a bedroom and perhaps given a few light chores. She hadn't thought beyond that.

Somewhere deep in the house a bell rang. It was the front door. Gloria guessed it was William.

'Do, now,' Olga said, with real venom in her voice at the further delay. 'Or it will be bad for you.'

She strode out of the room. Gloria heard a rattle of keys, then the door being locked.

There was clearly no alternative. Feeling self-conscious she took off her jacket of the grey suit she was wearing and began unbuttoning her blouse. She unzipped her skirt, let it fall to the floor, then stepped out of it. In anticipation of what she *had* expected she was wearing her best lacy white teddy. It had been too hot to wear tights.

Gloria looked around the room. It felt odd to be locked in, deprived, so quickly, of her liberty. She tried to tell herself that it didn't matter, that she had made her choice anyway but it wasn't true. The locked door bothered her.

Trying to take her mind off it she studied the storage unit, trying each of the doors and drawers in turn. Each was locked. She noticed that two sturdy metal hooks had been bolted to one of the walls. They were at head height and about three feet apart.

She sat on the examination table. The room was warm and the black leatherette stuck to her skin.

It was half-an-hour before she heard the key being turned

in the lock again. Olga bustled in.

'What is this. This is not good. I give you an order. All clothes I say.' Her voice was angry.

'I thought . . .'

Olga strode over to the storage unit and used one of her keys to unlock a long, thin cupboard door. When she turned around again she had a slender leather riding crop in her hand. She lashed it down against the black leatherette. 'You do not want this,' she said.

It was true. Gloria remembered only too well how the weals had appeared on William's buttocks and how it had radiated heat. She certainly didn't want to subject herself to that experience. Quickly she hopped off the table and reached down between her legs to unclip the gusset of the teddy. She pulled it up over her head, trying to ignore the way this bullying stranger was looking at her body. She pulled off her shoes and stuffed all her clothes into the plastic bag.

'Is good,' Olga said, examining her minutely. 'Jewellery too and watch. All.' She tapped Gloria's wrist with the leather loop at the end of the whip.

Gloria unbuckled her watch and took off the two rings she had on her right hand. She was wearing small silver earrings through her pierced ears which she also removed. She put the jewellery in the pocket of her jacket.

Olga took a tag from the pocket of her dress and tied it tightly around the neck of the bag. The tag had a label which Gloria couldn't read.

'Now, lie on the table,' she ordered tapping the leatherette with the whip. As Gloria obeyed Olga opened the door and set the black plastic bag down outside.

When she returned she was smiling again. She stood at the side of the table, her eyes roaming Gloria's naked body. The expression on her face made Gloria shiver and she started when she felt Olga's small, rather fat fingers fasten over her left breast. The big woman kneaded it for a moment, then transferred to the right, giving that the same treatment. Gloria tried to hold herself in check, restraining the impulse to slap Olga's face and run out of the room.

Olga's hand descended to Gloria's belly, rubbing against it in circles. 'Open your legs,' she ordered.

Gloria obeyed. There was no room on the table to accommodate them in this position so, from her knees down, they hung over the side awkwardly.

Olga's finger parted her nether lips and butted against Gloria's clitoris. It reacted to this intrusion with a pulse of feeling that took Gloria by surprise. Just as surprising to her was the fact that, as Olga's fingers ploughed the furrow of her labia, she could feel her own wetness, despite the revulsion she felt for the woman. As Olga pushed one chubby finger into her vagina, there was no resistance, Gloria's sex instinctively prepared for penetration.

'Over on your belly now,' Olga said pulling her finger out.

Gloria obeyed, bringing her legs up again and turning over. The black leatherette pressed against her breasts. She turned her head to one side away from Olga, resting her cheek on the table. Immediately she felt the woman's hand on her neck. It traced down along her spine, taking detours to the side every so often to squeeze and knead her flesh. When it reached her buttocks she felt her other hand too, pulling them apart, no doubt to get a better view of the puckered dip of her anus.

'You have been buggered?' she said.

The question was so unexpected Gloria did not know how to answer. 'I . . . er . . .'

Olga slapped one hand down hard on Gloria's left buttock. 'Yes or no.'

'Yes.' It had only happened once.

'You like this?'

Gloria wasn't sure what to say. The man who had got her drunk enough to allow him to try it had certainly wanted it very much, but she couldn't say she had enjoyed it particularly. But then her reaction to all sex had been muted.

Olga took her hesitation for disobedience and slapped her again. 'Answer.'

'It didn't hurt.' Gloria said truthfully.

Olga appeared satisfied with this reply. Her fingers delved into the cleft of Gloria's pert buttocks and for a moment Gloria thought she was going to penetrate her anus but she didn't. Instead she leant over the table and squashed the weight of her body into Gloria's back.

'I like very much,' she said. 'I look forward, very much, to being with you.'

The words chilled Gloria but apparently her sex felt differently. She felt her clitoris spasm, responding, she knew, to the weight of Olga's bosom pressing against her naked back. In her mind she had decided to get through this experience with the minimum of fuss, trying to hold herself above it all; obviously her body had a different agenda.

And then Olga was gone. Before she realised what had happened Gloria heard the door close. She felt another chill as she heard the key being turned in the lock.

Not at all sure what she should do, Gloria sat up. Olga's ministrations had left her body churning. Her nipples were so hard they felt heavy, so puckered they seemed to have pulled the rest of the flesh on her breasts taut. Her sex was alive and she could feel a wetness seeping from her labia over the black leatherette. Everything Olga had touched seemed to have been sensitised by her fingers. She could feel the journey they had made down her spine and where they had rested to lever her buttocks apart. Her mouth was dry and her heart pounded.

At any moment she expected Clarissa to walk through the door. It was the only reason she could think of for being stripped and handled like this. Clarissa was going to finish what she had begun in the study downstairs.

What had happened in her study only twenty-four hours ago had affected Gloria sexually more than anything else ever had. She knew what had happened last night had been caused by Clarissa too. That was the only way she could explain it. She could never remember wanting a man more in her life. Not wanting, but needing, like a man in a desert needs a drink. At least she had thought that's what she needed. How she could have gone from the super-heated frenzy of desire she had felt to the benumbed impotence she had ended up with she did not know. Though she didn't understand it properly Gloria was sure the way her feelings had been cut off so suddenly was related to the way Clarissa had treated her in her study, leaving her hanging on the brink, taking her to the point where she desperately wanted to explore the feelings Clarissa had created in her, but not being allowed to. What she had done was quite deliberate. Clarissa was a calculating and sophisticated woman whose sexuality was as complex as it was Machiavellian. She knew what she wanted and had many and various ways of getting it.

Gloria got to her feet. The black leatherette glistened where she had been sitting. Olga had not locked the cupboard door and Gloria peeked inside. Carefully racked, like guns in a gun cabinet, the cupboard contained eight whips, all of a different design, one with a long leash wound into a neat coil, one with a leather handle sprouting from which were six slivers of what looked like whale bone, and others like the riding crop but with minor differences. Hanging from two hooks on the back of the door were two silver chains. At the ends of each chain was a circle of black metal the centre of which was an iris like that on the shutter of a camera. Gloria stooped to examine them more closely.

'Would you like to try them?'

Clarissa stood in the doorway though Gloria had not heard the door being unlocked or opened. She was wearing a tight sleeveless white top with a neckline that plunged all the way to her waist and a black skirt that clung to her hips but was short enough to reveal most of her thighs. Her long legs were veiled in shimmering black tights and she was wearing black boots with high heels which had the effect of shaping and firming the muscles of her calves and buttocks.

'I asked you a question.' Her voice was cold and unemotional. Gloria noticed the way her mane of chestnut hair seemed to reflect the light.

'I don't know what they're for,' Gloria said weakly.

'Then I think I should allow you to find out. Bring one of them over here,' Clarissa said. She closed the door and stood by the examination table looking at the patch of wetness where

Gloria had been sitting, but not commenting on it.

Gloria unhooked one of the chains from the door. It was heavier than she'd expected. She walked over to Clarissa, and saw the way she watched her body, how her thighs moved against each other and her breasts jiggled up and down. Without her high heels and with Clarissa in her boots, Gloria was at least a foot shorter than her boss. She handed Clarissa the chain and their eyes met. Once again Gloria experienced a unique sensation as Clarissa's eyes held hers steadily in an unblinking gaze. It felt as though she was floating, suddenly freed of everything corporeal, aware only of her emotions, which were swamped with excitement.

'Sit up here,' Clarissa said after what was probably only a few seconds but, as far as Gloria was concerned, might have been hours. Snapping out of her reverie Gloria obeyed. Clarissa was not wearing a bra and Gloria could see the outline of her large breasts under the white top. She could see the darkness of her nipples too, nipples that were clearly already hard.

'Sometimes I use these for punishment,' Clarissa said. 'But pain is a two-way street isn't it Gloria? What is painful in some circumstances is exquisitely pleasant under others. Is that not so?'

'I don't know.'

'While you are in this house I want you to address me as Ms Peacham. Is that clear?'

'Yes.'

'Yes, what?' Clarissa snapped.

'Yes, Ms Peacham.'

'Let's see . . .' Clarissa's long fingers took the circumference of one of the circles in her hand. Gloria hadn't noticed the two tiny black extrusions on the outer rim. Clarissa pressed them inwards and the iris opened. With her other hand she grasped Gloria's left breast, squeezing it tight so her nipple was projected even further forward than it already was. She positioned the opening of the iris over the tight, corrugated flesh, then released it. The iris sprung closed, trapping the nipple at its centre.

Gloria felt a surge of sensation. She had expected pain but there was none, at least none that was not so striated with pleasure that she could not distinguish the one from the other. She heard a noise, so strange and strident it sounded like the screech of a wild animal, though she was sure she herself had made it. Her eyes closed involuntarily.

'You've got lovely tits,' Clarissa said, cupping her hand over Gloria's other breast.

When Gloria opened her eyes again she saw Clarissa had pulled her right breast from the front of the plunging neckline. She opened the iris on the other end of the chain, centred it over her own, much larger nipple, and released the spring, allowing the iris to close on the puckered flesh. Gloria saw the thin edge of the metal iris dig in. She saw Clarissa's eyes glaze with the same melange of pleasure and pain she had just experienced. And she could feel it too, as though the chain that joined their breasts was capable of transmitting the electricity of feeling.

'You make me very hot,' Clarissa said in a husky voice, swaying her body back until the chain was taut. The tautness made the thin edges of the irises dig deeper into their nipples. Both women moaned in unison. Again the chain transmitted the feeling from one to the other, more intensely this time, as the string stretched between them.

Opening her eyes, Clarissa plucked the ring from her nipple.

She opened the iris and centred it over Gloria's right nipple. 'You love it don't you?'

'No, Ms Peacham,' Gloria said not because it was true but because she didn't want to admit the truth. The truth was her sex had flooded with juice, so much so that she could feel it spreading on the black leatherette, her buttocks and the tops of her thighs squirming against it. Clarissa looked into her eyes as she released the iris on the second clip. One had provoked a wave of instant pleasure, two more than doubled it. Gloria moaned loudly. The chain hung down in a loop from Gloria's jutting breasts. Clarissa picked it up and swung it gently back against Gloria's body. A new wave of sensation coursed through her.

'Lie back on the table now,' Clarissa said with a gentleness in her voice she had not used before.

Gloria obeyed, every movement making her breasts quiver, provoking new sensations in her imprisoned nipples.

Clarissa was unlocking one of the drawers in the storage unit. Gloria heard it slide open.

'You must answer all my questions truthfully. Do you understand that?' Clarissa said.

'Yes . . .' Gloria had forgotten the sobriquet. 'Yes, Ms Peacham,' she said hurriedly.

'I want you to tell me when you last had a man.'

'A man?' Gloria wasn't at all sure what she should say.

'Yes.'

There was no point in lying. 'Last night.'

'And what did you do with him exactly ?'

'I . . . we . . . he fucked me Ms Peacham.' Gloria could not think of any other way to put it.

Clarissa laughed. 'And who was this man?'

'A stranger.'

'Do you make a habit of fucking strangers?'

'No . . . I just . . .' Gloria didn't know how to explain it. 'I needed a man. I needed a man badly.'

Clarissa walked back across the room. She stood by the examination table and looked down at Gloria. 'And why was that?'

'I don't know. What you did to me I think,' Gloria said as it was the truth.

'And did you enjoy it?'

Gloria had the strange feeling that Clarissa knew all the answers to the questions she had asked including this one. 'No,' she replied.

'No, of course not. What did you expect? You had to save yourself for me, Gloria. We had left something unfinished, hadn't we?'

'Yes, Ms Peacham.'

Clarissa's hand touched Gloria's arm, stroking it gently. 'Do you want me to take the clips off?' she said.

'No . . .' Gloria said rather too quickly.

Clarissa smiled a knowing smile. 'Very well.' Her other hand caressed the tops of Gloria's thighs, then ran over the bush of her pubic hair. 'Open your legs for me would you? Just a little.'

Without letting her legs fall to each side of the table, as they had done with Olga, Gloria managed to ease them apart. Immediately she felt something hard and cold sliding between her thighs and onto her labia. She wanted to look to see what it was but dared not do anything without permission.

'I want you to come for me Gloria. I want to see it. Do you understand? I want you to have an orgasm for me,' Clarissa said.

Gloria could see Clarissa's eyes roaming her body. The cold object between her legs nudged into her labia and up against her clitoris. It began to vibrate powerfully, a muffled humming reverberating around the small room. Gloria moaned, the vibration affecting her instantly, her clitoris already swollen and sensitised by all that had gone before.

'I think there's something special about you Gloria. It's too early to be sure, of course but I just have this feeling . . .'

'Oh, Ms Peacham.' A wave of sensation washed over Gloria. She looked at Clarissa and felt it intensify. She had not put her breast back in the blouse and it hung out obscenely, the tight material all around it pressing against her flesh. The short skirt revealed most of her thighs and Gloria's eyes feasted on them, the tight glossy nylon that sheathed them giving them the appearance of being wet. Gloria could hardly control her desire to touch. She had never wanted a woman before but now, as in Clarissa's study, she felt a profound need to push her hand between the other woman's thighs, and sink her mouth onto Clarissa's fleshy lips.

Instead she concentrated on obedience, on giving Ms Peacham what she said she wanted. It was not difficult. The incredible sensations the nipple clips were producing were multiplied by the vibrations that spread up from her sex. What she had felt last night, the overwhelming need for sex, was foremost again but this time it was not focused on a man. She knew this time too, there would be no barrier to her feelings; she could come effortlessly.

'Yes, I can see it,' Clarissa said.

'God, God,' Gloria gasped. Squeezing her legs together she pressed the phallus tighter against her clit. At that moment Clarissa turned her face to look straight into Gloria's eyes, and this time the look she saw there, instead of preventing fulfilment, enabled it. Her body exploded with feeling, an orgasm broke like none she had had before. Though it was physically exquisite, Gloria knew it was also an emotional experience caused by the way the beautiful chestnut eyes were looking at her.

Before the climax had run its course Clarissa's fingers were circling the nipple clips. With a double bout of intense feeling that made Gloria's body arch off the black leatherette, the chain fell to the floor. Gloria's body trembled uncontrollably. She had never felt anything like this in her life, the feeling in her nipples pitched her orgasm into another level of intensity.

But Clarissa had not done it for Gloria's pleasure.

'Come with me, quickly,' she said, pulling the door open and diving through it almost at a run.

By the time Gloria had recovered her senses sufficiently to climb off the table and walked into the bedroom, Clarissa was lying on the big double bed, her legs wide open, the phallus she had used on Gloria jammed into her crotch. Gloria could see she wasn't wearing panties under the shimmering black tights.

'Come here,' she said. 'Kneel on the bed here, take this.'

Gloria hurried to obey, despite the fact her body was still trembling with a myriad of tiny pleasures.

The phallus was large and black, shaped to resemble an erect male penis complete with the acorn shape of the glans at the top and the sac of the balls at the bottom. Gloria reached down and took it from Clarissa's hands. She had never used a dildo before. She could see Clarissa had jammed the tip up into her labia at the top and onto her clitoris, though it was veiled by the shiny nylon.

'Here,' Clarissa said. As soon as her hands were free she reached into the top drawer of the bedside chest and came out with a pair of nail scissors. Her need was apparently too urgent for her to undress. She didn't want to wait. 'Cut the nylon,' she said.

Gloria held the dildo firmly in one hand and carefully probed the point of the scissors into the nylon, with the other. The scissors made a long ladder appear immediately. As soon as the hole was wide enough Gloria threw the scissors on to the floor and tore at the nylon with her fingers. The ladder spread upward revealing Clarissa's sex. Though her labia were thick with hair, the hair was wet and plastered back and the entrance to her vagina was clearly visible.

'Put it in me. Right up me for Christ's sake.'

Gloria hesitated. She had never done anything like this, never even seen a woman's sex at close quarters before, but she wanted it quite as much as Clarissa obviously did. She hesitated, not through fear but because she was struggling to cope with the waves of pleasure that threatened to overwhelm her.

'Do it,' Clarissa snapped.

And Gloria did. She moved the head of the dildo down and thrust its large, broad shaft into Clarissa's vagina. She watched as it pursed to accept it, her labia thinning, stretched by its breadth. Gloria felt a spasm deep in her own sex as if it were imagining what the dildo would feel like.

'Fuck me girl, fuck me with it,' Clarissa muttered, tossing her head from side to side, her hands clawing at the silk counterpane.

Gloria was not at all sure what she was supposed to do. She withdrew the phallus until she could see the ridge at the bottom of the glans then pushed it back again. Stretched by the dildo Clarissa's labia had parted to reveal the little pink promontory of her clitoris. Acting on instincts she had no idea she possessed, Gloria leant forward and pressed her mouth against the upper part of Clarissa's sex, flicking her tongue out until she could feel the swollen nub of flesh against it.

'Yes,' Clarissa said at once. 'Do that too.'

In time to the pumping action she had established with the dildo, Gloria nudged the clitoris from side to side, as she had always loved men to do to her – though few had mastered the art. With her other hand she groped upward and clutched at Clarissa's one naked breast, squeezing it in her fingers until she found the nipple, then pinching on that. It was the nipple Clarissa had clipped in the metal ring and it responded immediately to Gloria's touch. Gloria sensed the moment when the trinity of feelings, from nipple, vagina and clitoris, became one. Clarissa's body arched off the bed and she came, the headlong rush into orgasm seeming to go on forever.

'Oh God,' Gloria whispered, her mouth moving against Clarissa's sex. Kneeling with her legs together, her clitoris trapped, her tenderised nipples brushing against the material of Clarissa's skirt, rucked up around her hips, she felt her own body lurch towards orgasm again. A wave of sensation seized her and her body curled around it. Her mind was in turmoil, she was so new to all this. As she succumbed to the final impact of orgasm, her mind registered the extremes of pleasure and compared them, inevitably with what had gone before. It told her, confidently, that she had never experienced such pleasure with a man.

WILLIAM

'What the hell do you think you're doing?' Clarissa unhooked the towelling robe from the back of the bathroom door and picked up the phone that hung on the wall beside it. She punched a single number into the key pad. 'Olga, come up here at once,' she said slamming the receiver into its chromium cradle. She turned back to William her eyes burning with anger. 'You didn't answer my question.'

William stood, feeling pathetic, the towel she had made him wipe her back clean with, still in his hand. 'I just couldn't help myself. You looked so beautiful, you felt so good . . . I'm sorry, I really am.'

'You will be sorry. Do you really think I'm interested in your opinion of me? I allow you to come into this house out of the kindness of my heart, as a way of giving you another chance. And what do you do to repay me? You behave like some dirty little schoolboy who can't control himself. I should have you thrown out.'

'You were . . . the way you were . . .' William tried to find something to say. He knew she had provoked him deliberately but that was no excuse for his lack of control. He had never felt more ashamed of anything in his life.

'Well you're going to pay for it. My God you're going to pay for it! If you can't behave like a man, if you behave like a

101

dirty little schoolboy, then I'm going to have to treat you like one aren't I?'

'Yes, Ms Peacham.' He was too chastened to argue. He saw Olga appear in the bathroom doorway, still wearing her grey uniform and black boots.

'Do you know what this pig did?' Clarissa said at once.

'He's been bad, yes?'

'I give him the special privilege of being in my bathroom, I allow him to dry my body and how does he repay me? He practically raped me.'

'Very bad,' Olga said shaking her head.

'Get him out of here. Is Hildegard coming tomorrow night?'

'*Ja.*'

'Good. She can deal with him. A session with her should teach him some manners. Now get him out of my sight.'

Olga took William's left arm and started to lead him out of the bathroom. Suddenly Clarissa grabbed his right so he was stretched between the two women. 'You're very lucky,' she snarled at him. 'You're very lucky I don't have you thrown out right now. Do you understand that William?'

'Yes, Ms Peacham.' He understood it only too well.

'If you cannot control yourself, if you have no self-discipline, then you are no good to me. I'm going to give you one more chance, that's all. Just one. Well? Are you going to thank me?'

The look in Clarissa's eyes burned into him, like the rays of the sun focused by a piece of glass.

'Thank you, Ms Peacham. I just couldn't . . . I couldn't help . . .' William felt as if he wanted to cry. He tried to fight back the tears. He was completely confused, his gratitude that she was not going to throw him out, mixed with the shame and regret at what he had done. He wished he could have explained to her what had happened but he didn't understand it himself.

Clarissa's fingers released their grip on his arm and he was led away. She made sure he did not see the smile of satisfaction on her lips. Like a puppet he had been made to dance to her tune; she had pulled the strings and he had behaved with absolute predictability. It was what she loved to see. It gave her almost as much pleasure as Gloria had done. Almost.

Olga did not let go of William's arm. She dragged him across the bedroom to the lift, crowding into it with him and pushing her body against his. She grinned as the lift door closed, reached down between his legs and squeezed his flaccid cock.

'Bad boy,' she said. 'She makes you a bad boy yes?'

'Yes . . .no.' Oddly he wasn't sure any more. His shame was colouring his judgment. Perhaps she hadn't provoked him deliberately at all. Didn't she have the right to expect he would have better control over himself?

'You will be punished,' Olga said cheerfully.

The lift arrived in the basement and Olga pulled him out. They walked down the corridor and she pushed him into the cubicle marked with the number five. Inside, she took a key from the bunch and locked the door. From the pocket of her jacket she took a small black leather strap. With practised ease she caught his cock in her hand, dropped to her knees in front of him and wrapped the strap around the top of his shaft and under his balls. She buckled it tight. At each side of the buckle was a metal D-ring. She took a small padlock from another pocket and threaded the staple through both rings before snapping it shut.

'Is necessary,' she said. 'Bad boy.' She grinned at him again. 'Now you make me feel like bad girl too,' she whispered conspiratorially. He saw her rub her hand down between her legs. The expression on her face was shy and coquettish like a girl deciding how far she would let a man go on the first date. It did not match the rest of her appearance at all, nor the situation. 'Get on the bed,' she ordered. 'On your back.'

William had no idea what to expect but saw no alternative to doing what he was told. He certainly didn't want to be reported to Ms Peacham for disobedience, not after what had just happened. To his horror, Olga unbuckled her belt and stripped off her jacket.

'You give me good time, yes? Very good time, yes?' she said. She was wearing a white bra, its large conical cups needing the support of a harness of straps to hold them in place. The bra pushed her huge breasts together to form a long, dark cleavage, flesh billowing up on either side. She pulled her boots off and then her breeches. Her legs were plump and meaty, her stomach rotund, and her buttocks were as vast as her bosom. She wore no panties or tights. Nestled in the middle of all this pulchritude he could just see her sex, sparsely covered with wispy brown pubic hair.

She left him in no doubt what she wanted. Kneeling on the bed facing William's feet she swung her massive thigh over his shoulder and dropped her sex directly on to his mouth. At the same time she slapped the side of his thigh with a stinging blow as if to tell him there would be more of the same if he did not begin.

William plunged his tongue into the furrow of Olga's rather thin labia. He had never had sex with a woman of her proportions, and had never imagined doing so, but, to his surprise, the softness of the flesh that enveloped him was instantly arousing. As he extended his tongue up to find her clitoris he felt his blood forcing its way past the leather strap and into his cock. As his excitement increased the strap bit ever tighter into his blossoming flesh.

'You like Olga yes?' she said as she saw his cock swell.

'Mmm . . .' he mumbled against her labia.

She took his cock in her hand and rubbed her fingers over the rim of his glans. His cock surged again. The strap was painful but it was the same sort of pain he had experienced from the metal ruler, a pain that was so bound up with pleasure he could not separate the two.

Olga wriggled her bottom, reminding him he was supposed to be paying attention to her. Another slap on the thigh, harder this time served the same purpose.

William found her clitoris, desperately trying to concentrate on her and forget about his own excitement. Like everything else about Olga it was big and bulbous. He pushed it back against the underlying bone. He had to make her come quickly. Though he could hardly believe it was possible after only just having come, his cock was pulsing with excitement, the strap wrapped around it giving it a whole new set of feelings to cope with. He did not want the shame of coming, unbidden, again.

He pushed her clitoris up and down and felt her body tense. He moved it from side to side to even greater effect and concentrated on this.

'Mmm . . . bad boy,' she muttered.

He brought one hand around to her big squashy buttock and found the entrance to her vagina. Surprisingly it was small and tight, so tight he could do no more than squeeze two fingers inside. She moaned loudly and ground down on him as she felt the penetration.

Unfortunately the silky wetness and tightness of her sex kicked his sexual reflexes into a higher gear. His cock strained against the strap. The larger he got the tighter the restraint and the tighter the restraint the larger he got. It was a vicious circle he had never experienced before. He imagined she had put the strap in place to keep him from coming. It was actually having the reverse effect.

He began to pump his fingers in and out of her vagina to the rhythm his tongue had established in pushing her clitoris from side to side. He could feel her excitement, the muscles under the layers of spongy flesh beginning to harden.

'Bad boy,' she said. Raising herself on her haunches she teased herself by pulling away from his mouth. 'Bad boy.'

Her body began to quiver. Reaching forward, she took his cock in her hand and looked at the reddened shaft, its veins standing out like cords of string, the leather buried in the straining flesh and felt her body pulse. She ground her sex back down on to his mouth.

'Bad boy, bad boy . . . oh *gotte in himmel*!' Olga came, her body rigid for a moment, every muscle locked around her clitoris and vagina as they exploded with sensation. Then, almost immediately, it melted like butter in the sun, her voluptuous flesh seeming to pour over him, drowning him. There was so much of it, all soft and yielding, he had to fight for air.

'Bad boy.' She slapped his thigh hard, then pulled herself off the bed, standing up, naked from the waist down, the triangle of her pubis hidden under the overhang of her belly. 'You like I think,' she said grinning and looking at his erection. 'You like big Olga I think. Is so?'

'Yes,' he said reluctantly.

'If I leave you like this I think you wank no? You must not wank. Is forbidden. You understand?'

'Yes.'

'Is good you understand. This sheet is brown. The carpet is brown. There would be stains. If I see stains in the morning then it is the end for you. The end. Bye, bye. Understand?'

'Yes.'

'Is good.'

Olga pulled up her breeches, put on her jacket and picked up her boots. She unlocked the cubicle door and looked back at at him as she opened it. Her eyes still sparkled with excitement.

'Hildegard tomorrow,' she reminded him. 'Bad boy,' and she almost giggled as she closed the door behind her.

Chapter Five

GLORIA

It was obscene. It was the most obscene garment Gloria could imagine. It was made from red satin, at least it looked like satin though in fact it was a modern material, stretchy and capable of clinging to every contour of her body. Olga had stood over her as she'd pulled it on. Basically it was a catsuit with full sleeves and a high neck but at the front two holes had been made through which her breasts protruded awkwardly. But that was not the worst thing as far as Gloria was concerned. Down between her legs the catsuit had been cut away from the top of her labia at the front to the cleft of her buttocks at the back, revealing, and making available, the whole slit of her sex.

To complete her outfit Olga had handed her high-heeled white ankle boots made from shiny patent leather. Olga had sat her on the edge of the bed and applied her make-up. Though there was no mirror in the cubicle Gloria could see the German was using colours much darker than she ever used herself. She also applied mascara, eye shadow and blusher that Gloria never used. She finished with a dark red lipstick she painted on with a brush.

Gloria had spent the morning of her first day in the house on Punishment Corner, doing very much what she had expected. After her session with Clarissa last night Olga had brought her down to the basement and locked her in a wooden cubicle not much bigger than the double bed it contained. The door of the cubicle was numbered with a metal six. There was a small shower room in the basement along the corridor from the cubicles and Olga had taken her there first thing in the morning, allowing her to wash and use the toilet. She had been given bread and fruit and water for her breakfast, then, dressed in a light blue nylon overall, had been taken upstairs to the kitchen. Washing up was her first duty and then she was moved next door to a utility room where she was set to ironing.

There was another girl, a pretty, petite blonde also wearing a blue overall, scrubbing the floor of the kitchen but Olga made it absolutely clear that they were not allowed to talk to each other, and neither of them made any attempt to break the prohibition.

At lunchtime she had been fed again and was returned to her cubicle. She had been left there all afternoon. What time it was when Olga had arrived, wearing an odd, grey military type uniform, Gloria did not know but she had been taken to shower again and then returned to her cubicle to be dressed and made-up.

Finally satisfied with her appearance, Olga had led Gloria to the lift. When they emerged into Clarissa's first floor bedroom it was dark outside though the heavy curtains had not been drawn. They walked through the bedroom and out into the corridor. Olga opened another door and led Gloria into a slightly smaller bedroom, though no less expensively decorated.

'Walk,' Olga ordered. 'You must walk up and down.'

Gloria rarely wore high heels and certainly had never worn any as high as the little white boots. She was having trouble keeping her balance. Obediently, she tottered the length of the bedroom and back again. Catching sight of herself in the mirror she could hardly believe what she saw. The woman in red looked like an expensive whore dressed for some fetishist client. Olga had made her face up to emphasise her dark brown eyes. They looked back at her from the mirror with astonishment. The sight gave her a tingling sexual thrill.

'Again,' Olga ordered. 'You must get used to this.'

Gloria set off again. The underside of her breasts chafed against the material that pressed against them so tautly. She glimpsed herself in the mirror again. Her breasts seemed soft and vulnerable in contrast to the tight material that surrounded them.

As Gloria walked back towards the bathroom the bedroom door opened and Clarissa stood in the doorway, a triangular cocktail glass in her hand, half full of a colourless, viscous liquid. She was wearing a simple, strapless, dark blue cocktail dress.

'Oh yes. You look very sexy Gloria. So subtle don't you think?' she said in a mocking tone.

Gloria felt herself blushing. 'Yes, Ms Peacham.'

'Turn around,' Clarissa ordered.

Gloria obeyed, knowing the catsuit revealed most of the cleft of her arse.

'Good,' Clarissa said apparently satisfied. 'I have some guests staying with me tonight. I want you to entertain them for me. You understand that you will do everything they ask without question?'

'Yes, Ms Peacham.'

'That is what you're here for after all, isn't it?'

'Yes, Ms Peacham.'

'Come here.' Gloria hurried forward still tottering in the shoes. Clarissa looked straight into her eyes, her expression critical, looking to see if Gloria meant what she said. 'Don't disappoint me Gloria. I have high hopes for you.' She trailed her finger down to Gloria's exposed breasts and flicked her fingernail against one of her nipples. Gloria shuddered, feeling a rush of sensation out of all proportion to the stimulus.

Without a word Clarissa beckoned to Olga to follow her, turned on her heels and left, with Olga bringing up the rear. The door closed and Gloria heard it being locked.

For a while she stood stock still. She had no idea what to expect, though it was obvious she had been brought to this room in such an obscene costume to have sex with one of Clarissa's friends. What was remarkable was that, after her experience with Clarissa, she had no idea whether the friend would be male or female. Even more extraordinary she found that she did not care which it was.

What had happened with Clarissa last night was still hard for Gloria to understand. She had expected it to happen and wanted it because of the intimacy they had shared in her study the day before. But that did not make the actual experience any easier to cope with. She had never dreamt of having sex with a woman, nor even imagined kissing or stroking a woman. Now the sight of Clarissa, the aroma of her perfume, let alone the touch of her hand, had set her alight again. She knew she was wet, the juices of her body leaking out from her labia. She knew, had Clarissa pressed her body against her – just that and nothing more – it would free all the images and dreams she had had last night lying alone in her cubicle, and would bring her to an almost instant climax.

What had Clarissa done to her? Was the reason she had found sex with a man so unsatisfying over the years because what she really wanted was sex with a woman? If that was the case why had it taken her so long to find out?

She didn't think it was. She could still imagine wanting men. Hadn't her first reaction to Clarissa's touch been a desperate desire for sex with a man? The fact it had been so unsuccessful was not through lack of desire. It had been unsuccessful because that was what Clarissa wanted and somehow, though Gloria still had no idea how, she had imposed that wish on her, as unlikely as that seemed. What Clarissa had done to her had not turned her into a lesbian. It might be that she had opened a door for her, allowing her to enjoy women as well as men. But it was just as possible that she had not. It could well be that Clarissa was the only woman she could enjoy.

Faced with the stark choice Clarissa had presented her with Gloria would have done anything to keep her job. But so far, apart from the domestic chores, she had no reason to regret her decision. Indeed, but for her summons to Clarissa's house, she might never have learned what her body was capable of sexually.

She wondered about William. She had not seen him. Wondering if his experience with Clarissa had been the same as hers, she remembered how he had come all over her desk. Did Clarissa Peacham have some strange ability to find and exploit sexual weaknesses, even weaknesses, as in her case, her victims had no idea they had?

Gloria's sexual excitement, intensified by the outlandish costume she was wearing and by the element of the unknown, coursed through her body in waves, so strong it was making her heart pound and her breathing shallow. Her nipples were so hard they projected from her exposed breasts like golf tees. She supposed this was what it was like to be a prostitute waiting for a client, dressed blatantly for sex. The sexual encounters in Gloria's life had been spasmodic and mostly she had never known whether, at the end of an evening, she was going to go to bed with a man or not. It would depend on her mood, and what she felt about him. Here, in this house, the element of doubt was removed. Sex was to be taken for granted. When a man walked through that door – if it was to be a man – he would be there for only one reason. Gloria found that exciting, very exciting.

It was a man. He was tall and broad, with thick brown hair and strong features, his face as lined and craggy as an outcrop of rocks. He was wearing blue slacks and a light blue shirt open at the neck. He was not fat but looked like a man who had once been very fit and was beginning to let himself go.

'Well look at that,' he said in a soft American accent. Gloria thought he was talking to himself, his eyes roaming her outrageous outfit. But he was not. A small auburn haired woman followed him into the room. She was certainly not much more than five feet tall but was perfectly proportioned, with a slender figure and shapely legs. Her face was round and a little chubby with rosy cheeks and a small nose. She was wearing a lime green cocktail dress with puffed sleeves, cinched tightly by a dark green leather belt so wide it was shaped like an old-fashioned waspie corset, emphasising the narrowness of her waist. The buckle on the belt, in gold plated metal, had been cast to resemble the shape of a leopard, the tongue projecting from its mouth. Her high heels were green too and her legs were sheathed in a very sheer creamy white nylon. On the second finger of her left hand was a large diamond ring and a thick gold wedding band.

'She's something all right,' the woman agreed. Like the man her accent was American but, while his was the cultured sound of the Eastern seaboard, hers had the definite twang of the mid-West.

The woman walked up to Gloria looking at her intently. She had beautiful eyes, a near emerald green, that were dancing with excitement, their lashes spectacularly long and curled.

'What's your name precious?' she asked.

'Gloria.'

'Well Clarissa sure knows how to pick 'em doesn't she Howard?'

'She's lovely,' Howard replied. He sat on the edge of the bed and began unbuttoning his shirt.

'You're real pretty.' The woman ran her hand down Gloria's buttocks. Her fingers delved into the opening of the catsuit and pried down between Gloria's thighs. 'She's wet already,' she announced.

'In that outfit I'm not surprised,' the man said stripping off his shirt. His chest was covered with a thick mat of hair.

'So what do you want to do?'

'I want to see her with you Mitzy. Remember the last time we were here?'

The words made Gloria's heart start to beat faster.

'Yah, but she wasn't as pretty as this one Howard. This

one's a princess. Look at those legs.'

'Look at that pussy.'

'Wet pussy. Lovely wet pussy. Have you been with a woman before Gloria? Some of Clarissa's girls haven't. That's kinda fun sometimes.' Her hand had come up to stroke Gloria's buttocks again. 'But then I like experience too.'

'I . . .' Gloria wasn't sure what to say. 'Yes,' she said. It seemed to be the easiest answer. She felt a surge of excitement as she said it because it was true.

'But you're not a dike right?' Howard asked, kicking off his leather loafers, pulling off his socks, then standing up to unzip his trousers.

'No,' she said. 'I've mostly been with men.'

'Well, that's just how we like it honey. Unzip my dress.' Mitzy turned and presented her back to Gloria as she unbuckled the wide belt and threw it aside. There was a long zip running the whole length of her back which Gloria undid. Mitzy pushed the material from her shoulders and allowed the dress to fall to the floor. She stepped out of it and picked it up, folding it neatly over a small bedroom chair. Her underwear was white, a lacy bra, a matching suspender belt and small bikini style panties. The triangle of material at the back of the panties covered little of her plump, balloon-like arse. The thin suspenders held the creamy stockings taut, their more than usually broad tops also made from white lace.

The man had removed his trousers. He was wearing small black briefs. Mitzy walked over to him and cupped her hand over the bulge in the material.

'Going to give me a good time, are you big boy?' she said talking to his cock as though it were a separate entity.

'He sure is Mitzy, if he knows what's good for him,' Howard said. He kissed her on the mouth. The difference in their height made him stoop to reach her. Gloria saw her hand grinding against his genitals.

'Come over here,' Mitzy ordered as she broke away from him. 'Take his shorts down.'

Gloria did as she was told. Her pulse was racing. She could hear it pounding in her ears. Her mouth felt dry too. It was quite obvious she was going to be required to have sex with both partners. She had never done anything like that before. She had never even been in the same room with another couple while they were being intimate, let alone this. At any other time the idea would have scared her. If it had been suggested to her she would have run a mile. But this was another world, with different rules and different standards of behaviour. Before social conventions and her own personal shibboleths would have made her react differently. But now she had no choice. She had entered into a bizarre contract with Clarissa and had every intention of fulfilling it. Oddly, the very fact she was obliged to do whatever Clarissa planned for her, freed her to behave in a way in which she would never have allowed herself to behave in the real world. She could abandon convention and her personal inhibitions because she could tell herself she had no choice. And what she was left with was raw emotion, sex at its most basic level, sex for its own sake with no social niceties getting in the way.

She knelt at Howard's feet. His legs were long and covered with almost as much hair as his chest. Mitzy's hand had given him a partial erection and Gloria could see it distending the cotton briefs. She reached up to their elasticated waistband and pulled them down over his cock. As it sprung free she caught it in her mouth despite the fact she had not been told to do so.

'She's a greedy little girl,' Mitzy commented.

Howard's erection grew rapidly in Gloria's mouth. She ran her tongue around his circumcised glans and sucked it enthusiastically.

'Oh she's good,' he said.

'Don't make him come,' Mitzy warned. She watched Gloria's cheeks dimple as she sucked even harder.

'Got to save myself,' he said, pulling himself out of Gloria's mouth.

'Tastes good,' Gloria said. She looked like a whore and was behaving like one and it thrilled her.

'So do I honey child.' Mitzy scrambled onto the bed and lay on her back. 'Come and get a good taste of me.'

Gloria felt a sharp stab of arousal, so intense it felt like an electric shock. She knelt on the bed.

'Take my shoes off,' Mitzy ordered raising her leg until the sole of her shoe was pressing against one of Gloria's exposed breasts. Gloria slipped it off her foot then brought the white nylon covered foot up to her mouth and sucked on her toes, just as she had sucked on her husband's cock. She looked up her leg to the crotch of the white panties, stretched tautly across the plane of her sex. 'That's good . . .' Mitzy muttered as Gloria pulled the other shoe off and subjected her other foot to the same treatment.

Mitzy lowered both her legs and put them together, raising her hips so Gloria could pull the panties down. As soon as they were clear of her ankles she scissored her legs apart, one foot nudging against her husband's thigh as he stood by the side of the bed, looking down at her. Her pubic hair was auburn and had been shaved into the shape of a cigar on her mons, its base pointing to the slit of her sex. Her labia, whether naturally or as a result of depilation, were completely hairless, every line and wrinkle visible. The outer lips were fat and rubbery, the inner more delicate. With her legs so far apart her vagina had opened and Gloria could see its scarlet maw, glistening with its own juices.

'Do you like it?' Mitzy asked. 'Howard spends a lot of time down there, keeping it trim.'

'Beautiful,' Gloria said almost to herself. Until Clarissa she had never seen a woman's sex exposed like this. But Clarissa's was covered in hair. Mitzy's was much more revealing. Gloria was having no trouble in responding sexually to the sight of a woman's vulva just as, in the past, she had responded to a man's cock.

'Get down on it then,' Mitzy said with a hard edge in her voice.

Gloria did not hesitate. It was exactly what she wanted. She dipped her head and positioned her mouth over Mitzy's sex letting her breath – her hot, panted breath – play against it. She had never done this before. She had tongued Clarissa's clitoris but her sex had been filled by a dildo. This was different. Mitzy's pulpy, wet sex was open like a mouth, a succulent, fleshy mouth. And Gloria kissed it like a mouth, pressing her lips against it then darting her tongue into her vagina. Instantly she felt her own sex react with a jolt of pleasure as she tasted Mitzy's juices and felt her velvety cunt. The jolt was strong enough to pitch her body into the first tell-tale signs of orgasm.

She had never responded so quickly with a man. She had

wondered if her experience with Clarissa was unique, whether she would only feel that way with her. Now she knew it wasn't. It appeared her body was capable of a whole range of sexual responses. She had no time to consider the implications of this discovery; the feelings coursing through her were too strong to shunt aside and too pleasurable.

'Very good,' Mitzy said, her hands tangled in Gloria's short black hair.

Howard knelt at Mitzy's head. Immediately Mitzy rolled her head around and sucked his cock into her mouth. She didn't take him very deep, just concentrating on moving her lips over the ridge at the bottom of his glans.

Gloria moved her tongue up to Mitzy's clitoris feeling it pulse wildly as she did so, her own clitoris, pressed tightly between her labia, experiencing exactly the same phenomenon. With the very tip of her tongue she circled the little promontory, as she snaked both hands under Mitzy's stockinged thighs until her finger tips were butting against her labia.

'Mmm . . .' Mitzy murmured without taking her mouth away from her husband's cock, wanting to tell Gloria she was doing the right thing.

Gloria pushed two fingers into the wetness of Mitzy's vagina and felt again a jolt of excitement at something she had never done before. It felt so silky and clingy. She pushed deeper, as deep as her fingers could go, feeling the spongy interior parting to admit them. The mental stimulation was as strong as the physical, the fact that this was the first time she had ever touched a woman like this, intensifying everything she felt. She made another discovery. Whatever she did to Mitzy she seemed to be able to feel in her own body. Her clitoris was pulsing as powerfully as Mitzy's and now her vagina responded too, just as though it were being penetrated.

The trouble was she was making herself come. The first inklings of orgasm had turned rapidly into a heavy, rhythmic throb, like the engines of a cruise liner deep below decks. Everything she did was carrying her closer to a climax, and more rapidly than she would have believed possible.

'My arse,' Mitzy said, pulling away from Howard's cock just long enough to say the words.

Gloria knew what she meant. Two fingers of one hand were already pressing up against the little puckered opening as the fingers of her other hand reamed Mitzy's vagina. The juices from Mitzy's sex had run down to make it wet. As she straightened her fingers to prod against the little ring of muscles she felt her own sphincter spasm too. The spasm kicked her closer to orgasm. As she felt Mitzy's sphincter relax and her fingers slid home on the copious lubrication, and the tight hot tube of flesh closed around her fingers, as she pushed all four fingers up deep into both passages of Mitzy's body Gloria could hold her orgasm back no longer. It exploded through her, an orgasm centred in her mind, as much as in her sex, the idea of what she was doing as thrilling as the actual doing.

Despite the intensity of it, or perhaps because of it, in the middle of the storm that raged in her body she could feel Mitzy come too, her sex contracting around the fingers that invaded it, as if wanting to suck on them. As Gloria strove to keep her tongue circling Mitzy's clit, she felt it leap, and this in turn seemed to kick her orgasm into another spiral, coiling it so tight she could do nothing but feel.

'Some performance,' Howard said, pulling his cock from

his wife's mouth where it had gagged her cries of pleasure.

'And how,' Mitzy said.

'Room for one more?' he asked.

Through the mists of passion Gloria felt the heat of his cock nestling into the cleft of her arse, so neatly exposed by the tight red, satin-like material. Instinctively she wriggled her arse against it.

'He's going to fuck you,' Mitzy said raising her head to watch. 'Do you want to be fucked?'

'Oh yes, yes, give it to me!' It was an exact repeat of her first time with Clarissa. After that experience Gloria had been desperate for a cock, any cock. Now she felt the same desperation, but this time what she needed was readily and instantly available.

Wriggling her buttocks from side to side she felt Howard's erection slide down between her legs. It was immediately anointed with her juices.

'She's so wet,' Howard said.

'She sure is,' Mitzy agreed.

Mitzy pulled Gloria's hands from her body and sat up. She reached behind her back and undid her bra, shucking it off her shoulders. Her breasts were small and flat but had nipples the size of cherries.

'Kiss me, honey,' she said taking Gloria's cheeks in her hands and pulling her face up. Her lips and tongue eagerly moved round Gloria's mouth, lapping up the wetness left there. 'Taste good, don't I?'

'Yes, very good.'

Howard bucked his hips and Gloria felt his hard, hot cock slide into her sex in one smooth, frictionless motion, right up to the hilt, so she could feel his navel against her buttocks and his balls hanging against her labia. He began to pump into her.

'She's got a tight little pussy,' he said to his wife.

'He's got a lovely hard cock hasn't he honey?' Mitzy said.

'Oh yes, so hard . . .' Gloria agreed feeling her sex contracting around it.

Howard filled her. He drove forward powerfully, every stroke seeming to open her up more, going deeper and deeper, until he was right at the neck of her womb. In seconds, less than seconds, she felt her body gear itself for orgasm again, the incident in the wine bar, the numbness that had descended so suddenly, seemingly banished from her vocabulary of response. Instead she felt a throbbing passion like nothing she had ever felt with a man. It was as though she could feel every inch of him, every contour and vein of his cock and every living pulse of it.

'Little bitch is on heat, she's coming again,' Mitzy said.

'Yes,' Gloria confirmed wanting them to know it was true. No man had ever had this effect on her. The unexpectedly sharp orgasm she had had with Derek was nothing compared to this. Every nerve in her body was focused on the sword of flesh buried inside her. Each inward stroke seemed to produce a new wave of sensation, stronger and more telling than the last.

'Does she feel good?' Mitzy asked.

'Great pussy,' he said breathily.

Mitzy reached up to Gloria's breasts and pinched both of her nipples at the same time. Gloria was already poised on the brink of orgasm and this plunged her over the edge. Her last conscious movement was to push back against Howard's body, digging his cock into her probably no more than an extra millimetre but producing a wave of feeling as though it were an extra metre.

She screamed, the sound echoing around the room. Now each thrust of Howard's cock penetrated the centre of an enormous hurricane of feeling, making it turn faster, whipping the winds to impossible speeds. And, like a hurricane, at the centre of Gloria's raging emotions, was a calmness, a realisation that she had crossed a threshold, that sex for her would never be the same again.

Slowly her orgasm released her. Only then did she realise Howard had not come.

'Now it's my turn,' Mitzy said, as Gloria felt the big phallus slide out of her vagina.

Still in a daze, she allowed Mitzy to push her over on to her back, spreading her thighs apart then kneeling between them. 'Such a pretty pussy honey,' she said, her fingers splaying Gloria's labia so she could see the pinkness of her clitoris and the scarlet opening of her sex. The action made Gloria tremble, her nerves over-sensitised by two shattering orgasms.

'What are you doing?' she said though it was obvious. She looked down her body, the red material still sleek and smooth, her breasts sticking out lewdly. Mitzy, naked now but for the lacy suspender belt and the white lace topped stockings, had an expression of undiluted lust as she dipped her head to kiss the flesh that only seconds before her husband had penetrated.

The impact of the sensation made Gloria drop her head back and close her eyes. Mitzy was licking up and down, as a child licks an ice cream, ploughing the furrow of Gloria's labia with the whole width of her tongue. At first it was soothing, her saliva balm on the tingling nerves. But it did not take long for Gloria's body to change gear again, for soothing to turn to needing, for balm to turn to bane.

Gloria felt a weight shifting on the bed. It was Howard. He had moved so he was kneeling behind his wife. Taking her hips in his hands he plunged his cock into the slippery wetness between her legs. Momentarily, as his phallus drove effortlessly into her vagina, Mitzy's head reared up from Gloria's sex.

'Give it to me you bastard,' she hissed between gritted teeth. 'You know what I want.'

'Love to see that,' he said, as Mitzy's mouth dropped back down to Gloria's sex, searching for her clitoris this time and butting her tongue up against it. 'Love to see you eating some little whore,' he said pumping into her.

Mitzy's body shuddered. She wanted to use her tongue on Gloria's clitoris, to push it to and fro but the strength of her husband's thrusts were just too powerful to be ignored. They took her over. Each forward stroke pushed her mouth against Gloria's sex, however, and her tongue against her swollen clit. She felt Gloria's body respond, just as she was responding, both women prone to the same stimulus though by different means.

By the same token, as Mitzy's orgasm began to break over the smooth, tumescent glans of Howard's cock, Gloria had the same reaction. Mitzy's mouth transmitted her feelings to Gloria's sex, every trill and thrill of pleasure, every electric shock of sensation, communicated perfectly until Gloria was writhing in orgasm too, an orgasm she would never have believed she could be capable of after what she had already been through.

'God, God,' she cried.

Howard looked down at the two women, the beautiful brunette provided for their pleasure, and his wife, her head buried between the stranger's legs. Her round bottom was fenced in by the suspender belt, the white lace cutting across her back, the suspenders running along the sides of her thighs, and the lacy tops of the stockings pulled taut at the tops of her legs. In contrast to the lace it looked impossibly soft and creamy; as soft and creamy as the velvety walls of her vagina.

He had reached the point of no return. He could feel Mitzy coming all over him, the contractions of her sex squeezing his cock as though trying to milk it of spunk. He would have liked to pull out, had the girl lick and suck him. He would have liked to kneel over her face and have Mitzy wank him while the girl sucked his balls so his spunk would spatter out over her breasts and the red catsuit. They had tried so many variations with Clarissa's girls. But he was too far gone. He drove one final time into Mitzy's seething sex and felt his shaft jerk determinedly, spitting out his semen against the silky walls that held it so tightly.

Chapter Six

It had been a terrible day. After being allowed to shower and eat his breakfast, Olga had given him a pair of nylon dungarees to wear and rubber boots. She had not removed the strap around his cock.

With no hint of a smile she had taken him to another part of the house and had set him to work cleaning the wooden floor of a room that looked as though it had been used as some sort of workshop. The floor was filthy, caked with dirt and paint. She had provided him with a small metal scraper and ordered him to get to work cleaning the wood, taking up position to supervise his efforts and discouraging the slightest relaxation with a well-aimed flick with a riding crop she obviously took great delight in finding an excuse to use.

Even with an electric sander the job would have taken a whole day, but by hand it was going to take days. He worked continuously with only a short break for lunch. Any idea that he had had that Clarissa's main purpose in bringing him to the house was to provide more intimate services was quickly dispelled by the backbreaking grind.

William had not seen Gloria. He had passed two other females on his way to the workshop, both in blue nylon overalls and both engaged in cleaning the house. Olga had warned him that speaking to any other servant was forbidden and they, in turn, had seemed to take little interest in him. Both of them had been attractive and both, he speculated, would be worthy of the sort of attention Clarissa had given Gloria. And both he thought he recognised, recruited he was sure, from the offices of Peacham Associates. Had Clarissa used the same means to command their compliance?

According to the time he glimpsed on Olga's watch it was five o'clock when she lashed him across the buttocks with the crop and told him to stop work. The weals from the metal ruler had still not entirely disappeared and this stroke seemed to land right across one of the deeper bruises making William gasp in pain, no sexual imperative to turn the pain to pulsing pleasure. She marched him back to the basement and told him to clean himself thoroughly, locking him in the shower room after taking the overalls away. It was half-an-hour before she came back to inspect him minutely and return him to his cubicle where he collapsed on the bed in exhaustion.

He must have dozed off to sleep because when Olga marched into the room again he started awake, so disorientated it took him a good minute to work out where he was.

'On your feet,' she said grinning broadly. He was astonished to see that her watch showed it was nine o'clock. She held a leather harness in her hand. 'Quick, quick. Be quick.'

William scrambled to his feet, standing in front of her. She immediately took him by the shoulders and twisted him around. She picked up his left wrist. The harness she had brought in consisted of two leather cuffs joined by a single metal link. She wrapped one of the cuffs around William's left wrist then secured it tightly by means of two buckles. She pulled his right wrist behind his back and looped the second cuff around it, buckling that equally tight too and thus binding his hands together.

'What are you doing?' he asked though it was perfectly obvious.

Olga swung him round and looked into his eyes. 'Hildegard's waiting for you. You must be punished. For what you did.' She took a silver chain from the pocket of the uniform jacket which she had worn all day. Hanging from it was a small key. She looped the chain over William's neck.

'Follow.'

They walked along to the lift. The racing of William's pulse was caused by a certain amount of fear, but mostly by an unaccountable excitement. He felt incredibly vulnerable, with his hands so securely bound behind his back, a vulnerability reinforced by his nakedness. It was not even possible for him to touch his own cock, to stop it bouncing up and down as he walked. For some reason he did not understand that inability aroused him and he felt his erection beginning to grow.

Olga noticed his condition as he got into the lift.

'What is this?' she asked looking at his genitals. 'What causes this?'

He made no reply but felt himself blush.

'Come on? What is? You like to be punished?' She tested her theory by slapping his thigh. There was very little room in the lift for her to swing her arm so the slap only produced a mild sting. Unfortunately the effect seemed to swell William's cock further, until he could feel the strap biting into his flesh again. 'Yes, that is it, I think,' Olga said delighted. 'And this.' She pulled on one of his arms to demonstrate that she meant his bondage. 'Many men find this makes them big, I think.'

The lift doors opened on the second floor. Olga led William down a corridor. There were several identical doors. Olga positioned him outside one of them and knocked on it twice.

'Wait,' she said turning back to the lift. In moments she was gone.

William could hear someone moving about behind the door. He tried to think of anything but his physical condition but his erection refused to wither. As before, the tighter the leather bit into him, the more his cock seemed to want to swell against it. Reflexively, forgetting the leather cuffs, he tried to pull the strap down slightly. The jerk that reminded him he was not free to do so sent a jolt of sensation through his body; the sensation was very definitely a peculiar, twisted pleasure. He had no idea why but the bondage was exciting him. Like the corporal punishment he had received, he had never imagined such a thing would affect him so powerfully. Obviously his sexual imagination had been severely limited. He apparently had the capacity to enjoy a whole range of experiences that previously he had dismissed as perverse.

After what he estimated to be fifteen or twenty minutes the lift door opened and Olga emerged. She was followed by a rather plump, petite blonde, one of the girls William had seen working in the house earlier in the day. She was wearing a black leather basque, black stockings, and shiny black patent leather shoes with heels so high she could only take diminutive steps. Around her neck was a studded leather collar attached to which was a chain like a dog leash. Olga led her down the corridor by the leash in the opposite direction from William. He could not resist looking at her despite the effect it had on his straining erection. She was wearing no panties and, as she walked, he could see the bush of her pubic hair between her legs.

Olga knocked on one of the doors. It was opened and a hand – too far away for William to be able to tell whether it was male or female – took the leash from her and pulled the girl inside. The door closed and Olga went back to the lift which was still open. She disappeared into it without sparing William a glance.

'In.'

The door had opened. A woman stood holding the handle, her eyes examining William critically. She was a blonde, probably in her mid-thirties, her hair permed into tight curls. She had a hard, unsmiling face, with a lantern jaw, small ice blue eyes and a thin, mean mouth. Her complexion was flawless, her skin fair and completely unblemished. She was wearing a knee length strapless dress in a crimson red, no more than a tube of material stretched tightly over her body. She had narrow snake like hips and small buttocks, with hardly any inward curves to her waist. The dress clung tightly to a full bosom.

'In,' she repeated.

William shuffled forward and she closed the door behind him. The room was decorated in shades of pink; a light pink carpet, flowery wallpaper in the same colour and curtains in a somewhat darker red.

'You are new,' she said. Her accent was the same as Olga's. 'You have no training yes?'

'Training?' he said.

'All men must be trained.' She looked at his cock and the leather strap that made every vein on it bloated and red. 'You do not know that you must kneel? Come on. Do it.'

William fell to his knees with a thump, finding it difficult without his arms for balance. Clarissa had told him to kneel for her; he hadn't realised it applied to all the guests in the house. Presumably he must also kiss her feet. He leant forward, anxious to show her he understood, and pressed his lips to her left foot. She was wearing flesh coloured nylon.

'So you do know this,' she said. 'Have you served other guests?'

'No.' He transferred his mouth to her right foot, licking and kissing her flesh through the nylon.

'*Ach so*?' She smiled. 'That is good. So you must learn many things. And I enjoy to teach.'

William covered all the available flesh. Knelt forward like this his cock was forced against his belly. It was throbbing, the constriction of the strap now so severe it was painful. Unfortunately it was the sort of pain that only served to increase his sexual need.

'Is good,' she pronounced. 'So, on your feet.'

Glad to be able to relieve the pressure on his erection William straightened up and got to his feet. Again he found it difficult without the use of his hands and almost stumbled over. The difficulty, like everything else that had happened to him, seemed to provoke him further. He looked down at his cock. It was as distended and red as he had ever seen it, the strap digging in around the base, a trickle of fluid running from the slit.

'Over here.'

Hildegard sat on the side of the bed. The counterpane and bedding had been stripped away to reveal a pink cotton sheet. On the bedside table was a long rectangular box which, according to the labelling was a catering pack of cling film.

'You are in a bad state, I think,' she said as William stood in front of her, his cock level with her breasts. 'You must be teased.' Her thin lips cracked into a smile. She extended her finger and touched the tip of the glans, smearing the fluid against it. 'You want I suck it?'

'No,' he moaned. Of course there was nothing he would have liked more, but he did not want to experience the humiliation he had suffered in Clarissa's bathroom.

'You must do as I say,' she reminded him.

'Please don't,' he begged.

The strap that held his cock so tightly was painful. But it was pain that stimulated an aching pleasure. It was a delicious torture like nothing he had felt before. Tendrils of feeling skewered into the sexual centres of his body, his nerves crawling with a feverish lust. His bound hands seemed to have the same effect, raising the temperature of the blood that coursed through his veins to boiling point.

But it was not just his physical situation that was affecting him. It was also what he felt, how he was being used, the way Hildegard was looking at him and the way, ultimately, he had been made to look at himself. He had never imagined being treated in this way would excite him. But it did, profoundly.

'Oh no, I think you want very much,' she said. She took his glans between her thumb and forefinger and pinched it hard enough to turn the flesh white. William moaned, desperately

133

trying to control the wave of feelings she had produced. 'Lean here,' she said indicating she wanted him to move his head down towards her. As he did she reached up and looped the silver chain off his neck.

'More, I think,' she said pinching his glans again. His body shuddered, his erection fighting against the strap.

'Please,' he said. If she didn't remove the strap soon he knew he would not be able to hold himself back. It was like a strong hand squeezing him constantly, magnifying every spasm of feeling, with no escape from its tantalising grip.

'I be good to you,' she said. With one hand she pushed his erection up against his belly, creating another wave of sensation, while the other found the padlock under the buckle and inserted the key. She opened the staple and undid the strap. It fell to the floor.

For a second William experienced a flood of pleasure so strong he thought he was going to come. His phallus throbbed wildly but he hung on desperately determined to control himself. In seconds the crisis passed and, to his relief, he found the lack of constriction eased the urgency of his need.

'You see, I am good to you,' she said. She got up off the bed. 'A little closer I think.' She took William's shoulder and manoeuvred him around so he was a foot away from the side of the bed with his back to it. 'Is good. Now you stand very still for me, yes? Very still.'

Fortunately the throbbing in his cock had subsided. It had been replaced by a dull ache, where the nerves, pinched for so long, began to re-awaken, and protest. They did not, however, affect his rock hard erection. He heard Hildegard opening a drawer in the bedside table, then she came up behind him, pressing her body against his back. She raised her hands to his head. Spread out between her fingers was an elasticated mask, made from black silk. She slipped it over his eyes. It fitted snugly, the silk contoured and padded around the eye sockets to exclude all light.

William shuddered. Three days ago he had been living a normal life, going to work, returning home. Since his divorce he had had a few girlfriends but most of his sexual activity had been masturbation. Now he was standing naked in a strange house, with a woman he did not know, his hands bound behind his back, a blindfold over his eyes, and an erection sticking out from his loins, obliged, he knew, to co-operate with whatever Hildegard wanted of him. The situation was so bizarre, it would have had a dreamlike quality but for the fact that he had never felt more wide awake.

The darkness the blindfold imposed made matters worse for William, concentrating his senses, narrowing his perception down to the compass of his own body, to what he was feeling, with no distractions from other things. He was intensely aware of the leather cuffs and the peculiar feelings they created. The blindfold itself provoked a similar response, its tight elastic digging into the flesh around his temples. The helplessness and vulnerability he felt provoked him quite as much as the extraordinary sensations he had experienced in Clarissa's study. How could he have been so unaware of this mine of sexual pleasure, its dark, rich seam apparently so close to the surface?

The blindfold seemed to intensify sound. He heard a sharp tearing noise. He felt Hildegard moving around his body. 'Very still,' she repeated.

Something cold and clammy touched his ankles accompanied

by another tearing sound. He knew what it was at once. As he felt the material enclosing his ankles and calves, winding around his legs, he knew Hildegard had taken the roll of cling film and was wrapping it around him, enclosing him like bunting around a maypole. The clingfilm was tight and unyielding, pressing his legs together.

Kneeling in front of him Hildegard passed the roll of film over the front of his legs with one hand, then reached behind him to take it with the other, pulling it tighter and tighter, several layers over each section of his flesh. She reached the top of his thighs, winding the film over his pulsing cock and balls, trapping them securely against his belly. She wound the transparent plastic around his buttocks and cock again, each loop increasing the pressure, the film clinging tightly to itself. He imagined what she could see – his cock through the folds of plastic, ironed back against his flesh, unable to move, the fluid from his slit slicked on the film.

William felt himself being engulfed, the clingfilm wrapping around his waist, over his already bound hands and wrists, roll after roll securing him completely. Hildegard worked it up over his chest and shoulders. For a moment she thought she was going to continue and encase his head but she stopped at the top of his arms and finished by rolling the film over his shoulders and diagonally over his chest forming a cross. She had created a mummy, a modern mummy, his living body swathed in transparent plastic film.

He sensed that she stood in front of him, admiring her handiwork. Then, with her right hand she pushed him in the chest. Unable to counterbalance himself with his limbs, William toppled backwards and fell like a dead weight on to the bed.

'Comfortable?' she mocked. She grabbed his ankles and pulled his legs around until his whole body was flat on the mattress.

In the darkness William listened intently for a clue as to what she was going to do next. If he had felt helpless before it was nothing compared to his situation now. Before he could have struggled and kicked and even run away. Now he could do nothing to protect himself. He remembered what Clarissa had said about Hildegard. She was to be his punishment. So far she had only succeeded in exciting him. His cock, pressed back against his own belly was throbbing again. The clingfilm enclosed his balls too, squeezing them tightly and further adding to his sexual arousal.

He heard a rustle of material. Hildegard must be peeling off her dress.

'What does it feel like?' she said.

'Tight.'

'No, what does it feel like to be . . .' she searched for the right word in English, 'powerless.' She bent over the bed. He could feel her breath on his ear. 'You can do nothing. Nothing. Try for me. I want to see you struggle. I like this.'

William tensed his muscles and pulled against the clingfilm, trying to open his legs. It was no good. The material gave not an inch. The only effect he had was to make his body rock slightly from side to side. He tried to move his arms but that was impossible too. Bound under his body as they were, forcing his hips to arch off the bed, they were already numb.

'Powerless,' Hildegard repeated with obvious delight. He felt her hand running down his chest. It moved on to his erection and stroked up and down. 'You have been a bad boy. Clarissa told me this. Is it true?'

'Yes.'

He felt her weight kneeling on the mattress besides him. 'Tell me what you did that was so bad?' Her hand continued to stroke his throbbing flesh.

'I . . .' He didn't know what to say. 'She made me help her dry herself. It was too much for me . . .'

'Too much? How too much?'

'I was too excited. She was so beautiful.' In the blackness he could see Clarissa's spectacular body, the wonderful curves of her rich buttocks, and those proud, supple breasts. The image didn't help the condition of his erection, as Hildegard's hand moved against it. 'You'll make me come,' he said pathetically.

'And what did you do?' she said ignoring him.

'I . . . she made me dry her sex. She pulled the towel away . . .'

'It is bad you say this,' Hildegard hissed in his ear.

'I mean the towel fell away. I was touching her then.' He could feel the soft, pulpy flesh of Clarissa's sex.

'And?'

'It was too much for me.'

'How too much?' Hildegard snapped angrily.

He was thoroughly ashamed of what had happened. He saw his semen spattering over Clarissa's lush creamy buttocks. He felt Hildegard's hand stroking his cock. The peculiar bondage seemed to have concentrated all his feelings on his erection, trapping them inside him, just as his body was trapped. It felt good, so good he didn't know what he was going to do to stop himself from coming again.

'Tell me,' she insisted, her breath travelling round the whorls of his ear.

'I couldn't hold back.'

'What did you do?'

'I came. I came over her buttocks.' He was one second from doing the same thing over the clingfilm. His body was rigid, as he felt the reins of control slipping away. 'Please, please,' he begged. 'You've got to stop.'

And she did. She moved around so she was facing his feet then swung her thigh over his shoulders. Instantly her sex dropped on to his mouth. Her labia felt thin and hairless against his mouth.

'Give it to me,' she said huskily, grinding herself down on his mouth so hard he had trouble catching his breath.

Her sex was wet, her excitement at what she had done to him making her juices flow. William plunged his tongue into the slit of her labia, and found the sticky, unctuous cavern of her vagina. He strained his tongue up as far as it would go, moving it from side to side inside her, glad of the distraction from his own condition.

'*Ja, ja,*' Hildegard encouraged.

He extracted his tongue and slid it up to her clitoris, then pressed the little nub of flesh back against her pubic bone. He felt her body tense, her thighs closing around his face reflexively. He worked his tongue around the little pink promontory, nudging it from side to side. The fact that he could not see made it easier to feel. In his imagination, in the blank screen behind his eyes, he could see her clitoris as the tip of his tongue pushed against it.

'*Ja, ja,*' she cried. She looked down at his mummified

139

body, his limbs so tightly wrapped. It was as though she had turned his body into one giant phallus, the head of which she was sitting on. She loved the feeling, her sex wet and open, squatting on her captive, helpless lover. He was powerless. She squirmed down on his face, burying his nose in the tight cleft of her buttocks, making it impossible for him to breathe. She held herself there counting the seconds in her mind, feeling his body writhe underneath her and his mouth gasping for air.

'You must learn to control yourself,' she said as she relented, easing up slightly to allow him to breathe before clamping down again.

But the one breath was enough. William went back to work on her clitoris. The pressure of her weight was pushing it hard against his mouth. He flicked it from side to side with his tongue, as fast as he could. He felt her react, the imperative to torture him overtaken by a more urgent need. Her body relaxed. He gulped in air through his nose as he continued to tongue her clit.

'Good . . . good . . .' she cried. He felt her muscles tense, then her sex melted over his mouth, a flood of juices escaping her vagina. Her labia turned pulpy, like a natural sponge soaked with her juices and squashed against his mouth. She squatted there for a long time, allowing the thrills of orgasm to fully run their course.

'Now then,' she said decisively as she swung herself off his face. He felt her get off the bed. Her footsteps walked to the bedroom door and he heard it open. It didn't close again. He thought he heard another door opening some way down the corridor.

There must have been a clock in the bedroom somewhere

because that was the only noise he could hear, the regular double note of a second hand. His face was wet. Sweat had run down from his forehead to mingle with the juices from Hildegard's body. The clingfilm made him hot and sweat had pooled under it, unable to escape, making his bondage even more uncomfortable. He tested his strength again, as a means of relieving the cramp that was creeping into his arms and shoulders, but made no impression on the rolls of clingfilm.

Unfortunately for him his body converted the feeling of constriction into a jolt of pure pleasure. His cock throbbed against its bindings. He had no idea why, but there was no doubt about the powerful effect – despite the discomfort – that the peculiar bondage was having on his sexual psyche. Had Clarissa known he would respond in his way, as she seemed to have known his reaction to being beaten? The source of this pleasure and what she had done to him in the study were, he suspected, from the same spring, the same basic impulse. Had she somehow managed to read his deepest secrets, secrets to which even he was not privy? Was that really possible? Or was it merely that she treated all her 'servants' the same way and his response just happened to be more extreme? He guessed he would never know the answer.

He heard the door creak slightly then close. Hildegard was back.

'Such a pretty picture,' she said. He heard her come over to the bed. 'So many things I could do to you.' She leant over and, with her hands on his hips rolled him on to his stomach.

It was a relief, his weight no longer pressing on his arms. But now his cock was trapped between his body and the mattress renewing his aching desire to come.

141

'I have been very lenient, no? But now . . .'

'Please,' he said though he wasn't sure why. The clingfilm around his cock had been lubricated by the fluid from his slit and his sweat, mixed together. It made the plastic slippery and William found himself moving against it almost imperceptibly.

'Please what William?' It was the first time she had used his name. 'You tell me you deserve punishment. If you do not wish to be punished you will be released from this house. That is correct is it not?'

'Yes.'

'And you wish to be punished then do you not?'

The peculiar thing was that William did wish it. The idea was making his blood boil. 'Yes.'

'Is good.' Almost before she got the word out he heard the whisper of something cutting through the air. A stripe of pain burnt across the meat of his buttocks. It was exactly the same feeling he had felt for the first time in Clarissa's study, stinging pain turning immediately to fiery pleasure. If anything it was more intense. 'Oh yes,' he heard Hildegard say, her voice husky with passion.

Again the whip fell, this time much lower, cutting across the bottom of his thighs just above the knees. Again the sharp tang of pain turned to a pleasure William had only experienced once before. Unconsciously, almost, his erection throbbing, he squirmed against the mattress.

Thwack. Another stroke, this one in the middle of his thighs.

'Lovely,' Hildegard said. 'So deep. Goes so deep.'

William wasn't sure what that meant. He heard her give a little gasp of pleasure, then the whip whistled down again and landed just under his buttocks. He bucked his hips driving his cock against the slippery clingfilm and the mattress.

'So good, so good,' Hildegard said with obviously mounting passion.

William knew he was going to come. He knew there was not a single thing he could do to stop himself, however humiliating it would be to spend his semen into the rolls of plastic. His cock was on fire, flames from the weals across his thighs licking at it, each new weal getting closer and the flames more intense.

'Feels so good,' Hildegard said hoarsely. Was she doing this to add further provocation? 'Yes,' she cried loudly. Another stroke followed in exactly the same spot as the last one, doubling the pain and, as night follows day, doubling the squirming pleasure too, the reverberation of it, trapped by the clingfilm, buffeting his balls. 'Yes, oh yes,' she cried even more loudly, as yet another stroke left a trail of fire, this time across the meat of his buttocks.

His cock jerked. His buttocks and thighs were alive, crawling with the sting of pain which produced sickly, sweet pleasure. He had never dreamt such pleasure was possible. He rubbed his cock against the mattress and pulled at his bondage, wanting to feel the constriction, knowing it would add an extra thrill to the incredible melange of feelings to which he was prone. His mind, starved of visual stimulus, had conjured up an image of Clarissa's body as she had peeled away the black satin robe to reveal her big round breasts and the black French knickers. But as his cock jerked and another stroke of the whip landed with unerring accuracy on the precise path of the last stroke, it was Clarissa's look of contempt and disdain that he saw, the final provocation as his spunk jetted out against the plastic.

It went on and on, semen pumping out in an endless stream, the feeling of its heat and wetness against his belly provoking him further. He had never felt anything like it. Never. He heard himself whimpering like a dog.

'Oh *ja, ja*,' Hildegard cried, her voice reaching a crescendo.

When William was conscious of anything other than his own feelings he could not understand what was going on. He thought her rising passion was related to the whipping she was giving him but there was more to it than that.

'So deep, oh it's so deep inside me,' she moaned. Then she growled, like an animal and screamed and he felt her hands fall forward onto the bed, to support her weight. 'Coming, coming, coming . . .' she cried, the mattress bouncing up and down.

It was then he knew there was something else in the room.

Hildegard's breathing was rapid and heavy. As it slackened, and returned to normal, William felt himself being rolled on to his back, the weals on his buttocks and thighs protesting at the contact with a tingling pain. A hand pulled the silk blindfold from his eyes.

Hildegard was leaning over the bed, one hand still supporting her as the other stripped the blindfold away. Behind, Clarissa was standing with her hand on the stub of a dildo the bulk of which was buried in Hildegard's sex. Her tall slender body was dressed in a tight fitting black silk and lace teddy, her big breasts tantalisingly covered by delicate lace cups, its legs cut so high the creases of her pelvis were exposed.

Clarissa's eyes were looking at him with the same expression he had remembered only seconds before, her contempt and disdain inspired by the white spunk that had spread across the clingfilm on his belly.

'Is there no limit to your disobedience?' She spat the words out at him, each one lashing him quite as efficiently as the whip had done.

GLORIA

'In here.'

Olga held open a door in the corridor on the second floor. She had collected Gloria directly from her domestic duties which was unusual in itself. The routine for the last seven days had been for her to be taken to the basement, where she had been allowed to shower first before being returned to her cubicle. She had not seen Clarissa, nor had she been taken to any guests.

She walked into a small bedroom decorated in blues and greys. There was a chest of drawers in mahogany and a wardrobe in the same wood. The door to an en suite bathroom, tiled in blue, was open.

'Shower. Wash your hair. Quick. Quick.' Olga ordered. 'Quick,' she repeated reinforcing the message with a slap on Gloria's rump when she did not move immediately.

Gloria trooped into the bathroom and stripped off her light blue nylon overall. She didn't know what this sudden break with the monotony of the last seven days meant but she felt a growing sense of anticipation. She ran the shower and washed her hair with the shampoo she found in the soap tray. She guessed that she was not being prepared for Clarissa or she would have been taken directly to her bedroom, but Clarissa had something in mind for her and she knew what *she* hoped it was.

With seven days of nothing but boring menial chores, Gloria had had plenty of time to think. Before she had been given to Mitzy and Howard her feelings had been confused but the experience with them had done a lot to clarify her reactions. What had happened initially with Clarissa, she had decided, had not changed her sexual proclivity. It was not that she had been hiding a lesbian tendency from herself but that Clarissa's attention had released something in her, had struck a spark which had ignited a fire within her. It had been *her* ability to respond sexually that before had been limited and unsatisfactory and that was what had changed.

Before Howard, if she had been alone with Mitzy, she might have been led to believe that what had started the fire was a lesbian impulse, but her reaction to Howard had been just as sharp and unrestrained. It was not to do with the object of her sexual attention but her own subjective response. That was the gift Clarissa had given her.

Over the last few days Clarissa had never been far from her thoughts. Clarissa had a sort of hypnotic power over her. Alone in her cubicle, unable to stop herself thinking about the extraordinary sexual energy her body had generated since she had been made to strip her clothes off in Clarissa's study, Gloria had twice tried to masturbate. She had masturbated regularly in her adult life, and had often found it more satisfying than her experiences with men. She had a routine, a ritual almost, which she followed faithfully. She began by running a finger along her sex to find her clitoris. She touched it gently, as lightly as she could to generate a wave of feeling that would lubricate her vagina. With two fingers of her other hand she would penetrate herself, increasing the pressure on her clit, until, ultimately, she was strumming it like the strings of a guitar. The technique had never produced a shattering orgasm but it had always brought her a modest climax. But not now. Both times the impulse had died almost before it had been born. Both times as the first stirring of pleasure had closed her eyes, there, waiting in the darkness for her was Clarissa, her face etched with stern disapproval, the implied prohibition absolute. She had tried in vain to shake the image from her mind, opening her eyes and looking at her naked body, but the more she toiled at her sex, the more benumbed it had become. It was exactly what she had experienced in the wine bar. Clarissa had a power over her. She did not understand it but she had to accept it.

Whatever she was being prepared for tonight, Gloria was anxious to renew her association with her body's new-found sexuality. If she was not allowed to masturbate, she reasoned, she was being saved for something else.

She dried herself on a large blue bath towel and walked back into the bedroom. The corridor door was open and the maid in the blonde wig stood in the doorway. She had a small make-up case in one hand. Closing the door she walked over to the dressing table by the window and pulled up a chair next to the one already standing in front of the mirror. Her eyes examined Gloria's naked body minutely.

Olga was sitting on the bed, her head propped up against the pillows, her feet up and her booted ankles crossed. 'Georgette is going to make you up,' she said.

'Over here dear,' the maid said. Her voice was rather gruff

and hoarse like someone who smoked too many cigarettes.

'Get on with it,' Olga said.

Georgette settled Gloria down, opened the make-up case and began applying eye-shadow. She was wearing exactly the same outfit as the first time Gloria had seen her, a black dress and white lace apron and opaque black tights. Her hands, Gloria noticed as they worked on her face, were large and ungainly.

'So what you think of this one Georgy?' Olga asked.

'She's got a lovely body. Wish I had a body like that.'

For some reason Olga found this funny and laughed. She got to her feet and came up behind Gloria, putting her hand on her shoulder and pinching at her flesh. 'She's had it too easy,' she said.

'Have you . . . ?' the maid asked Olga leaving the question unfinished.

'Not yet. But I'm sure my day will come.'

With that Olga turned and marched quickly out of the bedroom, leaving the door open.

By the time Georgette had applied the rest of the make-up, finishing with lipstick, painted on with a brush, Olga had returned. She dropped the clothes she was carrying onto the bed.

'She's ready,' Georgette declared.

'Put these on,' Olga said to Gloria. 'Boots first.'

Gloria got to her feet. Lying on the bed were a pair of high-heeled thigh-length, black wet-look leather boots. It was only when she picked them up she realised they were not leather at all but a sort of thick, stretchy rubber. She sat on the bed, and pulled one up her leg. It was hard work, squirming and wriggling the material up over her flesh until it was perfectly smooth. The top of the boot reached right up to her thigh, practically touching her sex on the inside. There was a strap inset all the way around the upper edge and Olga buckled it tight, holding the boot firmly in place, creating a shallow channel where it bit into the flesh of Gloria's thigh. The second boot took just as much effort to get on.

'Now this,' Olga said. She picked up a tiny triangle of a G-string in the same material. As Gloria drew it over her hips she felt the rubbery straps digging tightly into her sex and the cleft of her buttocks.

'It's very uncomfortable,' she said.

'Of course,' Olga said blithely. 'Turn round.'

Gloria obeyed. Georgette sat watching her intently, shifting rather uncomfortably on the chair.

'I should go,' she said.

'I thought you wanted to see it all,' Olga replied.

'I've seen enough.'

'Hurting is it?' Olga said.

'Yes.'

Gloria did not understand this exchange.

Georgette got to her feet and picked up the make-up case. Holding it out in front of her just below the level of her waist she waddled awkwardly out of the room.

Olga picked up another garment from the bed. It was a bra of sorts. Like a bra it had shoulder and back straps, which Olga fed over Gloria's arms and fastened for her, but at the front, though a wired cup curved around under each breast, the fabric did not cover them. Attached to the sides of each of these semi-circles was a series of shiny chrome chains, one on top of the other, that looped over her breasts. Gloria's nipples hardened at the touch of the cold metal and immediately made a gap for themselves, poking through the layers of chain.

Gloria glimpsed herself in the dressing table mirror. Once again she looked outlandish and obscene. The strap of the panties cut so deeply into her buttocks it was hardly visible, the clinging material of the boots extended right up to the lips of her sex. The view made her feel a surge of excitement. Like the red satin catsuit, she had been dressed for a purpose and there could be little doubt what that purpose was.

Olga took the last item from the bed. It was a thick leather collar, studded with metal stars. The German buckled it loosely around Gloria's neck. A chain hung down from the front like a dog leash.

Olga's hand seized Gloria's cheek. She brought her face within inches of Gloria's, and their eyes met. 'You've had it too easy,' she repeated. 'But that will change.' Her hand dropped to Gloria's breasts, stroking the chains, then continued down to her pubis, the thick hair barely covered by the tiny rubber triangle. She checked both the straps on the boots and briefly caressed Gloria's pert bottom.

Apparently satisfied that Gloria was ready Olga looked at her watch then sat back on the bed, putting her feet up again.

'Can I sit down too?' Gloria said, the heels on the boots cramping her calf muscles already.

'If I had wanted you to sit I would have said so,' Olga said.

'Where are you taking me?'

'You are not to ask questions,' Olga snapped. She looked at her watch again. 'It is nearly time.'

Chapter Seven

WILLIAM

The weals on his buttocks and the backs of his thighs had gone from scarlet to red to purple. They had remained painful for three days, reminding him every time he sat down of his experience with Hildegard. The stab of pain was therefore always accompanied by a sharp thrill of excitement as his body remembered what it had been subjected to.

It was the only reminder he was given. He had been made to work hard, finishing the wooden floor with the metal scraper at the end of his first week in Clarissa's house. But he had not been taken up to the first or second floors after his day's labour. It was probably just as well since each night, after food and a shower, he had collapsed on his bed in the cubicle and slept the sleep of the dead. Computer programmers were not used to manual labour.

At any minute he had expected – and hoped – to be summoned by Clarissa. The fact that he was not depressed him. As the days passed with nothing to occupy his mind but the monotony of work, he had plenty of time to think about her and what she had done to him. He imagined that his crime and subsequent punishment was a sort of initiation rite and that he was now condemned to more mundane chores – an opinion he became more sure of as the days passed.

It was a considerable relief therefore, when on the evening of the seventh day, after his shower, Olga had not taken him back to his quarters, but instead had marched him to the lift.

'You are to see Ms Peacham,' she told him as the lift arrived and she pushed him inside. She reached in, pressed the button for the first floor and retreated leaving him to travel up alone.

After seven days of neglect the words made William's pulse race as the lift rose. Just as the pain he had suffered at the hands of Hildegard had been so richly mixed with pleasure, so now his apprehension at what Clarissa might have in mind for him, was inextricably linked to a rising sense of excitement. Whatever she intended, nothing was as bad as her indifference. He wanted to serve her. He wanted to make up for what he had done. The last seven days had made him acutely aware of that fact. He was happy to be her servant. He only hoped she was equally happy to be his mistress.

The lift doors slid open at the little alcove that hid the lift from the rest of her bedroom. He heard the noise of a shower running in the bathroom. He stood where he was knowing better than to enter her bedroom without permission. The water stopped running. He heard the bathroom door open and Clarissa appeared in front of him, her body wrapped in a peach coloured bath towel.

'Good evening, William,' she said in a measured tone.

'Good evening, Ms Peacham,' he replied.

'Come through.' She walked into her cream-toned bedroom. The large bed was all mussed up. Lying across it on her stomach was a plump, tall redhead, her hair the colour of flame. William had seen her three or four times doing domestic chores about the house, dressed in the ubiquitous light blue nylon overalls, but she was not one of the girls he'd recognised who had originated from the offices of Peacham Associates. The girl's fleshy, pear-shaped buttocks were reddened, three distinct scarlet weals standing out against the general background of less marked abuse. A riding crop lay on the bed beside her.

William felt his cock stir. The girl's legs were splayed open and he could see her sex, fringed by red hair, nestling between her thighs. He could see that her labia were wet.

'I'm afraid I had to give Angela a lesson in manners, haven't I Angela?'

'Yes, Ms Peacham,' the girl said turning her head towards William.

'And is it a lesson you have taken to heart girl?'

'Yes, Ms Peacham.'

'Good. She's pretty, don't you think William? A little overweight, carrying a little too much fat, but pretty enough.'

'Yes, Ms Peacham.'

'Touch her. Kneel on the bed and feel her arse. Feel the heat. You can practically see how hot she is.'

William hesitated not sure she was serious.

'Go on, I insist,' Clarissa urged.

William did as he was told. He knelt on the bed and stretched out his hand, tentatively smoothing it over the camber of the redhead's bottom. She winced. Her buttocks felt as though they were on fire.

'Got her nicely warmed up.'

William's cock was unfurling rapidly. He tried to hide it with his other hand.

'Now feel her sex. Tell me what it's like,' Clarissa ordered standing at the foot of the bed looking down at her two 'servants', an indulgent look on her face like a parent with two naughty but irresistible children.

William slid his hand down between Angela's buttocks. She moaned loudly as the tips of his fingers touched her labia. They were soaking wet.

'Well?'

'She's wet, Ms Peacham. Very wet.' He felt his cock surge again, coming to full erection. The situation was so fantastic his mind was having trouble accepting it as reality. His body was much less fussy. His cock was as hard as a bone again.

'The little bitch,' Clarissa commented with no particular venom. 'Turn over Angela, I want William to see your tits.'

Angela rolled over. The contact of the sheet against the weals on her buttocks made her gasp. Her breasts were as plump and fleshy as her arse. Her stomach was large and round and there was a roll of fat on the top of her hips.

'She needs to lose weight don't you think William?'

'Yes, Ms Peacham.' William would have agreed with anything Clarissa said.

'But you obviously find her attractive.' She was staring into his lap. 'Don't hide it William. Put your hands behind your back.'

William did as he was told. He had blushed a deep red.

'Did I give you permission to get an erection?' Clarissa asked her voice hardening.

'No, Ms Peacham.'

'Haven't you forgotten something?' She was pointing at her feet.

'I thought . . .' he said, confused. He knew he should have dropped to his knees when he'd come into the room but he thought Clarissa's orders in relation to Angela countermanded the normal order of events.

'Don't think William. Do it now.'

William scrambled off the bed and knelt in front of her, dropping his mouth to her naked feet, the left first. He kissed it hard.

'All right, Angela, you can go. He's waiting for you. Put your panties on and go.'

As William transferred his attentions to Clarissa's right foot, Angela got to her feet. She pulled a pair of silky beige panties up her long legs and smoothed them out over her plump tummy. The colour of the material did not hide the thick red hair of her pubes. The panties were too small for her and stretched tautly over her tortured buttocks.

'It's the third door on the left,' Clarissa continued.

Angela started towards the bedroom door.

'Angela?'

'Yes, Ms Peacham?'

'Haven't you forgotten something?' Clarissa used her eyes to indicate the riding crop lying on the bed. 'I think you should take that with you don't you? Just in case he wants to warm you up again.'

'Yes, Ms Peacham,' Angela said with obvious reluctance, retracing her steps and picking the whip off the bed.

As she got to the bedroom door Clarissa asked her, 'What do you say Angela?'

'Thank you Ms Peacham, thank you for my punishment.'

'Good girl,' Clarissa said smiling and dismissing her with a wave of the hand. 'Get up,' she said to William immediately the door had closed again. 'Make the bed up. I was going to let you dry me but once again you have let me down. What do you mean by coming in here and letting your prick get into such a state?'

William leapt to his feet and began stretching the sheet tautly and tucking it under the mattress.

'Well?' Clarissa demanded.

'I can't help it Ms Peacham, it just happens. I can't control it. I really wish I could.'

'You can't help it. Who can then? You're not saying it's my fault are you?'

'No it's just . . . I can't . . . I mean with her and you . . .'

'You're pathetic William. I'm beginning to wonder if you are worth my time at all.'

Clarissa unwound the towel and used it to rub the rich curves of her body. William caught glimpses of her as he replaced the bedding and pulled the counterpane back over the bed, his erection refusing to do anything but throb harder.

'Well I can see I am going to have to teach you another lesson. Come here.' She was standing by the foot of the bed. She pointed at a spot immediately in front of her. 'I am going out. You're to wait here for me. But you must understand something William. Unless I give you permission, this . . .' she slapped his cock with the palm of her hand, 'must not happen. Is that understood?'

'I'll try, Ms Peacham.'

'Try? You'll do more than try.'

He wanted to explain that it was not something he could control, especially not when she made him do what he had done to Angela, but he knew it was pointless. 'Yes, Ms Peacham,' he said meekly.

'Because sooner or later I will get tired of punishing you.'

'I'm sorry, I just can't . . .'

'When I want your whining excuses I'll ask for them. I want you to sit on the floor with your back to the corner of the bed.'

As William hurried to obey he heard the drawer of the nearest bedside chest being opened. Something metal clinked in her hand but he dared not look around to see what it was. He found out soon enough.

Clarissa knelt by the side of him, her big melon-like breasts quivering. She snapped the metal loop of a handcuff around his left wrist and pulled his hand behind his back.

'Put your right hand back,' she ordered. She stretched the handcuffs behind the leg of the bed then clicked the second loop over his right wrist, effectively securing him to the bed.

She got to her feet and stood in front of him, her feet either side of his thighs. She stroked the forest of her pubic hair as though it were some furry animal. It was only inches from his face.

Without another word she walked away. He heard one of the three doors at the back of the room open.

She was back within minutes. She paraded in front of him, a clutch of clothes and a pair of shoes in her hand. She dropped them on the foot of the bed just behind him without giving him a second glance. Opening a cellophane packet she took out a pair of very sheer black tights. Standing slightly to one side of

157

him, she gathered one leg of the tights into a pocket around the toe, then raised her left foot, and inserted it into the pocket she had made. She pulled the nylon up above her knee, then made a pocket of the other leg and lifted her right foot into it. Then she pulled the sheer, semi-transparent, shimmering nylon up both her legs, smoothing it into position with her hands, stretching it against her crotch by pulling on the waistband and working her thighs up and down, as though marching on the spot. Obviously not satisfied that the nylon was taut enough Clarissa put one foot up on the bed inches from William's shoulder then bent and, starting at the ankle, used the palms of both hands to wriggle and smooth the nylon even tighter against her flesh. She worked up to her thigh, her long fingers rolling over the curves of her leg, rasping against the material. Raising her other leg she followed the same procedure, her big breasts squashed against her thigh as she bent forward, then gradually freed as she straightened up. Finally she worked her palms down between her legs and up over her buttocks, making sure the nylon was completely without wrinkles, like a second skin.

She picked up a lacy black bra and fitted it over her breasts, clipping it into position at the back. The big cups pushed her breasts together, the flesh billowing out above the restraining lace. The last garment on the bed was a one-piece trouser suit in a dark purple. She stepped into it and pulled the top over her shoulders. There was a long zip from her belly to her throat, hidden by careful tailoring. She pulled it up, sealing herself into the suit. The gusset of the garment fitted tightly against her crotch. She dropped the matching purple high heels on the floor and climbed into them. They increased her height by some four inches.

She disappeared behind his back. He heard her brushing her hair. It was some time before she returned but when she did she was fully made-up and her hair was set into soft waves that tumbled to her shoulders. This time she was holding a pair of pale peach silk panties in her hands.

'Look at the state of you,' she said quietly, with no anger in her voice. She raised her foot and touched the toe of her shoe against his cock. A tear of fluid had formed at the slit as he'd watched her put on her clothes. 'I don't know what I'm going to do with you William,' she said.

Clarissa raised her hand directly above his lap and dropped the panties. To William they appeared to float down lazily, like a parachute, the silk billowing out. He got a strong scent of Clarissa's perfume imprinted on the garment. They landed softly on his cock, the silk wrapping itself over his erection with a touch as soft as a butterfly's wing. The tear of fluid soaked into the silk, making the pale peach darker.

'Make sure they are still there when I get back,' she said, turning on her heels and walking to the door.

He watched her go, her magnificent legs striding out in the narrow, finely tailored trousers, their creases as sharp as the blade of a knife, the purple material defining every contour of her buttocks. She did not look back at him as she turned out the lights and closed the bedroom door.

GLORIA

'It is time,' Olga said, getting to her feet. She opened the bedroom door. 'Follow.'

Gloria followed her out into the corridor, the chain from the collar swinging across the chains that swathed her bosom, and making a tinkling noise. As they got to the top of the sweeping curved staircase she could see Clarissa waiting by the front door, her tall, elegant body dressed in a beautifully tailored, one-piece trouser suit in a dark shade of purple that looked as though its colour was copied from some exotic autumn foliage.

'Very *outré*,' Clarissa said as the two women descended the stairs. 'Very amusing.' Her eyes inspected Gloria minutely as Olga opened the front door. There was a black Rolls Royce parked in the street outside. A uniformed chauffeur sprung from behind the wheel and opened the rear door.

Gloria experienced a panic attack. 'What is this?' she said backing away from the front door.

'We're going on a little outing,' Clarissa said matter-of-factly.

'I'm not going out dressed like this,' Gloria said firmly her face colouring.

'You will do as you are told,' Olga said.

'I can't.' Gloria felt a wave of emotion sweeping over her.

'You must,' Clarissa said gently.

'Please, Ms Peacham.' Logically it was ridiculous Gloria knew. Since she had come to the house she had allowed herself to be manhandled shamelessly, dressed at Clarissa's whim and used by perfect strangers. But that was in the house, in the special world Clarissa Peacham had created. Outside the front door was the real world and the idea of exposing herself to the real world dressed like this filled her with horror.

'Close the door, Olga and leave us for a moment would you?' Clarissa said.

She felt no anger. She had trained many 'servants' since she moved to the house in Punishment Road. Most of them had experienced what she liked to call a crisis, when they refused to obey. It was usually occasioned not by being asked to do something outrageous and shocking, but by something comparatively simple. Often too the crisis occurred in the first week of their stay. Once the crisis had passed the 'servant' usually could be relied on to give no further trouble. Clarissa compared it to breaking in a horse; if she were subtle enough most horses could be broken no matter how fiery their spirit. Of course, there was a chance she would fail, that the horse could not be broken, but that, she thought, smiling to herself, was a very rare occurrence.

Olga closed the front door and marched off down the corridor. Clarissa put her arm around Gloria's shoulder. Gloria was shivering though it was not cold. 'I thought we'd established an understanding you and I?' she said. 'I thought I had come to mean something special to you.'

'Please, Ms Peacham,' Clarissa's tenderness made Gloria want to cry.

'You are special Gloria. Very special. You have given me a great deal of pleasure already, but I have allowed you your pleasures too haven't I?'

'Oh yes,' Gloria felt her body shudder at the thought.

'Then you must do this for me.' Her voice hardened slightly. She had used the carrot, now it was time for the stick. 'I'd hoped your time here was going to be pleasurable for both of us, but, of course, if you are not willing to obey me I have no choice but to let you go.'

Gloria's mind was in turmoil. She had wanted to see Clarissa so much, hoping she would take her into her bed again and now she was on the point of throwing it all away. She needed Clarissa. Clarissa had opened a door for her but she feared, if she lost her now, the door might slam shut again and she would never find anyone else who knew how to open it. She needed Clarissa to show her how to prop the door permanently open.

'It is your choice, Gloria,' Clarissa said removing her arm and taking two steps back. She looked in the Florentine giltwood mirror that hung by the front door and adjusted the collar of her suit. 'Well?' she said her voice less gentle.

'Please don't make me. I'll do anything else,' Gloria begged, the thought of setting foot outside the front door still filling her with dread.

'Very well.' Clarissa's face turned to stone. 'If that is your decision. Olga!'

'No, no, I'll do it, I'll do it.' Gloria cried. She had no choice. However hard it was she had to get a grip on herself and conquer her fears.

Olga had appeared. With no discernible change of expression Clarissa indicated that she should open the front door. As she did so Clarissa picked up the leash and pulled Gloria forward. It was no more than six steps but if Gloria took them she knew the crisis would be passed.

Gloria took a deep breath. She felt as though a thick steel shutter had come down in her mind, cutting her off from the feelings that had caused her to rebel. Her first step was hesitant, the second much firmer. By the time she crossed the threshold she was walking confidently. It had suddenly become clear to her, crystal clear. Nothing mattered. Her perceptions of what she wanted and didn't want were excess baggage to her life now. The only thing that mattered was what *Clarissa* wanted for her. Clarissa had opened the door for her, had handed her a key to a lock she hadn't even known existed. She had given her a gift, and it was a gift she must grasp firmly with both hands whatever the consequences.

Punishment Road was brightly lit by tall street lamps. As Gloria stepped onto the pavement, the chain leash in Clarissa's hand pulling her forward, two young men were passing by. They stopped and stared, their expressions changing from lust to contempt in a matter of seconds.

'Get in,' Clarissa ordered dropping the leash as they reached the car, its passenger door still held open by the chauffeur.

'What do you charge for her then?' one of the men shouted.

'You couldn't afford it,' Clarissa said coolly, following Gloria into the car.

The two men still stood staring as the chauffeur got behind the wheel, started the engine and pulled the car away from the curb.

The interior of the Rolls smelt strongly of leather, the comfort and silence doing something to calm Gloria's racing pulse. She had come so near to the brink she had been able to look down into the abyss and what she had seen had frightened her. Now she was doubly determined to re-establish herself in Clarissa's good books. From now on she would be the perfect 'servant'.

The driver wore a hat with a plastic cockade on its crest. He was a middle-aged man with a nose that looked as though it had been broken and badly re-set. Gloria saw him adjusting the rearview mirror with his gloved hand, angling it down to get a better view of her legs in the clinging wet-look boots.

They drove through the evening traffic. At traffic lights several pedestrians peered into the car, but the dark hid the details of Gloria's outfit and most were satisfied with a casual glance. Gradually the car left the more crowded streets and began driving through the leafier suburbs to the south.

According to the digital display on the walnut dashboard it was an hour before they pulled through two large brick pillars with open wrought iron gates and into the semi-circular drive of a large Victorian house. Several cars: another Rolls Royce, a red Ferrari, a Jaguar and an Aston Martin, were already parked at the side of the house.

The driver pulled up to the front door and got out. He opened the rear door on Clarissa's side. She got out and Gloria followed her.

'I hope you will not let me down,' Clarissa said picking up the chain leash.

'No, Ms Peacham, I won't,' Gloria said with absolute conviction.

Clarissa led her to the panelled front door, inset with stained glass that looked like it could be original. Lights lit up many of the rooms on the ground floor.

'Darling!'

A tall, broad shouldered woman in a shapeless red velvet dress threw open the front door before Clarissa had rung the bell. The dress fell, like a curtain, from her small bosom completely hiding the rest of her figure. Her hair was tied into a matching band of velvet, turban fashion, leaving little of it visible, though what Gloria could see was white. Her hands looked older than her face and were heavily beringed with everything from diamonds to sapphires.

'Beatrice.' Clarissa took the woman by the shoulders and they kissed on both cheeks.

'Well, she is adorable.' The woman's attention had turned to Gloria. Her voice was high and oddly falsetto. 'Come in, come in, everyone else has arrived.'

They walked into the hall and the woman closed the door behind them. The house was expensively decorated, an oak floor dotted with rugs, mid-green walls and a number of oil paintings, individually lit by brass lamps including a Sickert and a John Singer Sargent. There was a buzz of noise coming from a door on the left hand side.

'Go through,' Beatrice urged. 'You know the way.'

Clarissa opened the panelled oak door, leading Gloria by the leash. The room beyond was large with an impressive wooden carved fireplace and two wide box bay windows. It was dotted with chairs and sofas in various styles from modern to Victorian and more oil paintings decorated the walls. Three women stood in a circle by the fireplace drinking champagne from modern glass flutes. Each was extravagantly dressed though they were very different types. One was wearing an outfit that looked as though she had just come from being the master of a three-ringed circus, a black tail coat over a tight, white satin leotard with white fishnet tights and white high heeled boots, her long black hair pinned into a neat chignon on the back of her head. Another was in her fifties, her ample body obviously heavily corseted under a pink moiré silk dress, her bleached blonde hair permed into a mass of curls. The third woman was a blonde, the youngest of the three, and the shortest, her slender body clad in a shimmering catsuit that clung to her figure. It was patterned in leopard skin. Her suede high heels bore the same motif.

Standing to one side of the room was another group of three but they were not drinking. Like Gloria the two men and one woman in this group all wore studded collars attached to chain leashes. But there the similarity ended. The woman was wearing a black leather hood that was pulled down over her head so tightly it conformed to every contour of her face. There were oval slits which revealed her dark brown eyes and a small, pretty mouth. Her body was clad in a nylon leotard, the denier of the nylon so fine it hid little of the flesh underneath. Gloria could see her small breasts and nipples and the bush of her pubic hair which was jet black. The girl's arms were drawn behind her back and held there by leather cuffs wrapped around her arms above the elbow.

The two men were both strong looking and athletic. One had been dressed in a pair of leather chaps, like the sort of thing cowboys wore. The chaps were strapped all the way up the back of his legs, and as he was not wearing trousers underneath them, exposed his genitals at the front and his buttocks at the rear. His cock was strapped into a leather harness, a strap running around his balls and over the base of his shaft, attached to a series of leather loops at regular intervals down its length, the last in the ridge at the bottom of his glans. Not surprisingly he was erect and Gloria could see the straps bit into his flesh. The man's hands were bound behind his back in a pair of metal handcuffs.

The second man was probably the most bizarrely dressed of the trio. He was a strikingly attractive blond, naked apart from a stiff leather contraption strapped over his cock. It was a long fat cylinder on either side of which were two egg shaped ovals into which, presumably, the man's cock and balls had been stuffed. There were large gold rings piercing each of his nipples and a gold chain looped down from them over his chest. His hands, too, were handcuffed behind his back.

There were two other women in the room, both blondes, though one was an ash blonde and the other looked as though her colour came from a bottle. They were identically dressed in high cut gold lamé bodies with silky, transparent tights and gold high heels. The cut of the body revealed both cheeks of their very generous buttocks at the back and the crease of their pelvises at the front. The gusset of the garment was so narrow it only covered the centre of the plane of the sex and it was possible to see, under the nylon, the flesh on either side which had been carefully depilated. The wrap-over necklines of the bodies plunged to the waist and a great deal of their breasts were on display too, both girls having large, weighty bosoms.

One of these women was serving little canapés from a silver tray, while the other circulated with a bottle of Krug champagne, topping up the glasses of the three women. Clarissa led Gloria over to the studded collar trio and dropped her leash, then went to join the women by the fireplace. Beatrice handed her a champagne flute and saw that it was filled by the girl with the bottle. She picked up her own from the shelf of the mantelpiece.

'Nice to see you all again,' Clarissa said raising her glass and clinking it against that of each woman in turn.

'She's really lovely,' Beatrice said staring at Gloria.

'Gorgeous,' the leopard woman agreed.

'Is she new?' the ring master asked.

'Yes, very.'

'What do you think of mine,' the bleached blonde asked. 'I

love the rings don't you? He wants me to tattoo him next. He's totally besotted with me.'

Clarissa eyed the man with the pierced nipples. 'He's certainly a handsome brute,' she said. 'Does he fill that thing Andrea?' She was looking at the cigar-shaped cylinder that hung down between his legs.

The blonde laughed. 'Now that would be telling, wouldn't it?'

'Well, I don't know about you but I think we should get started.' Beatrice said. She signalled to one of the two girls who immediately put down the tray of canapés and walked to the other side of the room. She picked up a little stack of paper discs a little smaller than glass coasters. Coming over to the group of what Gloria had surmised were all 'servants' – each one belonging to one of the women by the fireplace – she separated out the discs and tore the backing off one, slapping it down on the hooded woman's shoulder. Gloria saw that the disc bore the number one. The girl stuck a disc on each of the other three of them, ending with the man with the pierced nipples. Gloria was number three. Finally the blonde went over to her partner in the gold lamé body and stuck a disc on her shoulder with the number five. There was one disc left in her hand. She stuck this on her own body. It too was the number five.

'Both?' the ring master said.

'I thought it would be a special treat,' Beatrice said in her high-pitched voice, smiling coquettishly. She reached up to the mantelpiece and took a tall wicker basket down. Gloria could hear something rattling in its base. 'Who would like to go first?'

It did not take a great deal of intelligence to work out what was going on, Gloria thought. Each of the four women had brought a servant to the party and each was going to draw a number from the basket and presumably would be paired off with whomever their number corresponded. The implications of this, that there were establishments like Clarissa's all over London, with women using 'servants' just as Clarissa did, were too much for Gloria to think about at the moment. She was having enough trouble coping with her feelings. Her heart was racing. She couldn't imagine what she would do if Beatrice drew her number. The thought of this odd, bony, rather lumpy woman pawing her body, let alone what she would be asked to do to her in return, filled her with apprehension. But it was an apprehension striated with a strange, almost sickly, excitement, that Gloria could not explain. There was a chance, of course, she would end up with the woman in the leopard print catsuit. She looked at the rich curves of the woman's slender body, the weight of her breasts, and the camber of her hips and felt a strong jolt of desire.

Clarissa stepped forward and put her hand into the wicker basket. It was so deep her arm disappeared up to the elbow. She drew out a small rubber ball on which a number was printed.

'Three,' Beatrice declared. 'You'll have to try again.' Three was Gloria's number. Clearly they were not allowed to 'win' their own servants. Clarissa replaced the ball and fished around in the basket again. She drew out a second ball.

'Five,' she declared, looking at the two girls in gold lamé with renewed interest.

'Damn you,' Andrea said.

'You next.' Beatrice pushed the basket out towards the woman in pink and Andrea's look of disappointment vanished when she drew the number one. 'Well that's not so bad,' she said looking at the hooded woman whose shoulder bore the corresponding disc.

The ring master stepped forward next and drew the number two which belonged to the man in leather chaps. Apparently he was her 'servant' and she had to draw again. This time she drew the number three. 'Well, so I'm the lucky one,' she said to Clarissa eyeing Gloria appreciatively.

The leopard woman was the last to dip her hand into the wicker basket. She came out with the number two. Beatrice had no need to draw. She was paired with the man with the pierced nipples.

'Very satisfactory,' she said. 'I got exactly what I wanted. More champagne girls?'

The two girls each collected a bottle of Krug to fill the guests' glasses, no one, apparently in any particular hurry to claim their prizes. Beatrice directed them over to the French windows at the back of the room through which a beautifully planted garden could be seen bathed in strong floodlights.

Gloria looked at the other three standing impassively beside her. She would have loved to question them. Was this a regular event? In what sort of establishments did they live? How had they come to be in the same position as her? But she dared not say a word. The two men refused to meet her gaze but the woman in the hood smiled at her wanly, the look of tired resignation in her eyes, tinged with a spark of excitement.

Not having looked at the ring master carefully when she came in, Gloria tried to catch a glimpse of her surreptitiously now. She had long legs, with strong meaty thighs. Her waist was thick and she had little in the way of a bosom but her face was striking with large features and big brown eyes. It was, Gloria noticed, heavily made-up, with a rather old-fashioned pancake base covering her cheeks and chin, and very noticeably false eyelashes. Unlike the leopard woman Gloria could not say she found her attractive.

Clarissa was the first to make a move. She came over to one of the two girls and put her arm around her, her hand immediately slipping down to the girl's buttocks. With her other hand she turned the girl's cheek to face her then kissed her lightly on the lips. As if by some pre-arranged signal the other girl put down the bottle of champagne she was carrying and slid up behind Clarissa, wrapping her arms around her body, and crossing them over Clarissa's chest to hug her large breasts. Clarissa strained her head over her shoulder to kiss the second girl on the mouth.

The other women watched. The two girls' hands snaked all over Clarissa's body, smoothing and caressing her, nipping and squeezing her flesh, their mouths working alternately on her neck, sucking at it or kissing it or licking it. Clarissa tossed her head back with pleasure, the long sinews of her neck corded like rope. One of the girls found the hidden zip and pulled it down, while the other's hands immediately delved inside the purple material.

Clarissa did nothing. She allowed them to pull the garment off her shoulders and wriggle it down her body. One of the girls knelt to help her out of her shoes, then pulled the legs of the trousers off one by one, as the other unclasped her black lace bra and let her big breasts escape.

'Such lovely tits,' Beatrice commented. 'Makes me so envious.'

'Oh me too,' the ring master agreed.

Clarissa was being eased back on to one of the big sofas, her tights pulled down her legs by the ash blonde as the other girl sucked at her nipples. The sight of Clarissa's thickly haired pubis was too much for Andrea.

'Come on,' she said to her prize, grasping the leash of the hooded woman and leading her smartly back into the hall. The leopard woman too moved to stand next to the man in leather chaps. His cock was straining against the straps that held it so tightly, the ballet of the three women played out in front of his eyes renewing his erection. The leopard woman took his cock in her hand.

'Is it uncomfortable?' she asked.

'Yes.'

'But you like it don't you?' she said. Gloria saw her hand grip his shaft tightly, her eyes sparkling. There was a cruel smile playing on her lips that made Gloria suddenly grateful she had not, after all, picked her in the draw.

The man did not reply as leopard woman picked up the chain leash and led him out of the room.

The ash blonde in gold lamé had knelt between Clarissa's open legs and was dipping her head to her sex, while the other began to pull off her clothes, shucking the gold leotard from her shoulders and skimming it down her legs. Beatrice came to sit on the sofa opposite.

'Are you going to stay?' she asked the ring master without taking her eyes from Clarissa.

'No,' the woman said. 'I'm still inhibited about it.'

'I used to be. But no one cares, Vivienne. Stay, it would be fun.' Beatrice snapped her fingers at the remaining man, indicating that he should kneel at her feet, which he did at once. She raised her foot and pushed it against the long leather cylinder that held the man's cock. 'You can start with my feet and work all the way up,' she said. 'And take your time.'

The man took her foot in his hand and lifted off her shoe. He bent forward and began kissing it. As he slowly worked his way up her leg he pushed the red velvet up ahead of him until it was over her thighs. Beatrice decided to give him more scope and laid lengthways on the sofa, pulling her skirt up over her hips. As Gloria caught sight of her crotch, she could not believe what she saw. Nestled in a neat little package under the tights was a small flaccid cock. Beatrice was a man!

The ring master caught Gloria's leash in her hand, before she had time to examine Beatrice any further and tugged her towards the door. In the hall she turned and mounted the long straight staircase, leading the way and keeping the leash taut between them. At the top of the stairs they turned down a corridor to the right. As they passed the first door Gloria heard a thwack of leather and a loud groan. Two more followed in quick succession, each accompanied by a howl of pain.

The ring master stopped at the third door along. It was open and she marched Gloria into a normal bedroom, with a double bed, a wardrobe and a chest of drawers, with bedside tables and lamps on either side of the bed. There was a small suitcase on top of the chest of drawers. The bed had no bedding with the exception of a white undersheet, and two pillows. Vivienne dropped the leash and it swung back against Gloria's breasts.

'I really wanted one of the men,' Vivienne said almost to

herself. She went to the chest of drawers and opened the suitcase, propping the lid back against the wall. 'You know what's required of you?'

'I'm not sure,' Gloria said truthfully.

'You must do everything I ask.'

'I will,' Gloria said with conviction, her determination not to offend Clarissa again after what had happened in the hall still unshaken, despite the increasingly bizarre circumstances.

'Sometimes they prefer it if you don't. Beatrice has some very imaginative ideas when it comes to punishment. She likes to entertain us. There's a special room at the back of the house.'

Vivienne took a small, cream coloured dildo out of the case. It was sticking out from a triangular pouch rather like a G-string but made from a rigid pink plastic. Each corner of the triangle was attached to a strong elasticated strap.

'Put this on,' Vivienne said. There was a door to one side of the bed. It was open and Gloria could see a bathroom beyond. The ring master walked into the bathroom and closed the door.

Gloria unravelled the straps and discovered the dildo could be pulled on rather like a pair of panties. She tugged the straps up her thigh boots and over the G-string she already wore. The plastic was curved slightly to fit snugly over her pubic bone. The straps could be adjusted to hold it firmly in place.

The bathroom door opened and Vivienne emerged dressed only in a pair of silk panties and a small matching bra, both in a dark burgundy red. Without the support of the tight leotard her body looked loose and lumpy with a thick waist and small buttocks. She switched the bathroom light off.

Only one of the bedside lamps was turned on. As she lay

down on the bed she reached over to turn it off. 'I don't like the light,' she said, as the room was plunged into darkness.

Gloria heard rather than saw her slipping her panties down her legs.

'Have you worn one of those before?' she asked.

'No.'

'I want you to fuck me with it.'

There was a little light filtering in from around the door. As Gloria's eyes adjusted to the gloom she saw that Vivienne was lying with her legs open. She had no idea what she was supposed to do but started to swing herself on to Vivienne's body. The brunette pushed her away immediately.

'No, she said, 'just lie there. I get on top.'

But for a moment she made no attempt to move, just lying there in the dark staring up at the ceiling. Then she swung her thigh over Gloria's hips and knelt above her.

'See, like this,' Vivienne said, the phallus poised between her legs.

'What do you want me to do?'

'Ssh . . .' the woman said leaning forward to kiss Gloria full on the mouth. Her mouth was big and her tongue hot and Gloria felt her excitement leap. She thought of Clarissa downstairs on the sofa being taken by the two blondes. She wished Vivienne had wanted to stay and watch. All this was beyond anything she'd ever experienced before, or even imagined, but she found her response to it was unqualified. The kiss inflamed her feelings, making her whole body tremble.

'Feels so good,' Vivienne said her voice betraying her own mounting enthusiasm, as the thrills of sexual passion began to run through her.

Gloria could see her silhouette in the dim light as she reached behind her back to release the clasp of her bra. She leaned forward and let it drop onto Gloria's chest. Even in the gloom Gloria could see her breasts were no more than inverted saucers of flesh.

'You're very beautiful,' Vivienne said. 'Beautiful body. I'd love to have a body like yours.' Her hand groped under the chains of the bra and fingered Gloria's breasts. 'Do you like women?'

It was too complicated to explain so Gloria simply said, 'Yes.'

'And men?'

'Yes,' Gloria repeated.

'Equally?' Vivienne asked.

'I think so.'

Vivienne reached up to the pillow and took something from underneath it with her right hand. Gloria could not see more than a faint shadow of what looked like a cylindrical tube. Vivienne unscrewed the cap of the tube and raised herself on her haunches so the dildo was clear of her body. Her hand disappeared behind her back.

'That's better,' she said, throwing the tube to the floor. Very slowly, holding the dildo firmly with one hand, she sunk down on it. As it got deeper she moaned. 'Oh so good,' she said her voice husky with passion.

Gloria felt her thighs come to rest on her hips. She knew the dildo must be buried in her but as it was inert she had no way of feeling it. She could feel the triangular plastic base however. It had been cunningly designed. On the inside was a small ridge which squeezed between her labia and butted against her clitoris as Vivienne pressed down.

'Feels good, feels like I'm getting fucked,' Vivienne said bouncing up and down. Gloria bucked her hips too, as much to work her clit against the inner ridge as to help the brunette. Her body responded with a jolt of pleasure. They began a rhythm together, Gloria arching her body off the bed, Vivienne pushing it back again, the dildo pushed even higher and deeper.

Gloria caressed the woman's thighs with the palms of her hands. She moved her fingers over towards her pubes, but Vivienne slapped her hand away.

'Don't do that,' she snapped angrily.

'I was only . . .'

'Just do what you're doing sweetie. That's all I want.'

She had wanted a man Gloria remembered her saying and she was using her exactly as if she was one. This was nothing like her encounters with Clarissa or Mitzy. She had taken pleasure in their meltingly soft bodies but Vivienne's was hard and unyielding. Nevertheless it was exciting by virtue of its strangeness. They were battering at each other relentlessly, the dildo affecting both women.

'You're making me come,' Vivienne said. 'Love what you're doing. Fucking me, fucking me . . . so strong, so masculine.'

Gloria could see her eyes were tightly shut. There was nothing masculine about her body, except the prosthesis attached to it but clearly Vivienne was imagining in her own fantasy that Gloria was a man.

Suddenly Gloria felt Vivienne's body tense. She sunk down on the dildo one final time with all her weight, not allowing Gloria to buck her back up again and wriggled on it from side to side.

'You're so deep,' she said. 'Yes, yes.'

It was a physical shock, a bolt from the blue. Spattering out across her stomach, and over the chains of the bra, Gloria was stung by gobs of wet heat. For a second she hadn't the faintest idea what they were and cried out in surprise.

'What's going on?'

And then it dawned. She raised her head and strained to see Vivienne's crotch in the darkness. There, no more than a dark shadow, was a small cock. She had not felt it before because it rested on the wide plastic base of the dildo. The hormones that had created Vivienne's nascent breasts had also shrivelled her penis because like Beatrice downstairs, Vivienne was a man.

Chapter Eight

WILLIAM

It was terribly uncomfortable. He could not move around too much for fear of dislodging the silky peach panties in his lap, but his buttocks were numb and cramped and he had to try and relieve them by shifting his weight from one to the other, in the process making the panties slide perilously close to the side of his thighs. If they fell he would never be able to retrieve them, not in this position, with his hands stretched out behind his back and cuffed to the leg of the bed.

The panties were soft and incredibly silky against the ultra sensitive skin of his glans. They exuded a strong aroma of the perfume Clarissa always wore and he knew she must have been wearing them for most of the day. The thought made him throb. He saw the panties, in his mind's eye, pressed into her crotch at the top of those long legs. They had delicately decorated, scalloped edges and the material was flounced. He could imagine how it would give glimpses of her labia and her chestnut coloured pubic hair.

His cock pulsed. As he moved his buttocks it rubbed against

the silk. It was a delicious torture, exactly, he was sure, as Clarissa had intended.

If he twisted round to his right he could just see the luminous dial of the small clock on the bedside chest. It had been eight-thirty when he had been left like this. Now it was one o'clock in the morning.

The house was silent and so was the street outside, so silent that when the car drove up to the front door he heard it quite clearly. He heard the front door being opened too and footsteps coming up the stairs.

The bedroom door opened. Clarissa switched the lights on, blinding him temporarily. As his sight returned she went into the bathroom, leaving the door open. He heard her running a shower and cleaning her teeth. He heard her pee and the toilet being flushed.

She came back into the bedroom naked, apart from the black satin high-heeled slip-ons she favoured. She walked over to a large cabinet that was built into the wall. She opened it. William saw a fridge on one side and bottles and glasses in racks of shelves on the other. Clarissa took a balloon glass and poured herself a glass of Vieux Antique Hine brandy from an ornate pot-bellied bottle. She took a large swig of the golden liquid before walking back to the bed.

She stood at his side, her feet almost touching his hip. 'I'm going to allow you a special privilege tonight,' she said, 'even though you have done nothing to deserve it. You may begin by kissing my feet.'

He did nothing, expecting her to set him free.

'Come on,' she said irritably, taking another swig of the brandy and kicking at him with the toes of her left foot.

William tried to push his head down to get to her feet but it was impossible with his hands tied so far behind him, 'I can't,' he said.

'You're useless,' she said. The words stung him.

He wriggled harder, rolling on his side and trying to double himself up. But he was still inches away. Relenting she moved her feet to where he could reach. Instantly he sunk his mouth on to her left foot, and kissed it hard, the humiliation of what he was doing entirely forgotten in the rush of gratitude he felt at her having moved to help him. He knew that was a warped perspective but that was how he saw it. It was a strain to reach her right foot but he pulled at the handcuffs and ignored the pain this caused.

'That's better,' she said. The amelioration of her tone did not last long. 'Come on, you can do better than that.' He increased his efforts, kissing every inch of her foot.

Apparently satisfied she walked away and sat on the bed beside him.

'Get up,' she snapped. 'You look ridiculous.'

He wriggled into a sitting position again finding it more difficult to achieve than it had been to roll over. The peach panties had fallen to the floor at his side.

'Where are my panties?' she asked though she must have been able to see them on the floor by her feet.

'There, Ms Peacham,' he said indicating them with his chin.

'I thought I told you to make sure they remained in your lap.' Her voice was cold but not angry.

'I did, I mean they did. They only just fell off when I . . .'

'I don't want to hear your excuses William. That's all I ever hear from you isn't it? You abused me in my own bathroom, you disgraced yourself with Hildegard. I give you a simple task, the simplest of tasks, and you can't even do that.'

It was quite extraordinary. Though William knew it was silly, though he knew everything Clarissa had done was deliberately intended to belittle him and that her complaints were ridiculous, he felt, at another, deeper level, that he had genuinely let her down. Whatever she had done to him in the last few days had served to destroy his self assurance and made him feel an almost childlike dependence on her. When he had first come to the house, when she had humiliated him in front of Gloria with all that had happened in her study, he had told himself he was doing it for one reason and one reason alone: he wanted to keep his job. But as the days had passed that reason seemed to have become blurred and confused. Another raison d'être was taking precedence. He wanted to obey, to fulfil the letter of her commands, however outlandish they were, because he wanted to please her. Conversely, as now, her displeasure wounded him, not because he feared retribution or punishment, nor because he might be thrown out and lose his job, but because he could not bear the thought that he had disappointed her. How she had achieved his transformation in him, he did not know. What's more he did not care. His attitude was self-sustaining. It needed no justification from the outside world, no reason or logic. It needed only her presence and her approval.

Clarissa got to her feet. He watched anxiously as she walked over to the bedside chest, her sex visible in the gap at the very top of her thighs. He felt a jolt of desire that made his erection ache. She put her brandy glass down and picked up the key to the handcuffs and turned to walk back. This time his eyes feasted on her big breasts as they bounced on her chest. They were firm and supple, her broad nipples corrugated into buds so hard they were dimpled at their centre.

She dropped onto her haunches in front of him.

'Did I give you permission to look at me?'

'No, Ms Peacham.'

She reached behind his back, her left breast pressing into his shoulder, and inserted the key into the cuff. It sprung free. 'You can do the other one yourself,' she said standing again. 'Then strip the covers off the bed. And pick up my panties. Don't leave them lying on the floor.'

William found it difficult to stand. His legs refused to obey him and he stumbled, pins and needles invading the numbness in his muscles. He picked up the panties and managed to totter to the head of the bed, pulling the counterpane and the top sheet back and folding them neatly at the foot of the bed.

'At least you can do something right,' Clarissa said. She dimmed the lights by means of a switch on the wall by the bed then sat on the edge of the mattress. 'Get me another brandy.'

He picked up her glass and went over to the cupboard to pour her drink. Bringing it back he was conscious of her eyes staring at his erection.

'That's better. Why can't you be so well behaved all the time William?'

'I try, Ms Peacham,' he mumbled.

Clarissa swallowed a large gulp of brandy then lay back on the bed. 'I've had a long day,' she said. 'Kneel by my side William.' She patted the bed on her right.

'What shall I do with your panties, Ms Peacham?'

'Here,' she said. She took the silk from his hand and

slipped it over his cock, tying it loosely in a bow. 'That looks pretty.'

William walked around the bed, his cock trembling against the silk, and knelt beside her, trying not to look at her body.

'Stroke my leg for me. Nice and gently. I need soothing.'

Tentatively William reached out to caress Clarissa's thighs, his heart in his mouth, and his pulse racing. As he ran his palms as softly as he could down her long, silky thighs she moaned, arching her body off the bed very much as a lover would do. She closed her eyes and smiled her pleasure.

'Lovely,' she said.

He stroked right down to her ankles, then up again, moulding his hands to the curves of her flesh. Her legs had been together but now she scissored them open, allowing him to run his hands down onto her inner thighs. Inevitably his eyes fell to her sex. Her pubic hair was still wet, whether because she had not dried it after her shower, or from some other cause he did not know, but it was plastered back against her labia and he could see the opening of her vagina.

Trying to concentrate on what he was doing, he circled both his palms against her thighs, his finger inches from her sex.

'Lovely,' she repeated. 'Now my belly.'

He did as he was told, moving his hands up to caress her almost concave stomach. Her hip bones stuck out prominently on either side of it.

She moaned loudly.

'I'm going to allow you to do my tits William,' she whispered without opening her eyes.

He could not believe this. She had allowed him no physical intimacy with her before, except to taunt him. Now she appeared like a lover, languid and relaxed, instructing him to take untold liberties.

As he moved his hands higher, to the foothills of her breasts, his cock jerked against the silk that enfolded it. It felt as soft as her thighs had been. He opened his hands, stretching his fingers out to gather in the flesh of her breasts, her nipples pressed down against his palms. Closing his hands he watched as his fingers dug into the spongy flesh creating their own valleys. Her breasts felt wonderful. His cock jerked wildly.

'Now use your mouth William. I want to be licked and kissed. You'd like to do that wouldn't you?'

'Oh yes, Ms Peacham.'

'Start on my legs.'

He abandoned her breasts with reluctance but his pulse was racing. There was only one way this encounter was going to end he told himself. She was going to tell him to fuck her. She needed it. She wanted it. He could sense it in every inch of her body. He could see it in the way she was moving, subtly undulating to a sensuous tempo. He would hear it in the way little moans and gasps of pleasure escaped her lips. He was sure that is why she had left him bound to the bed all evening, knowing he would be waiting for her, anxious and ready, when she got home.

He shifted down the bed slightly then bent his head forward. He sunk his mouth to her ankle, then used his tongue to lick it. Slowly he worked higher, up over her knee, along the escarpment of her thighs, then down on to the soft inner flesh, until his mouth was so close to her sex he could see it quivering with pleasure and could inhale the musky aroma it produced. He moved over to the other thigh then repeated the process in reverse, ending up at her ankle.

'At last you've done something right,' she whispered.

He licked his way up again, this time staying on the top of her leg, then following the crease of her groin to her hip. He licked his way across her stomach. It was time to climb her breasts. She made no objection as his lips started the ascent, his tongue lapping at the creamy skin. He approached the nipple slowly, licking around the narrow band of the areola first, all the way around it, before closing his lips on the nipple and sucking it into his mouth.

'Oh William, you've got hidden talents, haven't you? Do the other one.'

He obeyed, following the same procedure, licking the areola first, before descending on the nipple. This time he dared to use his teeth, nipping the bud of flesh just a little. Clarissa moaned.

He *knew* what would come next. 'Fuck me William,' she would say. Or would she be more subtle? 'Now use your cock on me William?' What exactly would she say? It was an intriguing puzzle.

'Down over my belly, lick down there.'

He obeyed immediately, kissing and nipping down to the thick bush of her pubic hair.

'Lovely, lovely,' she said.

He approached her pubes.

'A little lower,' she encouraged.

William strayed into the thick curls of hair. Her legs were still wide open and he could see her labia. Now there could be no doubt, the wetness with which they glistened was the result of her own excitement.

'All right, that's enough,' Clarissa said in an entirely different tone of voice, all hint of passion gone.

The words hit William like a slap in the face. 'What!'

'I said that's enough William. I've had enough.'

He was so astonished his reaction came without thinking.

'You're not going to let me fuck you?'

'Fuck me! How dare you? How dare you? What could possibly give you the idea that I would let you fuck me?' She rolled over onto her side and picked up the phone, punching in a single number. 'Get up here,' she said as soon as it was answered.

William was trembling with frustration. 'Why did you let me . . .' He couldn't think of what to say. He couldn't believe she had led him on in this way.

'Stand up,' Clarissa barked. 'I said stand up,' she repeated when he did nothing.

'You can't treat me like this.'

'I can treat you in any way I choose. Now stand up. Do I have to remind you of the consequences if you don't?'

'How could you do that?' He was still seething. 'How could you let me touch you like that and not, and not . . .'

'William you are to stand. Now.' Clarissa's voice was so forceful it penetrated the maelstrom of emotion he was experiencing. He managed to control himself enough to get to his feet. The loose knot of the panties slipped free and they fell to the floor. 'You see, this is what happens. I give you a privilege and you immediately abuse my kindness. I give you an inch and you take a mile.'

'I thought . . .'

'That's the trouble William, you are not here to think. You

187

are here to do what I tell you to do.'

Suddenly William felt his anger evaporate. It turned to regret. She was right. It had all been his fault. He should have realised she was never going to allow him to have sex with her. The idea was ridiculous. He wasn't worthy of her. She had given him the privilege of stroking her body and he had abused it.

'I didn't mean to . . . I promise next time . . .' He wished he could have thought of something to say, something that would explain how he had come to make such a fundamental mistake, but he didn't know the answer himself.

There was a knock on the bedroom door and Olga entered without waiting to be called, a towelling robe wrapped around her large body.

'Get this thing out of here,' Clarissa said.

'He has been bad?' Olga asked. She was looking at William's erection as though it would give her the answer.

'He has no control. I've tried to teach him, God knows I've tried to show him what is required but I think I've failed. Just get him out of my sight.'

Olga grabbed William's arm and marched him towards the alcove that concealed the lift. He put up no resistance and said nothing more. He felt suddenly tired, terribly, terribly tired.

GLORIA

'Come in, Gloria.'

Clarissa was sitting behind the desk in her study. Just as on her first visit to this room Gloria saw she had a bottle of champagne in a wine cooler on her desk in front of her. Gloria walked in through the open door escorted by Georgette who had dressed her and brought her up from the basement. That was remarkable in itself, for Olga usually performed that function. It was also unusual that the maid was not dismissed but instead stood with her back to the door.

Clarissa sipped her champagne, regarding Gloria with a critical eye. She had ordered the maid to lace Gloria into a tight white leather corset. Gloria already had a narrow waist but the boning of the corset reduced it to almost hour-glass proportions. Gloria's breasts ballooned up out of the equally tight bra cups of the garment and were pinched together to form a firm cleavage. Long white leather suspenders snaked over her thighs at the front and side pulling the white tops of her stockings taut. The white ankle boots were also laced, their heels high and spiky. She had not been given panties to wear.

'You look most attractive, doesn't she Georgy?'

'Yes, Ms Peacham.' The maid replied in her gruff voice.

Gloria knew it was true. She had been allowed to do her own make-up and hair and had applied it more thickly and with darker colours than she ever had at home. She had never thought much about her appearance before, but Clarissa had made her realise she was capable of looking quite stunning and she liked the way that made her feel. When she got home, she had decided already, she was going to give a great deal more attention to what she wore and how she looked.

'Sit down Gloria, please.' Clarissa indicated the uncomfortable steel-framed chair Gloria had used on her first visit to the study. Gloria sat down, the narrow seat cutting into her naked rump. 'I've brought you here to tell you how pleased I am with you. Vivienne called me yesterday. She was delighted with you. Ecstatic in fact. Isn't that nice?'

'Yes, Ms Peacham.'

'Vivienne has certain . . . shall we say difficulties. Apparently you handled them with great aplomb. I am very pleased with you.'

'Thank you, Ms Peacham.' The praise was making Gloria blush.

'We all have our problems. Take Georgette. She has been with me since I started this little . . . what shall we call it . . . *incentive* scheme. Well I discovered Georgette had a natural penchant for being a maid, so I allowed her to stay.'

Gloria didn't understand what this was all about. When she had been dressed so provocatively she had not expected to be brought here to Clarissa's study. She'd hoped the surroundings would be more intimate. After the strangeness of her experience at Beatrice's house three days ago she yearned for a more satisfying sexual adventure and more particularly for one involving Clarissa.

'Occasionally I like to give her a little treat. She'd have loved helping you put your pretty things on. Isn't that right Georgette?'

'You're very kind to me, Ms Peacham.'

'Go and get her then will you?' Clarissa said to the maid.

The maid turned and shuffled out of the room, a little awkwardly, Gloria thought.

'That is not the only reason you are here. I've decided I'm going to let you help me out. A little problem . . . a most interesting case. I fear this might be her last chance.' She sipped her champagne. 'Will you do that for me?'

'Of course, Ms Peacham.'

190

It seemed that Clarissa's body produced a physical reaction in Gloria. She felt herself getting hot and slightly breathless. Pictures, graphic images of what Clarissa had done to her, swarmed into her mind. Her sex moistened. There seemed to be nothing she could do to suppress it.

'Were you disappointed?'

'Disappointed?' Gloria didn't know what she meant.

'Disappointed by Vivienne?'

Gloria thought about that carefully. 'Yes,' she said. The experience with Vivienne had been bizarre. Gloria had been excited by the prospect of experimenting with another woman but it was not the fact that Vivienne had turned out to be a man that was disappointing but that neither as a man or as a woman had he/she made any attempt to satisfy Gloria's needs.

'Do you still want to be fucked?'

'Yes, very much,' Gloria said. 'But . . .' The corollary was more difficult for Gloria to say.

'But what, Gloria?'

'I very much want to . . . to have a woman again.'

Clarissa smiled. 'I'm pleased with you.' There was a knock on the study door. 'Come in,' Clarissa ordered.

A petite woman with extremely long, light brown hair tied in a pony tail, entered the room followed by Georgette. She was naked apart from black high heels. Her body was slender, her breasts small but shapely and her legs short and compact. Her sex was so completely hairless it had obviously been shaved, the first inch or two of the slit of her labia clearly visible. The woman's arms were bound behind her back by means of two leather cuffs strapped above the elbow and joined by a single metal link, exactly like the harness that had bound the hooded girl at Beatrice's house.

The woman's face was neat and pretty. She had a very straight nose, large blue eyes and a small round chin. Her mouth was small though her lips protruded slightly as though permanently pouted.

'Good evening, Polly,' Clarissa said.

'Good evening, Ms Peacham,' the woman said with obvious defiance.

'Have you had a chance to consider what I said?'

'Yes,' Polly said in the same tone.

'And?'

'What choice do I have?'

'Oh dear Polly, that is not the attitude I wanted to hear,' Clarissa said. Georgette was standing by the door looking uneasy. 'Georgette, I told you,' Clarissa said. 'I want you to stay.'

'If you're sure Ms Peacham.'

'Close the door.'

Georgette did as she was told, closing the door and leaning against it as she had done before.

Clarissa turned to Polly again. 'I was hoping you would have seen the error of your ways.'

'I have, I told you, I don't have any choice.'

'All right if that's how you want to play it.' Clarissa sipped her champagne and then got to her feet. She was dressed in a scarlet velour minidress. It had a plunging V-neck and was sleeveless, its skirt so short it barely veiled the apex of her thighs. Clarissa's spectacularly long legs were sheathed in sheer flesh coloured nylon tights, the leather of her high heels matching the colour of the dress. 'Bend over the desk here,' she said, as she came up alongside Polly. She put her hand on the girl's neck and pushed her forward until her torso was leaning across the walnut top, her face turned to one side, her long hair streaming over the wooden surface. 'Well?'

'Well what?' Polly replied.

'I want to hear you say it Polly.'

The girl's jaw was set, her teeth grinding. 'Please . . .' she spat the word out. 'Please punish me for what I have done.'

'Thank you Polly,' Clarissa said brightly, 'I shall do as you suggest.' She went back to her desk and, opening one of its drawers, took out a long, chrome tube. Attached to each end of the tube were two leather cuffs, identical to the ones already strapped around Polly's arms. 'These go on her ankles. Do it Gloria will you?'

Gloria picked up the tube. It was heavier than she expected. She knelt by the girl's feet and strapped one of the cuffs around her left ankle. She found herself staring directly into the girl's hairless sex, pursed almost vertically between her buttocks. Gloria felt a surge of excitement. Her desire to press her mouth against the girl's labia was almost irresistible. Instead she concentrated on the task in hand and tried to tug the girl's other ankle to one side so it would fit into the second cuff. But the girl kept her foot stubbornly where it was.

'Move it,' Clarissa chided seeing what was happening.

Polly moved her foot to one side. Gloria wrapped the strap around it and buckled it tightly, forcing the girl's legs apart.

'Better,' Clarissa said as Gloria stood up. 'Do you remember what you did to William?'

'Yes, Ms Peacham.' Gloria remembered it graphically. How could she ever forget? It had been the beginning of everything, her initiation into a world of feelings and sensations she would not have believed possible. Though it was only a matter of days, it seemed like a lifetime ago.

'Take this then,' Clarissa handed her the metal ruler from her desk. 'She is to have six strokes.'

'You bitch,' Polly hissed under her breath.

'No, eight strokes.'

Gloria felt her sexual temperature rise dramatically. She was a servant like this girl and should feel sympathy for her. But she felt none. The idea that Clarissa was giving her a chance to administer punishment was thrilling. She knew it was a privilege. But it was not that fact that excited her most. It was the thing itself, the chance to relive the feelings she had experienced when she had done it to William in this very room. She remembered the way the vibrations she had caused in his body had somehow transmitted themselves to hers.

She raised the ruler and stroked it down on Polly's upturned arse without the slightest hesitation, producing a tremor in her flesh. The girl did not make a sound. A red weal appeared across both buttocks. The second stroke was harder. As it landed Gloria felt a jolt of sensation coursing through her body like an electric shock. Her face flushed. She liked this, she wanted this. The power excited her. The physical sensation excited her. The way that Clarissa's knowing eyes were looking at her also had their effect.

Thwack. The sound reverberated through the room. *Thwack.* On the fourth stroke Polly moaned. On the fifth she gasped. On the sixth she screamed. 'No, no, please, not again.' Her buttocks were criss-crossed with weals.

As Gloria raised the ruler again she saw Clarissa shake her

head. 'Take your time. Feel her first,' she said like an adult teaching a child a new skill. 'Feel what you have created.'

Gloria thought that was a wonderful idea. She smoothed her palm over the camber of Polly's buttocks and was amazed at the heat they were producing. The touch of her cool hand made Polly moan. Her fingertips butted into Polly's sex. It was just as hot there, and wet, a river of juices washing out from her vagina and onto her thighs.

'She loves it doesn't she?' Clarissa said. She was standing behind Gloria and could see Polly's glistening sex.

For some reason Gloria glanced over her shoulder at Georgette. She was astonished at what she saw. The maid had pulled up the front of her black maid's dress to reveal a pair of white, very frilly French knickers, white suspenders and the tops of her opaque black stockings. She was rubbing her hand up and down the front of the knickers and under it Gloria could see the outline of a small but distinct erection. Like Vivienne and Beatrice, it seemed that Georgette was a man.

'Now you know,' Clarissa said, following Gloria's gaze. 'Vivienne and Beatrice can afford to live like women, Georgette couldn't, so I took pity on him.'

Gloria raised the ruler again, not in the mood for distractions. Hard and accurately she delivered the final strokes, each one making Polly gasp, each one affecting her own sexual psyche just as tellingly.

'What do you want to do now?' Clarissa said, again like a teacher leading a pupil along the path to knowledge. 'Follow your instincts.'

Gloria did just that. She dropped to her knees, wrapped her arms around Polly's thighs and brought her mouth up to her sex. The girl's whole body was trembling.

'No, no . . .' Polly gasped but it was the sort of no that meant a heartfelt yes.

Gloria forced her tongue up between her labia, stabbing it into her vagina. It was awash with the milk of her sex. She moved on to her clitoris, which was swollen and large, pushing it from side to side. Polly shuddered against her bonds, as if the discomfort was adding in a peculiar way, to the pleasure.

'Please, please,' the girl begged.

'Please you want her to stop?' Clarissa asked.

'No, no, please don't stop.'

'I think she should, I think that should be your punishment,' Clarissa insisted. 'You don't deserve to come.'

'I'll do anything, anything. You were right. You were right. Please . . .' Polly tried to twist her head round to look back at Clarissa, to use her eyes to convince her she was in earnest.

'I'll let you decide what to do with her Gloria,' Clarissa put her hand on Gloria's shoulder as a way of confirming what she said.

Gloria flicked her tongue from side to side again, and felt her own sex respond as though it too were the object of an intimate assault. She felt Polly's body tense.

Follow your instincts, isn't that what Clarissa had said. She pulled her mouth away.

'Oh no, oh no,' Polly cried, wriggling her buttocks as if trying to find Gloria's mouth again.

'You want it don't you?' Gloria said, taking her lead from Clarissa, enjoying the power she had been gifted.

'Oh yes,' Polly said. 'Please . . .'

Gloria's sex throbbed. She squeezed her thighs together to

put pressure on her own clitoris. It responded with a sharp stab of pleasure. She stared into the girl's sex. Her labia were puffy and red, her legs not far enough apart to open her vagina. With the tip of one finger she pushed at Polly's clitoris and saw her sex contract. The idea that the girl was entirely at her mercy thrilled her to the core. She pushed her finger into the girl's vagina, then extracted it, watching the way the labia folded back into place.

With one hand she stroked her buttocks again, feeling the heat they still generated. Polly gasped and trembled. She could leave her like this, of course, but Gloria suddenly felt her own needs asserting themselves. She plunged her mouth back on to Polly's sex kissing it at first as though it were a mouth, squirming her lips against it before she pushed her tongue out again to search for the girl's clitoris. The first contact made Polly's sex pulse strongly and her body tense. Gloria felt a gush of juices against her chin and the girl gave a long low moan, as Gloria's tongue worked the little swollen promontory from side to side again, as regularly as a metronome.

Then the girl let out a piercing cry, a cross between a growl and a scream. Her whole body went rigid and she pulled against her bondage, not as a means of escape but as a way of extending the orgasm that flooded over her, the feeling of constriction as provoking as the weals of fire on her buttocks and the delicate, hot tongue that prodded against her clitoris.

Gloria pulled away slowly. She turned to Clarissa to see if she had her approval.

'Take her back Georgette,' Clarissa said. Georgette was pulling down the skirt of the dress, covering a damp stain that spread over the front of the French knickers. The maid quickly unbuckled the ankle cuffs and led the girl away.

Clarissa refilled her glass of champagne as Gloria still knelt on the floor. She came and stood right in front of her and handed her the glass.

'Have some,' she said.

Gloria took the glass and drank. 'Thank you,' she said handing the glass back.

Clarissa stroked her hair, then pulled her face against her thighs. The dress rode up and Gloria could see Clarissa's sex covered in the flesh coloured nylon, its pubic hair ironed down by the material.

'You're a natural,' she whispered. 'I knew you were special.' With that she took her hand, brought Gloria to her feet and led her up the sweeping staircase to her bedroom.

Chapter Nine

WILLIAM

It had been a miserable two weeks. He had been worked from dawn to dusk. Olga had shown true inventiveness in finding him menial, unnecessary and back-breaking tasks to perform. She had had him scrub the large kitchen floor with a nail brush. He had been made to clean every bathroom in the house, and there were many, with the same implement. Usually she decided his work was slip-shod and he had been made to do it all over again.

The attic of the house had proved fertile ground for her. Years of disuse had seen an accumulation of cobwebs, dead flies and insects – surplus to the spider's requirements – and a thick coat of dust encrusted with insect droppings. William had been made to clean and polish every inch, then start on the disused and discarded furniture and junk that littered it.

In the evening the shower had run black, his hair, face and arms caked in grime. His fingers were sore and his hands blistered. He had several splinters and bruises and grazed flesh where, in the confined space, he had knocked himself against the sloping roof or fallen over. Olga had overseen his work frequently and had seen many – often fictitious – reasons to add to his discomfort by stroking the whip she always carried down on his arms and legs and buttocks.

But he did not mind the hardship. He welcomed it. Since his last encounter with Clarissa, it matched his mood perfectly. He hoped that if he performed all the physical tasks he was set, however unnecessary and demeaning they were, Olga would report to Clarissa that he was trying to make amends.

Fortunately at night he was too exhausted to do anything but sleep because Clarissa had decreed that he was to be prevented from masturbation. Clearly other 'servants' had been treated in the same way as an electronic device had been developed for this purpose. Olga had padlocked two straps around his wrists, and a third under his balls and over the shaft of his cock, very much like the one he had been made to wear with Hildegard. There was an essential difference however. Each strap was fitted with a small transponder. If he put either hand within two inches of his cock the transponder sent a signal to a small unit set in the ceiling of the cubicle which immediately admitted an ear-piercing shriek. The alarm would be repeated in Olga's room.

At night Olga would often take her time attaching the strap to his cock, pulling it this way and that and pretending to find the whole operation difficult. Her attentions would frequently result, as they were no doubt intended to, in William developing a throbbing erection which he had no means to satisfy.

In the mornings too he would wake with a throbbing hard-on, his mind full of images of Clarissa's naked body, and the expression on her face, her words – '*How dare you?*' – echoing endlessly in his ears.

It was no longer a question of serving out his 'sentence', of taking his punishment so he would not be thrown out of the house and consequently lose his job. He had been very close to that, he knew, but his priorities had changed. He wasn't sure he wanted his job any more, or his former empty life. What he wanted, beyond anything else, was to serve Clarissa, even if, as now, in the most menial of ways. He wanted merely to be in the same house as her, to know that, though it might be days, even weeks, she could eventually call for him, and that a crumb of comfort would fall from her table in the form of a minute of her attention.

He did not know how it had happened, but he was completely in her thrall. A part of him could not understand how he could feel like this about a woman who had been so callous and cruel, but most of him simply didn't care. The thought of kneeling in front of her, of bringing his lips down to kiss her feet, made him instantly erect whatever he was doing. He knew he had made a terrible mistake the last time he had seen her, not only because he had gone too far but because he had not realised that having sex with Clarissa would never be an option for him. He was not and would never be worthy of her. She had given him an opportunity, a priceless opportunity as he saw it now, to soothe and caress her body, to serve her in the most private way, and he had abused her trust. He had come to realise his desires and feelings didn't come into it, they were not of the slightest importance. His role was purely to serve, to do precisely whatever she wanted him to do.

Now that truth *had* dawned and he knew what he must do, he yearned for the opportunity to demonstrate it to her. He knew that the endless days without seeing her were his punishment for what he had done, a greater punishment by far than his work load. Hopefully, soon, she would decide he had been punished enough.

It was exactly fourteen days since his last encounter with Clarissa when his wish came true, in part at least. As usual he had been allowed to shower, was given food and then returned to his cubicle by Olga. She had fitted the three straps to his wrists and his cock, the latter with her customary difficulty, and had locked him in for the night. Ignoring the erection her fumbling had given him he had fallen into a deep sleep by the time Olga unlocked the door and turned the light on again.

'Up,' she said.

Blinking against the light he scrambled to his feet, his heart thumping against his ribs, as much from shock as excitement. He was disorientated by being woken so suddenly. 'It's not morning is it?' he said.

'You are required upstairs,' she said.

The words made William's heart thump faster. Had Clarissa decided his time in purdah was over?

Olga unlocked the electronic transponders. 'Follow,' she said.

They went to the lift. Olga was wearing her familiar grey uniform and William's naked body pressed against it in the small cage of the lift. She looked at him with disdain, his manhood, the lack of spirit he had shown in the last two weeks, the lack of even the smallest act of defiance, beneath her contempt. He was disappointed when her short fat finger punched the button marked with a two. It meant he was not being taken to Clarissa.

Olga led him along the corridor on the second floor. They

were almost at the end of the passage when she stopped him in front of one of the doors.

'Hands behind your back,' she said, taking a pair of metal handcuffs from her jacket pocket.

He wanted to tell her that they were not necessary, that whoever was behind the door would get no trouble from him, but he remained silent. Clarissa obviously still didn't trust him and he knew it was up to him to earn that trust again.

Olga snapped the cuffs over his wrists then knocked firmly on the door and opened it, pushing William inside. He felt a surge of adrenaline make his heart leap, when he saw Clarissa sitting in a small armchair upholstered in chintz. She was wearing a leaf green, suede trouser suit, its tight jacket buttoned all the way up to her throat where it was fashioned into a mandarin collar.

Sitting on the bed opposite her was another woman. She was young with frizzy fair hair, an attractive, well proportioned face and high cheekbones. Her eyes were a bright emerald green. She was wearing a pair of black thong style panties and a matching black bra. Her figure was slim and curvaceous, her belly flat and her breasts round and firm.

'Well, I'll leave you to it,' Clarissa said getting to her feet. 'Do you want Olga to stay?'

'Don't worry, I can handle him,' the girl said as Olga put the key to the handcuffs on the bedside table.

'Whatever you want,' Clarissa said, going to the door. She did not give William so much as a glance. Her indifference stung him as much as any whip.

'Oh, I know exactly what I want,' the girl said smiling broadly.

Clarissa walked out into the hall followed by Olga. The door closed. Immediately William sunk to his knees experiencing the same awkwardness he had done when his hands had been bound before. The girl appeared to be quite familiar with the ritual. She got up and walked over to him so he could reach her feet. He bent forward and kissed both of them. Unfortunately the action had an instant effect on his cock. He felt it unfurling rapidly. He wished he could have hidden it with his hands.

'I've heard all about you,' the woman said. 'Such a bad boy.'

'I didn't . . . I tried . . .' He couldn't think of any reply.

'You're not going to be bad with me are you?'

'No.'

'My name is Hilary Laing. You must call me Ms Laing.'

'No, Ms Laing,' he said.

'That's what I like to hear William. So we'll start shall we? I want you to take my knickers down.'

William looked at her, then rattled the handcuffs behind his back, trying to show her his hands were not available for such a task, as if she hadn't noticed.

'Use your teeth,' she said petulantly.

William stared at the tight panties and tried to work out how to do it. He leant forward, and nudged his mouth against the top of the waistband, inhaling a wonderful scent from her body, and feeling a rush of pleasure from physical contact with another human being again. Trying to ignore his cock rising like the Indian rope trick, he worked his tongue under the elastic then gripped it with his teeth. He started to tug the material down. His first attempt tore the material from his grasp and he had to fish for it with his tongue again. Clenching his teeth tighter he tugged again. Unfortunately, though the front of the panties slipped lower, the back remained firmly in place.

Hilary caught his cheeks in her hand and squeezed them to make his mouth release its grip. She turned and walked back to the bed.

'Not a very good start,' she said. With her back to him she skimmed the black panties down her shapely legs. He could see her sex, tufted with pubic hair, nestling between her buttocks as she bent down to loop the panties off her ankles. With the panties still in her hand she reached behind her to unclasp her bra, allowing it to fall from her breasts. She turned to face him. Her breasts were pendulous, elongated by their own weight. She had very little areolae around her nipples which were small and a very dark red. Her pubic hair was thick and surprisingly long.

'Come here,' she said.

He started to struggle to his feet.

'No, on your knees,' she insisted smiling. 'I like to see that.'

William shuffled forward, his erection sticking out from his loins. As soon as he was in range she rubbed the silky panties over his face.

'They smell of me don't they?'

'Yes, Ms Laing.'

'Do you think I'm attractive? Do you think I've got a nice body?'

'Very nice, Ms Laing,' he said sincerely. Her body was lovely.

'Good. That'll make it easier for you then. I want you to give me a good time. I need it. I need to relax.' She sat on the edge of the bed, opened her legs and indicated with her finger that he should kneel between her thighs. He shuffled forward. 'Lick it for me William,' she said in a low voice.

As William dipped his head towards her sex Hilary lay back on the bed, bringing her legs up over his shoulders then crossing her ankles over his back, so her thighs were splayed apart. William found himself staring into her sex. It was oddly shaped, projecting prominently like a mouth pursed to be kissed, her labia round rather than oval.

'Come on,' she said wriggling it towards him.

William plunged his tongue into the tight furrow and searched for her clitoris. It was already swollen. He licked it briefly then moved down to her vagina, using his own saliva for lubrication as she was quite dry. Pushing inside her sex he heard her moan. He plunged his tongue as deep as it would go, probing the velvety walls of her cunt. Instantly he felt her produce a sticky wetness.

He pressed his mouth against her sex harder, ironing her labia flat against his lips, so he could get his tongue higher. The walls of her sex clung to him, and he could feel it throbbing.

Slowly he slid his tongue out and up to her clit. He pushed it this way and that then began to circle it with the tip of his tongue.

'Yes, like that,' she cried.

He felt her legs clasp together reflexively trapping his head between them. His own sex was pulsing. Any man would have been excited by what he was doing to this beautiful woman but he knew his excitement was more profound than that. The image he could see of himself kneeling before her, his hands bound behind his back, his lips pressed to her sex, playing obeisance to her body, obliged to obey her slightest whim, touched something deep in his psyche. He had never known it was there before but now that he knew, it felt as though he had found himself.

He could feel her coming. Her sex was contracting, her clitoris pulsing wildly, her thighs around his head rigid. He moved his tongue faster and harder and heard her moan. She ground herself against his mouth, the opening of her vagina wet and slippery on his chin, then went from total rigidity to absolute relaxation, her legs suddenly listless and loose, her sex like some syrupy guava squashed against his mouth.

'Don't move,' she ordered as the aftershocks of orgasm seized her and her body trembled anew.

Eventually she unwound her legs from around his back and sat up. 'Well so far so good,' she said her eyes sparkling. 'You know I've never done anything like this before I met Clarissa. Such an interesting woman. Quite as capable as any man don't you think? She's given quite a few of her female friends the chance to express themselves, I mean find out what they really want. We're so bound by convention when it comes to sex. Women I mean. It's so nice to have the chance to throw over the traces . . .'

She got to her feet and went to the bedside table. She opened the single drawer and extracted two dildoes, both made from cream plastic and one much smaller than the other. She laid them on the bed then delved in the drawer and extracted a long cylindrical tube of KY jelly. She placed this on the sheet by the dildoes.

'Clarissa tells me you have been prevented from coming for some while now. Is that true?'

'Yes, Ms Laing.'

'How long?'

'Fourteen days.'

'Oh dear. That must be terribly frustrating. No wonder you're so big and hard. I'm surprised you haven't jumped on me. That's why they had you cuffed I suppose. In case you were tempted.' She walked behind his back. He heard the wardrobe door open and close. 'Get to your feet William,' Hilary ordered, clearly fully enjoying the power she had over him.

William staggered to his feet, his knees protesting.

'Clarissa also tells me you have something of a penchant for being whipped. Is that true?'

'No, Ms Laing,' William said though he wasn't entirely sure that was true. He glanced over his shoulder to see that Hilary had taken a short riding crop from the cupboard. His cock jerked violently belying his words.

'No? Your cock seems to think differently.'

'I was . . . it was . . . I'd never . . .' He blushed a deep red, ashamed at what had happened in Clarissa's study and even more upset that Clarissa had related it to others.

'I understood you enjoyed a little flagellation. In fact I was told it can make you produce, how shall I put it, spontaneous combustion? Is that not true William?'

'I just . . . it was the first time . . . I . . .' He couldn't think of a way to explain what had happened because he didn't understand it himself.

'Bend over the bed. We're going to try a little experiment.'

'No, please Ms Laing.' William felt a wave of panic take hold of him. He feared he would not be able to control himself.

'No? Did you say *no* William?'

Hastily he bent over the bed, his tethered hands uppermost, perched unnaturally on the small of his back.

She said the words he feared most. 'This time you'd better control yourself. Is that understood?' Before he could answer Hilary cut the crop down across his buttocks. The lash burnt into him. He felt the familiar searing pain making his nerves dance. The pain created long fingers of sensation which raced through his body and curled around his cock. He felt it pulse violently. He had only experienced this extraordinary sensation twice before but it seemed to have become inextricably bound with his sexual gratification.

Thwack. The leather whip lashed across his naked buttocks.

'This is what you like isn't it?' Hilary said her voice breathless with exhilaration.

'No, no,' he moaned not wanting to admit it to himself or to her.

Thwack. Thwack. Four red weals striped his bottom. The pain from them, the sensation that flowed through his body, was routed directly to his cock, making it swell and pound. He simply could not distinguish the pain from the pleasure it gave him.

'Isn't it?' Hilary insisted slicing the whip down for a fifth time.

He couldn't stand another stroke. His cock was pulsating, full of spunk. Another stroke would bring him off, just as it had with Clarissa and Hildegard. 'Yes, yes it is, it is. Please – you have to stop.'

Hilary laughed. She threw the whip on the bed satisfied that she had achieved her aim. William knew there was no doubt from the state of him, his body trembling uncontrollably, sweat running down his back, that he was on the brink of orgasm.

Quickly Hilary lay on the bed, picking up the smaller of the two dildoes and anointing its shaft with lubricating jelly. She opened her legs, her left foot touching William's thigh, and arched her buttocks off the bed.

If William had cared to look he would have seen her prodding the tip of the torpedo-shaped dildo against the little crater of her anus, then, with hardly a pause, pushing it home. He dared not look, however, for he was fearful of the effect such a spectacle would have on his over-wrought erection. He closed his eyes and opened them again immediately. The images that lurked in his mind, images of Clarissa, were just as potent.

Hilary slid the second dildo into her cunt with no need for extra lubrication. He could not help but see this. As the cream plastic nosed up into her body, he saw her compact, pursed labia stretch around it. It slid home effortlessly making a slight squelching sound.

'Come and kneel here,' she said patting the sheet by her side.

He obeyed, his erection sticking out directly over her belly, his hands still firmly manacled behind his back.

One by one she turned the little gnarled knobs at the base of the dildoes. A loud humming filled the air on two frequencies. William saw her eyes close, as she was momentarily overcome by the impact of the dual vibration. He saw her fingers pushing both dildoes deeper as her body writhed down on them.

She opened her eyes again and turned to look at him.

'In five seconds, William,' she said in a calm voice. 'You are to come in five seconds. Can you do that? Have I prepared you properly?' She moved her hip slightly so it touched his knee. Instantly he felt the vibration from her body. It spread up his leg and into his cock. 'One.'

She made no attempt to touch him. She used her free hand to grip her right breast and pinch at its nipple.

'Two.'

She expected him to come without any other stimulation, to combust spontaneously, as she had put it. And he knew he could. The fire in his buttocks and the sight of her was quite enough. The problem was waiting until the count of five.

'Three.'

His cock was spasming. He felt his spunk pumping up to the last barrier, like water behind a crumbling dam, waiting to burst through. He was beginning to have delusions. He started to imagine he was coming, so strong were his feelings. He looked down at his cock and was astonished to see that no semen was spurting from it.

'Four. Don't let me down William. I could make up all sorts of terrible stories about you to Clarissa if you do.' Her eyes closed. He saw her body trembling, one breast squeezed between her fingers the other quivering.

'Five.'

He thought the first spurt of his spunk jetted out of him just before she said the word, but it didn't matter. A string of white hot spunk followed, arcing out of his throbbing, pumping cock, and over her belly and thighs, gobs of it landing in her pubic hair.

She gasped, pushed the dildoes in with one final effort and

came, her body responding to the vibrations, and the hot spunk that had lashed across it, but most of all to the sense of power, that she was able to make a man perform like this. William guessed that that was what Hilary loved most. Clarissa had given her the ability to have what she had always wanted.

She seemed reluctant to bring herself down to earth, but slowly she allowed the dildoes to slide out of her body of their own accord, the silky wet flesh of both her passages gradually expelling them.

William knelt, waiting for instructions. His wrists ached where, unconsciously he had pulled against the metal cuffs. After so long without coming his orgasm had left him weak. As to what she had made him do, he wasn't sure whether to feel proud or terribly ashamed.

GLORIA

Gloria watched Clarissa get into the black Rolls Royce parked outside the front of the house. She felt a strong surge of desire as she saw her long legs sheathed in sheer, shimmering nylon, her short skirt, as usual, revealing most of her beautifully contoured thighs. She watched as the chauffeur closed the rear door and walked around to get behind the wheel. She didn't allow the curtains to fall back over the window until the car had completely disappeared across the other side of the square.

After the encounter with Polly, Clarissa had ordered that Gloria be moved from the cubicles in the basement to a small bedroom on the second floor overlooking the front of the house. It was a considerable privilege. All the other 'servants' were quartered in the basement and the second floor was reserved for Clarissa's house guests, but it seemed that she had decided it would be more convenient to have Gloria – her star pupil – close at hand. In addition, Olga had been instructed that Gloria was not available for anything but the lightest of domestic chores. Clarissa wanted to save Gloria's energies for other purposes.

Four times in the last two weeks Gloria had been taken to Clarissa's bedroom late at night. Each visit had given Gloria a renewed taste of her own blossoming sexuality and her orgasms were as sharp and fulfilling as any she had already experienced under Clarissa's tutelage. That is how she had come to think of it. Clarissa was a master and Gloria her willing, previously naive, pupil.

Her new privileges did not extend to being allowed the run of the house and when she was not required the bedroom door was locked. Nor was she allowed any clothes.

As she walked back to the bed, almost before the curtains had stopped swishing against the window, the key turned in the lock and the bedroom door swung open. Olga stood in the doorway, a broad grin spreading over her face.

'Ms Peacham is leaving you on your own this evening, yes?' She strode into the room and closed the door. Like the first time Gloria had seen her she was wearing a dress, a full flowing cotton print in blue and lilac with a button front. She began to unbutton it.

Gloria shrunk against the wall. 'Have you got Ms Peacham's permission to be here?' she said. She was sure that she hadn't. Clarissa had given her no reason to believe that she would be subjected to Olga's unwelcome attentions.

Olga slipped the dress off to reveal a white satin bra, its

large cups and thick straps struggling to contain her mountainous bosom. She was wearing voluminous French knickers in the same material but no tights or stockings.

'You are having things rather too easy. Now it is my time. I will teach you a lesson you will not forget.'

'Does Ms Peacham know you're here?' Gloria persisted.

'No, and she will not find out. Do you know why? Because if you tell her what happens here tonight I will make the rest of your time in this house a misery. Do you understand this?'

'If I tell her you'll be fired.' Gloria said defiantly.

Olga laughed. 'Fired? Fired? You think she could fire me with all I know about what is going on here? No, I do not think so. I will not be fired. I will be here to see that you suffer. So, it is better you co-operate, yes?'

She had thought it all out. Gloria saw she had no choice.

'Good,' Olga said, taking Gloria's silence for victory. She sat on the foot of the bed and prised off her shoes. 'First I warm you up. Here. Come here.' She indicated the top of her meaty thighs. It was quite clear to Gloria she wanted her to bend over them.

'What are you going to do to me?' she asked.

'What should have been done earlier.'

Gloria stepped forward. She clearly had no choice. Olga was strong and could soon overpower her. It seemed sensible to take whatever was coming to her with as little fuss as possible. The odd thing was a buzz of excitement was beginning to affect her.

Olga grasped her by the wrist and forcibly pulled her over her knees. She held her there with one hand on the back of her neck while the other caressed the firm curves of Gloria's buttocks and the tops of her thighs. 'So soft,' she said.

With no warning Olga raised her arm and brought the palm of her hand slapping down on to the middle of Gloria's right buttock. Almost immediately an equally swingeing blow struck her left cheek. The sting of pain was accompanied by a flush of heat that spread right across her arse.

'Please . . .' she gasped not knowing what she meant by it.

Olga's left hand pressed firmly on her neck as she raised her right again. Two more slaps were delivered, harder than the first and lower, towards the bottom of the buttocks. The sound of flesh smacking against flesh reverberated around the small room.

'Got you nice and warmed up, I think.'

The heat in Gloria's bottom was intense. She could feel it radiating out as Olga's hand went back to caress and stroke her buttocks. But that was not all she could feel. As Olga's hand soothed the fire it had created she felt her body change gear, the excitement she had felt becoming noticeably stronger. She could not stop herself from wriggling sensuously against Olga's hand. She remembered William's reaction and Polly's. Is this what they had felt?

'Oh yes,' Olga said at once. 'You like.'

She slapped Gloria twice in quick succession, this time producing a sharp throb of pleasure deep in her sex. Gloria squeezed her thighs together, the cheeks of her buttocks clenched, husbanding the sensation, not wanting it to dissipate.

'You little bitch,' Olga said. 'You want more?'

'Yes,' Gloria muttered. Each new sting of pain had increased the intensity of her pleasure. She had applied the whip willingly and enjoyed the thrill it had produced in her. It seemed her sadism was a coin that could be flipped to masochism with equally satisfying results.

Olga spanked her twice more, treating each buttock equally, then smoothing her hand against the reddened flesh.

'Oh God, God.' Gloria was not sure which was the more provocative, the smack or the caress.

But Olga had her own agenda. 'Get to your feet,' she ordered.

Gloria obeyed, her buttocks stinging as they were fanned by the air.

Olga knelt on the bed, pulling the white satin knickers to her knees then positioning herself on all fours. 'Now you will give me a good time. You've had a lot of practice in this so make it good. Understand?'

'Yes.' There could be little doubt what Olga wanted her to do. Olga's hairy sex, trapped between her mountainous buttocks, was already wet.

'Come on then,' Olga said impatiently.

Gloria knelt on the bed behind Olga. She grasped the white satin and tried to pull it down over her knees.

'No, like this,' Olga snapped irritably.

It was awkward. Gloria straddled Olga's lower legs and pushed her mouth against her sex. She extended her tongue and licked the runnel of her labia. She was surprised to find, at the bottom, it was possible to insinuate the tip of her tongue against Olga's clit. Like everything else about the woman her clitoris was large and fat.

'Like that,' Olga said.

Gloria concentrated on the little nodule of flesh, flicking it from side to side then tapping it hard with her tongue. She ran her hand down over the vast curves of Olga's buttocks and pushed her fingers into her vagina, not penetrating far but, instead, scissoring her fingers apart to stretch the entrance wide open. Olga moaned.

Suddenly the big woman swung around, pulling herself away from Gloria's mouth. With surprising agility she jack-knifed her legs into the air and pulled her knickers off, throwing them aside. She made no attempt to pull off her bra.

'Now,' she said, the spark of excitement that danced in her eyes becoming even brighter.

Her strong hands took Gloria by the shoulders and pushed her down on to her back, her hands smoothing over Gloria's breasts, squeezing them gently. Then she crawled down to her feet and grasped both Gloria's ankles in her hands and stretched her legs wide apart. For a moment she stared at her sex.

'What are you going to do to me?' Gloria said, her voice wavering with her excitement.

Olga did not answer. Instead she let go of Gloria's ankles and pushed her left foot up under Gloria's buttocks, quite forcibly, so Gloria was thrown to one side and the stinging in her reddened bottom was renewed. She continued to extend her leg until her foot was level with Gloria's shoulder blades. At the same time she thrust her other leg up over Gloria's belly, and extended that up until her right foot was under Gloria's chin, her body squeezed between Olga's legs. Similarly Olga's body rested between Gloria's legs.

At once Gloria could feel the heat of Olga's sex. In this position their sexes were no more than an inch apart, both necessarily open. Quickly Olga caught Gloria by both wrists and pulled her down, with a considerable jerk. For the first time in her life Gloria felt her sex slammed against the sex of another woman. It was an incredible sensation. It felt like Olga's sex was sucking on hers, drawing it in. She could feel her clitoris throbbing violently and realised she could feel Olga's doing the same. They were pressed together, clitoris on clitoris, their labia joined too, like hungry mouths hot and wet.

'Oh God, God!' Gloria cried.

'You see my little friend.' Olga ground her sex down on Gloria's, wriggling her hips from side to side. 'I can teach you too.'

The big woman allowed their bodies to part slightly, then pulled them together again, jerking on Gloria's arms. There was a noisy, squelching sound as their sexes smacked together.

'Yes,' Gloria gasped at the jolt of sensation this produced.

'Yes, you want?' Olga asked, needing no answer, then repeating the process, letting their bodies slide apart then slamming them back together again, the impact producing a suction effect that made them both tremble. 'You want . . .' She jerked forward again.

Gloria was coming. Not only was her clitoris pulsing wildly but her whole labia seemed to be alive, pushed back, then sucked outward as their sexes parted. What's more she could feel exactly the same effect in Olga's body, her sex was just as active.

At exactly the right moment, the desires and needs of both women so precisely matched, Olga pulled them together for the last time. Their bodies melded against each other, the soft, pulpy flesh throbbing with an ever increasing tempo. As Gloria felt her orgasm explode, she felt, just as acutely, Olga's body lurch too. Their thighs squeezed each other in a vice-like grip as their sexes convulsed. Like an echo the orgasm bounced from one to the other and vice versa until they were simply incapable of feeling any more.

Chapter Ten

WILLIAM

'Well at last I have a good report about you,' Clarissa said. 'It seems you are beginning to learn at last.'

'Thank you, Ms Peacham.'

'Hilary was most complimentary. It appears you obeyed her to the letter.'

'Yes, Ms Peacham.'

They were in her bedroom, William kneeling waiting to be allowed to kiss her feet. He noticed his hands were trembling slightly, his excitement at being in her presence again, at long last, difficult to contain.

Clarissa came to stand directly in front of him. She was wearing a black lace slip with spaghetti straps. It floated around the black tops of her very sheer black stockings, held taut by ruched black satin suspenders. He could not see her suspender belt but caught a glimpse of the silky black panties that covered her sex. Her high heels were black too, the toes encrusted with diamanté. He inhaled her familiar musky scent as he dipped his head and pressed his lips against the sheer nylon on the arch of her left foot.

'Very good,' she said as he moved his lips over to her right foot. Her voice was soft and soothing. He sensed something was different about her tonight, and not just in the fact that her attitude to him was more benevolent. 'I have no desire to punish you William. It gives me no pleasure. You understand that don't you?'

'Yes, Ms Peacham.'

'There are certain standards I have to insist on. I'm glad that you seem to have come to your senses. Let's put you to the test shall we?'

Clarissa walked over to one of the sofas and sat in the corner of it, crossing her legs. 'Come here,' she said.

He knew better than to get to his feet without being told. He 'walked' across the carpet on his knees. Clarissa extended her right foot straight out in front of her, resting her ankle on his shoulder. He could see the whole plane of her sex tightly covered in black silk. The silk was dimpled, sucked up into the furrow of her sex.

'Can you see my sex?'

The question struck fear into his heart. He knew he hadn't been given permission to look at her. But lying would only make matters worse. 'Yes, Ms Peacham.'

'And the tops of my stockings?'

'Yes, Ms Peacham.' She was not reacting as he had expected.

'I always think that stockings seem to make the flesh above them seem so much more creamy in contrast. Do you agree?'

'Yes, Ms Peacham.'

As much as he had prayed it wouldn't, William felt his cock beginning to unfurl.

'Get up. Go to the bathroom. There's a pair of my panties

on the floor, the ones I've been wearing to work. Bring them here.' She returned her foot to the floor and William jumped to his feet, practically running to the bathroom. A peachy bra and matching bikini panties lay where she had dropped them by the bath. He picked up the panties and rushed back to her, sliding to his knees again. He held the panties out for her to take.

'No,' she said. 'I want you to rub them against your face.'

'No,' he moaned under his breath, afraid that his control might break.

'Get a grip on yourself William,' she warned sternly.

He brought the peach silk up to his cheek. It smelt strongly of her perfume.

'What can you smell?'

'Your perfume, Ms Peacham.' He felt his cock harden, at full erection now.

'Nothing else?'

He sniffed the silk. There was an unmistakable odour of sex.

'I had sex today William.' There was a dreamy distant look in her eyes. 'A friend of mine came to my office. He's big and strong, a real man, very forceful and powerful, very dominant. He locked the office door and took me over my desk, thrust his big, hard cock into my soft, wet cunt. Oh, it was so exciting.' He saw her body shudder as she re-lived the memory. 'He wouldn't let me take my panties off, he just pushed them aside. Those panties William. I've been leaking his spunk into them all afternoon.'

William felt his cock spasm. She was undoubtedly telling the truth; the panties were damp. The story was not made up for his benefit but it was a test. He ground his teeth.

Clarissa extended her high heel and dug the toe into his erection.

'You see, William, I'm turned on by big powerful men, ones who know what a woman needs. You're not like that. You could never give me what I need, could you?'

Four weeks ago, in this situation William might have been tempted to throw himself at her, used her taunting as an excuse to be as forceful and powerful as she said she wanted. But now he did not move. The odd thing was that he hadn't the slightest desire to ravish her. He only wanted to obey. The thought of having sex with her had been removed from his psyche, extracted like a rotten tooth. What she said was true. He could never give her what she wanted. He was her servant, her slave. And that is what *he* wanted to be. He realised, with a sudden brilliant insight, that is *all* he wanted to be.

'No, Ms Peacham,' he said earnestly.

'I'm glad we're agreed about that at least. Take my panties. Wrap them around your cock.'

He did as he was told. The touch of the silk made him quake.

'Does that feel good?'

'Oh yes, Ms Peacham. Very good.'

'If you had behaved yourself better, I would have given you more treats like this. I would have let you watch, William, let you watch me being fucked. But now your time is almost up.'

'I'm sorry, Ms Peacham.'

'Would you like to see that? See me with a man?'

'Anything you want, Ms Peacham.'

'What about with a woman, what about with your friend Gloria? She's a very special woman William. Very adept. Very feminine.'

'Anything, mistress.' He hadn't called her that before but the word seemed so right. She was the mistress of his fate.

She was stroking her breast under the silk slip. '*Anything* William?'

'Anything, Ms Peacham. Ms Peacham, mistress please don't send me away. I couldn't bear it.' It had never occurred to him before he actually said it, but he realised it was absolutely true. He could not stand to go back to the real world. This was all he wanted now. Like some patients with a psychiatrist, he had become totally dependent on her. She was his life. She was everything. He only wanted to be allowed to stay here, to be with her however infrequently, to hear her voice and see her and occasionally bathe in the warm, fulfilling glow of her attention, however short its span. He had no family and no friends. He had nothing to go back to. He just wanted to serve her.

'Stay here?' she said. 'After your month is up?'

'Please, Ms Peacham. I realise it's a lot to ask.'

'I'll have to think about that William. Do you think you could behave yourself as well as you've done tonight?'

'Yes, Ms Peacham.'

His heart was pounding. He tried to will her to agree. He looked up her long legs.

'I would have to give you a test. A severe test.' He could see she was thinking. Then she smiled. 'All right, you may go now. Use the lift.' She got to her feet before he could and walked to the phone, the hem of her slip flouncing up over the top of her stockings. She picked up the phone to tell Olga he was on his way.

William shuffled over towards the lift feeling completely

drained. He wanted to say more, he wanted to try and tell her how he felt, to express in words the depth of his feelings, but he simply dared not.

'Thank you, Ms Peacham,' he said instead, but she did not acknowledge him or glance at him again. She picked up the black cocktail dress that had been laid out on the bed.

With a final longing look William stepped around the corner and into the lift.

At the bottom Olga was waiting for him.

GLORIA

The party was lavish and grand. The outfit Gloria had been given to wear by Clarissa was from Versace and was undoubtedly the most expensive she had ever worn. It consisted of a long sleeved canary yellow jacket buttoned to the neck by big gold and black buttons but short, leaving her midriff bare. The skirt was black and had a high, tight fitting waist, then flared out to a hem that finished well above the knee. The slinky material was also slit in the front right up to the apex of the thighs and here the skirt had been embossed with a cluster of large glass beads, shaped to look like a bunch of grapes. Her open-toed high heels were striped in yellow and black. She wore no bra or panties, only a pair of ultra sheer flesh coloured tights that, from a distance made her legs look almost bare.

It was a far cry from the drab colours and workaday suits that Gloria had habitually worn only four weeks before.

Clarissa's black cocktail dress was just long enough to cover the tops of her stockings. Its box neckline gave an intriguing view of the deep cleavage and the impressive swell of her breasts. On her wrist Clarissa wore a silver, diamond and emerald bracelet. Attached to it was a silver chain, the links beaten into rectangular shapes no more than an inch in length. There were eight links in the chain which was attached, on the other end, to an identical bracelet on Gloria's wrist. Both bracelets were locked in place by a silver padlock the key to which hung from a thin silver thread around Clarissa's neck. The two women were thus manacled together.

It was definitely the talking point of the party. Clarissa told everyone who cared to ask that Gloria was her 'slave'. The fashion for using the fetishistic images of bondage as icons of style made most of the women envious of Clarissa's daring, not guessing the truth of her relationship with Gloria.

The party was being held on a small sound stage where Clarissa's advertising agency filmed many of its commercials. It was to celebrate the film company's tenth year of business and was studded with guests from the world of film and fashion, as well as many of Clarissa's rivals in advertising. All the men were dressed in black tie, all the women in extravagant creations from Bond Street couturiers.

Champagne, and every other drink, flowed like water. Food: lobsters, oysters, smoked salmon, and silver buckets filled with Beluga caviar, was piled high on white linen covered trellis tables under the steel lighting gantries.

Manacled to Clarissa, Gloria had no choice but to stay at her side. She seemed to be looking for someone.

'Hi!' He had come up behind them and clasped Clarissa by the shoulders. 'Is this the new police restraining device?' His hand slid down to the silver chain and picked up both their wrists.

'Charles!' Clarissa said. From the expression in her eyes Gloria could see this was obviously the man she had been searching for. And she could see why. Charles was tall and attractive, with broad shoulders and a stomach as flat as a board. He had long blond hair and deep, deep blue eyes, his complexion that olive colour that suggested a Mediterranean background.

They kissed on both cheeks.

'This is Gloria,' Clarissa said.

He hardly gave her a second glance.

'Do you want to go next door?' he said. His eyes sparkled with life. He was wearing a blue silk shirt that reflected and enhanced their colour.

'What's next door ?' Clarissa asked.

'My flat. I had a door knocked through.'

'Very convenient. Charles owns the studio,' she explained to Gloria.

Charles was looking at the silver bracelets. 'Where you go she goes right?'

'I thought the idea might excite you,' Clarissa said. 'If not . . .' she fingered the silver chain around her neck.

'It does,' he said simply taking her free hand.

They manoeuvred through the crowd, acknowledging the greetings of friends and acquaintances, occasionally forced to stop and chat. Gloria was towed along in their wake.

Eventually they reached a door, heavily sound-proofed like the walls that surrounded it. Charles took a key from the pocket of his cream flannel slacks and unlocked it. As it opened Gloria saw a narrow, steep staircase on the inside.

Charles locked the door behind them, then led the way

upstairs. At the top was a door which opened into a large studio room, a kitchen, sitting room and bedroom all contained in the pillared space of what was clearly a converted warehouse. The floor was stripped oak and the furniture minimalist and ultra modern, the two sofas upholstered in bright primary colours, book shelves constructed from black tubular steel, two huge futuristic speakers connected to an equally large stack of hi-fi components by spirals of black wire. The frame of the double bed was also steel, the mattress covered with a black counterpane.

Charles took Clarissa into his arms and kissed her full on the mouth. Clarissa wrapped his arms around his back, pulling Gloria's hand up too.

'I thought, after lunchtime . . .' Clarissa said when the kiss ended.

'Lunchtime only made me more hungry for you,' Charles said. He went over to the bed and threw off the counterpane. There was a black silk sheet underneath. Gloria could see an erection tenting the front of his slacks. He began unbuttoning his shirt. His chest was contoured with muscles but was almost hairless. He was slim enough for Gloria to be able to count his ribs.

'Unzip me,' Clarissa said to Gloria.

Gloria obeyed. She should have known what was going to happen from the conversation downstairs but it was not until Clarissa stepped out of the dress that the realisation really hit her. They were going to have sex in front of her. She felt her pulse begin to race.

'You'll have to hold it,' Clarissa said to Gloria. The dress was hanging from the chain of the bracelets. Gloria gathered it in her hand. 'Do you want her to undress?' Clarissa asked as Charles kicked off his loafers and peeled away his cream coloured socks.

'She's your idea. What do you think?' He pulled down his slacks and little white briefs. His cock was large: long and broad and circumcised.

'There's no time.' Clarissa stepped out of her black slip. Like the dress she handed it to Gloria as it would not come off over the chain.

'Well look at you. Quite the little whore aren't you?' Charles said, looking at Clarissa's lingerie, the scalloped edged, three quarter cup bra from which her large breasts spilled, and the panties and suspender belt that banded her hips and belly. He lay on his back on the bed, his cock sticking up vertically. 'Come over here and fuck me,' he said. 'Take your panties off this time, and leave your stockings on. They look good.'

'Thought you'd like them,' Clarissa said, stripping her panties down her long legs, forcing Gloria's hand to follow hers down to her ankles. 'Undo my bra,' she ordered.

Gloria found the clasp and unfastened it her hands trembling slightly with her own excitement, the sight of Charles's big cock affecting her just as much as she knew it was Clarissa. Clarissa's big breasts tumbled from their constraints.

'I didn't see your tits before,' Charles said.

'You were in too much of a hurry weren't you?'

'You're not complaining are you?'

'I didn't say that. As a matter of fact I loved it. But you know that don't you, you bastard?'

Clarissa took Gloria's cheeks in the palms of her hands and

kissed her full on the mouth, plunging her tongue between her lips.

'Come over here and fuck me. I'm not interested in all your lesbian shit.'

Clarissa broke the kiss immediately and pulled Gloria over to the bed. They both looked at Charles.

'I want you,' Clarissa said.

'Take me then.'

Clarissa sprung onto the bed, straddling his hips. Her sex was poised above his cock, her left hand pulled across the bed towards Gloria's.

'Sit on the bed,' she snapped.

Gloria obeyed, though it still meant Clarissa's hand was stretched out to one side.

Charles reached up to Clarissa's thighs caressing the tops of the stockings and the creamy flesh above. He turned his head to look at Gloria for the first time.

'She's pretty,' he said.

'You can fuck us both,' Clarissa said.

'No,' he replied firmly. His fingers dug into her thighs and pushed her down onto him as he bucked off the bed, his big cock sliding into her vagina, lubricated by her copious juices. 'I want to fuck *you*,' he said. He began a rhythm, pulling Clarissa down on him then pushing her up again, his hips powering his cock into her. Gloria saw Clarissa's body tense.

'You're so big,' she muttered.

'Too big? Do you want me to stop?'

'No, no, don't stop. It's too good.' She was being bounced up and down on him her breasts jiggling on her chest.

'Of course it's good,' he said, increasing his pace.

Gloria could see his phallus sliding in and out of Clarissa's sex, her labia pursed around it, her juices making it glisten.

'You're making me come.'

'You'd better come,' Charles said between clenched teeth. 'You'd better come for me.'

'You're so deep, so big.'

Clarissa's body shivered. They had shared so much together Gloria could almost feel the waves of pleasure that were coursing through Clarissa's body. She saw her eyes close and her thighs move further apart as she ground herself down on the phallus buried inside her, wriggling her clitoris against Charles's pubic bone. This produced the desired effect. As the big cock drove into her once again Clarissa's orgasm broke.

Gloria watched as Clarissa's body convulsed. Then she saw it melt, the rigidity in the muscles turning to jelly. Her own sex was throbbing and she could feel its moisture making the gusset of the tights damp. She could imagine exactly how this big, bone hard erection would feel inside her.

'Turn over, on your knees,' Charles ordered.

'Oh Charles,' Clarissa breathed. She pulled herself off him, his cock leaving her body with a loud plop, producing an aftershock of feeling that made her momentarily unable to do anything. When she came to her senses she turned around, facing the foot of the bed now, and coming up on all fours, the only way she could do it without making Gloria walk all the way around the bed to the other side. Clarissa's buttocks pointed at Charles.

'Make yourself useful,' he snapped. It took a second for Gloria to realise he was talking to her. 'Suck it for me.'

He got on his knees behind Clarissa, but twisted to one side to point his cock at Gloria. Immediately she leant forward and sucked the glans into her mouth. The taste of Clarissa's body was familiar. She ran her tongue around the pronounced ridge at the bottom of the glans and felt it jerk in her mouth. She could see his hands caressing Clarissa's pouting arse.

'That's enough,' he said almost angrily.

Gloria pulled away. He centred his cock between the fleshy folds of Clarissa's labia. She watched intently. The labia parted for all the world like a mouth parted to welcome him with a kiss. Her own sex was seething, her nipples as hard as stone. Charles did not push forward, he just held himself there.

'Come on, I need it,' Clarissa said, her body re-asserting itself, her first orgasm only the beginning.

'Oh I'm going to give it to you baby,' he said but did not, teasing her by making her wait.

Clarissa wriggled her hips from side to side. 'Please,' she said.

'Pretty please?'

'Don't tell me you don't want it, don't tell me you're not turned on by Gloria?' Clarissa said trying to make him lose control. 'Look at her. Look at the way she's looking at you.'

As if by way of reply Charles thrust forward. Gloria saw his cock being swallowed up by the folds of Clarissa's body until it disappeared completely. She saw the muscles of his buttocks dimple as they drove it in and his fingers clawing at Clarissa's hips. He began to pump into her, hard and fast, so fast his cock was a blur of motion.

'Is this what you want?' he hissed.

'Yes, for Christ's sake, yes.'

'Reach behind me, hold my balls,' he said to Gloria.

He slowed momentarily. With her free hand Gloria reached down between his legs. She found the sac of his scrotum and locked her fingers around it.

'Very good,' he said, pumping wildly again.

Gloria almost lost her precious prize but managed to hold on, even though each forward stroke almost wrenched it from her grasp. She could feel his balls pulsing.

Clarissa moaned loudly, the pounding she was receiving provoking another orgasm. Charles did not waver. His own completion was only seconds away. He looked into Gloria's eyes, then down to her body where the skirt was rucked up, revealing most of her legs.

'Show me,' he managed to breathe.

She wasn't sure what he meant.

'Show me,' he repeated looking at the top of her thighs.

She understood. She could not move her manacled hand far enough over to pull up her skirt, and did not want to take her other hand from his balls so she rolled on to the bed alongside them, raised her legs in the air and let her skirt fall back over her hips revealing the bush of her pubic hair under the tights. She parted her legs hoping he would be able to see enough of her sex. Exactly as she did so he thrust himself forward, pulled Clarissa's hips back with all his strength and, growling like an animal, all the muscles of his body locked and rigid, his cock spasmed in the silky, tight confines of Clarissa's sex.

They collapsed on the bed, Clarissa falling forward onto her stomach and Charles toppling on top of her. Gloria's hand was dragged along the bed, Clarissa's discarded garments trailing along on the chain, as Clarissa rested her head on her arms. She turned to the side to look at Gloria.

'Not fair is it?' she said. The tension in Gloria's body was all too clear.

'It's all right,' Gloria said.

'No, no, you've deserved a little prize. When we get back you can take your pick. Whatever you want.'

A bond had been established between the two women. It had started the first day in Clarissa's study as a purely sexual dynamic but over the weeks it had grown into more. Now, though sex still cemented them together, there was much more to it than the purely physical. Clarissa had given Gloria a self-confidence and assurance she had never felt before, but Gloria knew, in turn, that she had given Clarissa more than she had expected from one of a long line of servants. Despite the disparity of their positions there was a growing mutual respect.

WILLIAM

'Gloria? Is it you?'

William could hardly believe the woman who stood before him was the same woman with whom he had sat in Clarissa's study under four weeks ago. She was barely recognisable. She was wearing make-up that made her face seem more striking and her eyes darker, and her hair was styled differently. Certainly he had never seen her wearing such a beautiful and outrageous outfit; a tight yellow jacket displaying her midriff, the split in the flared black skirt right up to the top of her thighs. Had it not been for the glass beads that had been carefully crafted to resemble a bunch of grapes he would have been able to see the outline of her pubis. She was standing in the doorway of his cubicle with a riding crop in her hand.

235

'William,' she said coolly.

'Are you all right? What's happened to you? You look wonderful. What has Clarissa done to you?' The questions came tumbling out, the opportunity to talk to someone a rare event in the last few weeks. He was so used to his nudity he made no attempt to hide his genitals from her.

'Ms Peacham,' she said pointedly, 'has treated me very well. In fact, that's why I'm here.' She walked inside and closed the door firmly behind her. 'Haven't you forgotten something?'

'What?' He looked blank. It was not only Gloria's appearance that had changed but her attitude. Before she had been shy and self-effacing, now she was confident and imperious.

'Get on your knees,' she barked.

'What?'

'You heard me. Do it. I thought you'd been properly trained.'

He hesitated. She was a servant like him. She didn't have the right to demand such treatment. But the look in her eyes, the sort of look that until now he had only seen with Clarissa, brooked no argument. Still not sure why he was doing it, he slid to his knees.

But that, of course, was only part of the ritual.

'Go on,' she said, expecting him to complete the homage.

He leant forward and kissed the arch of her left foot.

'That's better,' she said. 'As you can see William, there have been some changes.'

'Yes,' he mumbled moving his lips to her right foot.

'I've learnt a lot in my stay here.' She watched him as he kissed her nylon covered flesh. 'Lick the leather William, like you did with Clarissa that day. Do you remember?'

'Yes.'

'Do it then.'

He licked around the leather of her shoe.

'What else do you remember about that day? It was traumatic for both of us wasn't it?'

'Yes.' He raised his head to look up at her. He could not avoid seeing the top of her thighs under the split skirt. She wasn't wearing any panties and he could see the dark bush of her pubic hair. 'It was humiliating for me,' he said.

'But not for me. Don't stop, you haven't finished. Do the other shoe.'

He dipped his head back to her feet.

'Clarissa's told me all about you William. She's told me how badly you behaved at first. How you let her down.'

'I didn't mean to,' he mumbled.

'Lick my legs, William. Up to my knees. Show me how good you can be.'

He didn't hesitate, transferring his mouth from the yellow and black striped shoes to her slender ankles. He felt his cock beginning to rise, pressing into his belly.

'But now, she tells me, you want to stay. Is that true?'

'Oh yes,' he muttered.

'I remember what happened to you that first day William. I remember it well. I'd never done that to a man before, or anything like it.'

He completed one journey up to her knee, then dipped his mouth to her ankle on the other leg, his cock growing rapidly.

'Apparently, you have more control of yourself now. Is that true?'

'Yes,' he mumbled as he worked up her calf.

'Good. You see William I was allowed a treat. I mean for the next few days I'm still a servant like you. With special privileges but still a servant. But tonight I've been allowed a little taste of freedom, of what I'll be able to do when I leave here, of what I shall demand of men when I leave here. And you, of course, if you are allowed to stay on. Clarissa is going to invite me back regularly as an honoured guest. Won't that be nice?'

'Yes,' he whispered against the nylon.

'So I get a little foretaste of the pleasures to come. You may go higher William, right up my thigh,' she said opening her legs wider.

He pushed his head up, his mouth just above her knee. He could see her black pubic hair flattened by the tight nylon. He kissed and licked at her thigh. She was very beautiful and his cock was rock hard.

'You're in quite a state aren't you? Do I excite you that much? Or is it this?' She stroked the tip of the riding crop against his back. He reacted as though he had been touched with a live electric wire. 'Oh I see that it is. Higher, William, lick higher.'

He felt Gloria move forward, pushing his face down between her legs so it was forced back horizontally under the plane of her sex and he found his mouth against her nylon covered labia. He kissed and tongued it through the material and heard her moan.

Suddenly she stepped back. She unzipped her skirt and let it fall to the floor, then unbuttoned the short jacket, peeling it off her naked breasts. She cupped her breasts in her hands, one bisected by the whip she still held.

'Pull my tights down William, there's a good boy.'

William obeyed, his hands trembling slightly. He did not know what had happened to Gloria in the past weeks but whatever it was he found her just as exciting as Clarissa. Her voice had the same cold, steely tone and her eyes expressed that same look of disdain and contempt for what he was and what he represented. He had seen the way Gloria responded to Clarissa's touch that first time; clearly Clarissa's effect on her had become more pronounced.

He skimmed the tights down to her ankles. She put her hand on his shoulder to steady herself as she raised each foot in turn to allow him to ease off her shoes, then pull away the sheer nylon.

'Do you know what I'm going to do now William?'

'No,' he said.

'No, Ms Price,' she corrected. 'Let me hear you say it.'

'No, Ms Price,' he mouthed.

'I'm going to use the whip on you. It excited me the first time. That was a surprise. I had never imagined such a thing. But it did. And I want to be very excited tonight. Then you're going to fuck me. And when I tell you, but only when I tell you, you're going to come. Do you understand?'

'Yes, Ms Price.' Being able to call her Ms Price somehow made it easy for William to accept Gloria's power over him.

'Bend over the bed then.'

He turned around on his knees and rested his torso on the mattress. Almost before he had put his head down the first stroke whistled through the air.

'Oh yes,' Gloria said, obviously excited. *Thwack*. The second stroke was harder. 'Oh yes,' she said again.

William's cock pulsed against the mattress. At first he thought he would lose control immediately. He was used to Clarissa's sternness but with Gloria it was so unexpected. There was something about the fact she was clearly so new to it all that made it especially exciting.

Thwack. Thwack. The third and fourth blows came together. Each produced an audible gasp of pleasure from Gloria as if the sight and sound of what she was doing and the stinging reverberations of the whip in her hand, were too much to bear. Despite the familiar heat spreading across his buttocks and the squirming pleasure it produced, William managed to control himself. His cock was hard, as hard as a poker, but he knew he would not ejaculate.

Gloria, however, could apparently take it no longer. She threw herself on the bed and opened her legs wide. 'Come and fuck me,' she cried.

William scrambled up on to the bed. He looked briefly at the scarlet channel of her labia framed by her jet black pubic hair. The entrance of her vagina was open. It was shiny and wet. He fell on her, pushing his cock home, her wetness allowing it to slide right up to the hilt.

'Oh God, God,' she mewed, her hands clawing at his back. Her whole body was alive. This was the end of a long evening of provocation, her mind already filled with images of what she had seen. She was boiling.

William stroked his cock back and forth.

'Like that, like that . . .' she cried, tossing her head to and fro, her hands clutching at his back.

He felt her sex convulsing around him, and her body arched off the bed, carrying him up with it. Every muscle in her body was rigid. He felt as if her sex was rippling, the silky walls moving against his cock. Her fingers were like talons, clawing into his buttocks to push him in deeper.

He was proud of himself, proud of his control. The provocation she had offered him was unbelievable, not only the whipping but the fact that this was the first time he had been in a woman's sex since he'd arrived at the house. But he held on because he knew he must, because a bad report from Gloria would affect his ultimate goal and nothing, nothing, was going to get in the way of that.

He felt Gloria's body change, the hardness thawing out. He didn't know whether she would allow him to come. Though every sense in his body screamed out for release he knew there was another level of his being, deeper and more profound, that would regard denial as just as meaningful, just as satisfying, as an orgasm. That was his nature, he knew now. Clarissa had mined a rich vein of masochism in him, exposed it and brought it to the surface.

It was with another sort of relief however, that he felt Gloria's body moving under him, wriggling and squirming on his cock, her need for a second coming as great as for the first. And it was only his spunk that would provoke it this time.

'Come,' she said breathing the word into his ear, as her body surged with pleasure. 'I need it.'

It was the perfect justification. And he did precisely what she wanted.

GLORIA

It was exactly one month to the day. Gloria left the house in

Clarissa's black Rolls, back to the office of Peacham Associates, but not back to her job. Clarissa had decided to promote her. She had told her that her knowledge and instincts were wasted and that she was going to put her on the creative team responsible for developing advertising strategies on products aimed at women. Gloria had, Clarissa felt, a special insight in that area.

It was going to be an exciting day. That evening there was to be a party at Clarissa's house. She would return there, not as a servant, but as a friend and guest. The small circle of friends she had already met would be there. And William, of course.

As she sat in the back of the luxurious car, she thought of William. He had changed quite as much as she had. At first she was astonished at the way he had allowed her to treat him. She could hardly believe a man, any man, would subject himself willingly to such slavishness, and obviously enjoy and get pleasure from it. It was an aspect of sexual behaviour – like so many others in Clarissa's house – that she had never encountered before. But, by the same token, she could hardly believe her reaction to it either, and the quite extraordinary pleasure she had felt in giving William what he so obviously craved. It was the pleasure she had first tasted in Clarissa's study on what she now thought of as her initiation into another world.

It seemed that was Clarissa's gift to her. Admittedly she had never had much sexual success with men, and may therefore have been ripe for a sexual awakening but had she not come to the house she doubted she would ever have had one. Somehow Clarissa had put her in touch with her own sexual feelings and allowed them to blossom. It was not a question of finding pleasure in a woman. It was both sexes. Clarissa had empowered her, given her the capability for what seemed like unlimited enjoyment.

She also knew that power was the operative word, certainly when it came to men. She was prepared to be the equal of a woman, but from now on, with men, she was going to be the dominant partner. The thought of treating a man, any man, the way she had treated William gave her a thrill in a way nothing else had. That was what she wanted. That was her nature. And Clarissa's gift was in giving her the ability to get what she wanted, as she would tonight.

She wondered if her new attitude would affect her work.

She wondered if she would find another candidate to be taken to the House on Punishment Corner.

WILLIAM

'Come in.'

He walked tentatively into the room. He was naked apart from a pair of peach coloured silk panties, Clarissa's panties, which she had decided he should wear.

They sat in a circle of armchairs, all apart from Olga that is, who stood by one of the other doors.

He knelt in front of Clarissa, bending his head and kissing her left foot.

'You must show obeisance to all my friends, William,' she said.

As soon as he had kissed both of Clarissa's feet, he crawled on his knees to the next woman on her right without the slightest hesitation, knowing tonight was the night his fate was to be decided. She was a tall rather lumpy woman in a long dark green velvet dress whose hair was done up in a matching turban. He kissed her feet. They were sheathed in opaque green nylon. Four other women sat in the circle. Gloria was the last. She was wearing a skin tight red catsuit that clung to every contour of her body. Around her waist was a wide leather belt laced up like a small corset. Her feet were encased in high heeled black boots. He kissed the leather.

'William has asked to stay here. As you know I don't usually allow my servants such privileges. There's Georgette of course . . .' Clarissa looked from the woman in velvet to a tall brunette whose hair was pinned to her head in a tight chignon, 'but he was a special case. However William may be a special case too.'

'He's a pretty little thing,' the turban headed woman said.

'Yes, Beatrice he is.'

'And enthusiastic.' One of the women, with permed bleached blonde hair was looking at William's cock which had already forced its way passed the silky waistband of the brief panties.

'So William, I have decided to put you to the test. If you really want to belong to me, because that's what it amounts to, you must agree to be marked.'

'Marked, Ms Peacham?' His voice trembled. For a moment he had an image of a branding iron. She surely couldn't expect him to stand that.

'Marked. Tattooed to be precise. Andrea here gave me the idea.' She smiled at the bleached blonde.

That information was hardly less daunting. He had heard tattoos were extremely difficult to remove. He would be marked for life.

'Property of Ms Peacham,' a lithe, cat-like creature with natural blonde hair, said.

'Yes, that sounds appropriate.' Clarissa agreed. '"Property of" on one buttock and "Ms Peacham" on the other. What do you think William?'

He simply didn't know what to say. The idea scared him but excited him too. He would never be a free agent again, not sexually at least. No woman would want him once they saw such humiliating marks on his bottom. But wasn't that what he wanted? Wasn't that what he had begged her for?

'It's your decision.' She looked at him steadily, her eyes seeming to look right through him, as they had always been able to do. 'Olga will bring the tattooist in. It'll be done in front of us all. Then one of us, the lucky one, will take you upstairs. We will draw lots.'

'I hope it's me,' Beatrice said in her husky low voice. 'He's just my type.'

'Or you can leave. As you will have seen your things are on the floor over there.' She indicated the labelled black plastic bag lying on the floor by Olga's feet. 'You have six seconds to decide William.'

'Ms Peacham, I can't . . . it wouldn't . . .' He simply did not know what to say.

'One,' said Clarissa.

'Two,' said Beatrice.

'Three,' said the bleached blonde.

'Four,' said cat-woman.

'Five,' said Andrea.

Gloria paused a long beat. 'Six,' she said finally.

There was a silence.

'I agree,' he said. Was there any choice? Of course not. There never had been.

Clarissa said nothing. She nodded to Olga who opened the door and ushered in a small, dark woman who carried a leather bag like a doctor. The woman appeared not to be surprised by William's appearance.

'So what's it to be dearie?' she asked in a strong Cockney accent.

Clarissa told her the words to be used.

'Very good. Get him to bend over that chair will you?' She indicated an upright wooden dining chair, then opened her bag and prepared her equipment, plugging a fat syringe-like pen into an electrical socket nearest to the chair.

'Do as you are told, William. Take your panties down.'

'Yes, Ms Peacham.'

William bent over the seat of the chair then wriggled the panties down over his buttocks. His flesh had never felt so vulnerable.

The door opened and Georgette entered carrying a tray of champagne flutes filled with champagne. The maid distributed them to the women.

'Well William,' Clarissa said, raising her glass, as the hum of the tattooist's pen filled the air. 'Here's to your future life.'

It was the end and the beginning, the end of one life and the beginning of the other. As he felt the first sting of the tattooist's pen, as the indelible ink of the first letter sunk into his epidermis, he felt no regret. He felt only excitement as his eyes roamed the six women and he wondered who would be taking him upstairs and what they would order him to do.

Headline Delta Erotic Survey

In order to provide the kind of books you like to read – and to
qualify for a free erotic novel of the Editor's choice – we
would appreciate it if you would complete the following
survey and send your answers, together with any further
comments, to:

> Headline Book Publishing
> FREEPOST (WD 4984)
> London
> NW1 0YR

1. Are you male or female?
2. Age? Under 20 / 20 to 30 / 30 to 40 / 40 to 50 /
   50 to 60 / 60 to 70 / over
3. At what age did you leave full-time education?
4. Where do you live? (Main geographical area)
5. Are you a regular erotic book buyer / a regular book
   buyer in general / both?
6. How much approximately do you spend a year on erotic
   books / on books in general?
7. How did you come by this book?
7a. If you bought it, did you purchase from:
   a national bookchain / a high street store / a newsagent /
   a motorway station / an airport / a railway station /
   other . . .
8. Do you find erotic books easy / hard to come by?
8a. Do you find Headline Delta erotic books easy / hard
   to come by?
9. Which are the best / worst erotic books you have ever
   read?
9a. Which are the best / worst Headline Delta erotic books
   you have ever read?
10. Within the erotic genre there are many periods,
   subjects and literary styles. Which of the following
   do you prefer:
10a. (period) historical / Victorian / C20th /contemporary /
   future?
10b. (subject) nuns / whores & whorehouses /
   Continental frolics / s&m / vampires / modern realism /
   escapist fantasy / science fiction?

10c. (styles) hardboiled / humorous / hardcore / ironic / romantic / realistic?

10d. Are there any other ingredients that particularly appeal to you?

11. We try to create a cover appearance that is suitable for each title. Do you consider them to be successful?

12. Would you prefer them to be less explicit / more explicit?

13. We would be interested to hear of your other reading habits. What other types of books do you read?

14. Who are your favourite authors?

15. Which newspapers do you read?

16. Which magazines?

17. Do you have any other comments or suggestions to make?

If you would like to receive a free erotic novel of the Editor's choice (available only to UK residents), together with an up-to-date listing of Headline Delta titles, please supply your name and address. Please allow 28 days for delivery.

Name   ....

Address   ....

....

....

A selection of Erotica from Headline

BLUE HEAVENS	Nick Bancroft	£4.99	☐
MAID	Dagmar Brand	£4.99	☐
EROS IN AUTUMN	Anonymous	£4.99	☐
EROTICON THRILLS	Anonymous	£4.99	☐
IN THE GROOVE	Lesley Asquith	£4.99	☐
THE CALL OF THE FLESH	Faye Rossignol	£4.99	☐
SWEET VIBRATIONS	Jeff Charles	£4.99	☐
UNDER THE WHIP	Nick Aymes	£4.99	☐
RETURN TO THE CASTING COUCH	Becky Bell	£4.99	☐
MAIDS IN HEAVEN	Samantha Austen	£4.99	☐
CLOSE UP	Felice Ash	£4.99	☐
TOUCH ME, FEEL ME	Rosanna Challis	£4.99	☐

All Headline books are available at your local bookshop or newsagent, or can be ordered direct from the publisher. Just tick the titles you want and fill in the form below. Prices and availability subject to change without notice.

Headline Book Publishing, Cash Sales Department, Bookpoint, 39 Milton Park, Abingdon, OXON, OX14 4TD, UK. If you have a credit card you may order by telephone – 01235 400400.

Please enclose a cheque or postal order made payable to Bookpoint Ltd to the value of the cover price and allow the following for postage and packing:

UK & BFPO: £1.00 for the first book, 50p for the second book and 30p for each additional book ordered up to a maximum charge of £3.00.

OVERSEAS & EIRE: £2.00 for the first book, £1.00 for the second book and 50p for each additional book.

Name ....

Address ....

....

....

If you would prefer to pay by credit card, please complete:
Please debit my Visa/Access/Diner's Card/American Express (delete as applicable) card no:

Signature .... Expiry Date..............